Couldn't he see she was flirting with him?

When Kane lowered his arm, Charlotte touched the tip of the sword tattooed on his biceps. "What does this one mean?"

"In some cultures," he said, his tone gruff, "it symbolizes judgment."

Judgment. She hadn't expected that. Had thought someone like him would've chosen a different emblem, something that meant power or perhaps antiestablishment. Power to the people and all that. A hand with the middle finger sticking up.

Maybe there was more to him than she'd thought.

"What are you doing here, Red?" He looked pointedly at her hand still on his arm, her fingers caressing the smoothness of his skin as if of their own will.

Good question. What *was* she doing here? Her first instinct was to leap back, to put as much distance between them as possible. But that would defeat her purpose, wouldn't it? She could do this. She would do this. Kane would be hers for one night.

She'd come too far to back down now.

Dear Reader,

One of the things I love most about writing is discovering my characters. It never fails: I start a book thinking I know each character's complete backstory, personality and the traits that will make them fully developed and realistic. I often have page upon page of notes outlining their strengths and flaws, how they'll react to others and what it will take to push them out of their comfortable—if not completely fulfilling—existence, and into the lives they were meant to live.

And then, as I'm writing, something always, *always* takes me by surprise. A previously cynical hero turns out to be shy and romantic. A heroine who was supposed to be a sweet-natured pushover fights her way through a story. It's these surprising insights that, I think, make my characters become people we want to root for and stick with throughout an entire book.

That's exactly what happened with Kane Bartasavich, the sexy bartender first introduced in *What Happens Between Friends* (Harlequin Superromance, August 2013). I thought Kane was your typical bad boy. He had the looks and the attitude, after all. He was, in my mind, a loner with a chip on his shoulder, someone no one could get close to.

Until his teenage daughter showed up at his apartment.

Yes, I was surprised by that development. But the more I wrote, the more I realized I'd initially shortchanged Kane by labeling him as just another bad boy. He's so much more—which Charlotte Ellison quickly realizes!

I loved writing Kane and Charlotte's story and revisiting the town of Shady Grove. Later this year my fifth book in the In Shady Grove series will be out, where charming playboy Leo Montesano meets his match. I hope you'll look for it!

Please visit my website, www.bethandrews.net, or drop me a line at beth@bethandrews.net. I'd love to hear from you.

Happy reading!

Beth Andrews

BETH ANDREWS

Small-Town Redemption

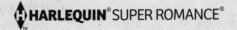

HARLEQUIN® SUPER ROMANCE®

Recycling programs
for this product may
not exist in your area.

ISBN-13: 978-0-373-60850-8

SMALL-TOWN REDEMPTION

Copyright © 2014 by Beth Burgoon

Printed in U.S.A.

ABOUT THE AUTHOR

Romance Writers of America RITA® Award winning author Beth Andrews writes contemporary romance for Harlequin's Superromance line, checks for her kids' college tuition bills and text messages that somehow end up on her kids' Twitter feeds. She loves coffee, hockey and happy endings. Learn more about Beth and her books by visiting her website, www.BethAndrews.net.

Books by Beth Andrews

HARLEQUIN SUPERROMANCE

*The Truth about the Sullivans
‡In Shady Grove

Other titles by this author available in ebook format.

To my wonderful editor, Wanda Ottewell.
Thank you so much for your insight,
encouragement and patience!

Acknowledgment

Special thanks to Taryn Maley, RN,
for her invaluable help.

CHAPTER ONE

CHARLOTTE ELLISON HAD a life plan.

She'd *had* a life plan, she amended as she stomped up the wooden stairs. She'd had it all figured out, had carefully planned how to achieve her goals and gone after them, no holds barred. And she'd achieved so much, had always done what she'd set out to do. Had always, *always* gotten what she'd wanted.

Until two weeks ago when she'd made a complete and utter fool of herself. When she'd kissed the man she loved, the man she was so sure was going to be the father of her future children, and he'd responded with a pat on the head and a kind *I'm just not into you.*

Bastard.

Her ankle twisted. Pain shot up her leg and she almost did a face-plant on the stairs before catching her balance. She glared at her shoes. Stupid four-inch hooker heels. And to think, they'd actually seemed like a good idea when she'd bought them. She continued on, resolute and limping, the sound of her footsteps bouncing off the walls, the echoes mocking her.

But worse than that humiliation? The next day

she'd discovered the real reason James Montesano didn't want her.

He loved her sister.

Tears stung Charlotte's eyes, tickled her nose. She sniffed them back. She was through crying. Done. It was time to move on. Back in the saddle and all that. But it grated—oh, how it grated—that she'd done everything right, every last damn thing, and still she'd failed in a stunning and spectacular fashion.

It wasn't fair.

Not when she'd worked so hard, planned so well and considered each and every possible outcome.

She pressed her lips together, bumped her fist against her thigh with each step. Okay, so she'd considered every possible outcome except the one that had actually happened. She could hardly believe she'd been so naive. So stupid.

Never again.

No more lists. No more worrying about the future. No more plans. She'd learned her lesson. From now on, she was following her instincts. Being spontaneous. Taking the road not taken.

That road led here where, in a matter of minutes, she'd prove she was a desirable woman worthy of a man's attention. Not just any man, either. A gorgeous, sexy man with a cool, hooded gaze, a hard body covered in tattoos and a perpetual smirk. A dangerous man. The kind who would induce panic in her mother, give her father nightmares and make all of her friends weep with envy.

The kind of man she'd sworn never to get involved with, had never before been interested in. The kind of man Sadie—her pretty, flighty, reckless sister—usually went for.

Biting her lower lip, Char stared at the warped wooden door. Behind it lay the key to her vindication.

Or her complete ruin.

She was putting her self-worth on the line here. Was tossing aside her morals and pride. He'd better be worth it.

She knocked, the sharp raps brisk and authoritative, as if her knees weren't shaking. As if she weren't terrified out of her mind.

When the door remained shut for the longest three minutes of her life, no sound of movement coming from behind it, she used the side of her fist to pound on the wood. Repeatedly.

His motorcycle was in the parking lot. He had to be home.

She wouldn't have the courage to come back if he wasn't, if she had time to think about this for too long.

The door was yanked opened, and there he stood. Not the man of her dreams—that title belonged to her as-of-yet-unknown future husband. No, the man before her was more like the star of her deepest, darkest, sexiest fantasies.

Well, look at him, she thought in exasperation. With a sharply planed face way too pretty for his—or anyone else's—good, Kane Bartasavich was tall, broad-shouldered and, at the moment, barefoot and shirtless. His wild mane of golden hair tousled around his face, the ends brushing his shoulders. His chest was smooth and leanly muscled, his arms well defined.

He had the word *savage*—in flowing script—tattooed above his heart. A swirling tribal tat covered his left arm from shoulder to just above his elbow. His right biceps sported a flaming sword, his right side the word *pride*. Below his navel, three Chinese symbols formed a triangle, the bottom two disappearing under the waist of his low-slung jeans.

Jeans, she noted, her eyes widening, he'd zipped but not buttoned.

Oh. My.

Warmth swept through her, fast and furious, stealing her breath, her thoughts.

She wished it would take her inhibitions, too. Her doubts.

Averting her gaze to somewhere less…dangerous…she worked moisture back into her mouth. Then checked out the symbols once more. Honestly, they were like a magnet, drawing her attention again and again.

Heat still stinging her cheeks, she opened her mouth to say something clever and charming, only to cringe when all that came out was a croak more often associated with Kermit the Frog than a highly intelligent, confident woman.

She tried again, this time managing a breathless, "Hi."

So much for dazzling Kane with her wit and tantalizing conversation. Good thing she wasn't here to talk.

He looked beyond her as if searching for the reason she was there. Finally, his gaze settled on her, his green eyes giving nothing away. "You lost, Red?"

Red. That was the tired and unoriginal name he'd christened her with upon their first meeting a few weeks ago. She supposed it was better than *Freckles.* "No."

"Then the building had better be on fire and you woke me to save my life." The implicit threat in his low words wasn't the least bit softened by the huskiness of his sleep-laden tone.

"It's after noon," she said. "Time to wakey-wakey."

"I work nights. I don't wakey-wakey until at least 2:00 p.m."

"I worked last night, too. But I'm up and dressed. And pleasant."

"This is you being pleasant?"

"I'm extremely pleasant," she snapped before getting herself under control. She inhaled, counted to five, then exhaled slowly. "I realize we haven't seen the best side of each other." Only because he brought out the worst in her. The man was infuriating. How Sadie could even tend bar for him was beyond Charlotte. "But suffice it to say, I'm an incredibly nice woman."

He stared at her, obviously not believing it. And he kept right on staring, as if he had all the livelong day to stand there.

She crossed her arms. Tapped her foot. Felt the minutes tick-ticking away.

Dropping her arms, she huffed out a breath. "Aren't you going to invite me in?"

"Hadn't planned on it."

Un-freaking-believable. Taking matters into her own hands—the best way to get things done—she shoved open the door and brushed past him. "Anyone ever tell you you're rude?"

One side of his mouth kicked up in a condescending smirk. "You're the one who barged into my apartment without being invited, little girl."

Little girl.

She stayed rooted to her spot, her scalp prickling, a lump forming in her throat. Sadie had called her *little girl* when they'd had their fight two weeks ago. It'd been a huge, ugly blowup. One Charlotte was afraid they might not be able to get past.

Then again, she was still mad enough she wasn't certain she wanted to get past it.

And she wasn't a little girl. She was a fully grown, competent, independent woman. Wasn't she here to prove that?

She couldn't let Kane get to her. Yes, he was an ass. An ill-mannered, overgrown rebel without a cause. He was everything she didn't want in a man. Cocky. Arrogant. Snide.

She didn't like him.

She didn't have to. Not for this.

Kane walked into the tiny kitchen, granting her a view of the Aztec tattoo on his broad back—a large bird, its wings outspread across his shoulder blades. Black flames dripped from the wings, licked along Kane's spine, which served as part of the narrowing tail. It ended in a sharp point between two finger-print-sized indentations above the waist of his jeans.

She rubbed the pads of her thumbs against her forefingers. Wondered what it would be like to press them there. To have all of that skin, those lean muscles under her hands.

Wondered if she had the courage to find out.

She rolled her head like a boxer preparing for round one. Guess she'd soon know.

Charlotte set her purse on the table by the door, then joined him in the kitchen where he poured distilled water into a large, and expensive, coffeemaker.

"Need any help?" she asked, trying for cheerful but falling somewhere in the vicinity of aggrieved.

He didn't even glance her way. "Don't make me call the cops to come and haul you out of here."

She puffed out her cheeks. The least he could do is look at her. She hadn't wiggled into these jeans for her health. Was probably damaging a few internal organs by wearing the tight denim. Not to mention how bad her feet hurt. But the overall effect was worth it. The stupid heels added to her considerable height and the dark jeans made her legs look endless, cupped her butt and gave the illusion she had hips—no easy feat. Her shirt was silky and cut low enough to give a glimpse of her black lace bra. She'd straightened her hair, taken time with her makeup.

She'd been cursed with too many cute genes to ever pass for beautiful, but right now, she looked hot. Sexy.

Kane was obviously too blind to notice.

Leaning back against the counter, she subtly arched her back, held on to the edge with her hands, pushing her chest out. "Your apartment is…" She glanced around. "Uh…nice."

Lovely. If you liked worn, beige carpet, walls that needed a fresh coat of paint—preferably something other than the current dingy yellow—and a kitchen straight from the 1970s, complete with orange Formica counters. At least it was clean. Then again, he kept O'Riley's, the bar downstairs, his bar, spotless.

A point in his favor.

"You're very neat," she blurted.

Biting the inside of her lower lip, she winced. Neat? Was that the best she could come up with? Next thing she knew she'd be complimenting him on his straight teeth and bringing up the weather.

Oh, sure, *now* he looked at her, when she was blushing and mentally kicking herself. Not just looked, either, he studied her, rather intently. "Are you off your meds or something?"

She giggled—giggled, for God's sake—the sound forced, high-pitched and way too loud. Why did flirting have to be so hard? It was as natural as breathing to Sadie. You'd think that was the kind of genetic trait that could be passed from sister to sister.

Charlotte swatted his arm, meant for it to be playful, but ended up hitting him hard enough to make her palm sting. He didn't so much as blink.

"Don't be silly," she said, seemingly unable to bring her tone back to its normal range. "I just meant that, well, you're so…" Rough. Hard. Dangerous. She gestured to him in all his bare-chested, tattooed glory. Let it go at that. "I thought you'd be—"

"A slob?"

"No," she breathed, the lie like a stone in her throat, choking her. "I mean, maybe I'd briefly considered you'd be…less tidy. With a motorcycle in the living room, a pet boa constrictor and a closet filled with scarred leather jackets."

"Stairway's too narrow for my bike," he said solemnly. "But who says the other two aren't true?"

She swallowed. He was probably kidding about the snake. Still, she stepped closer to him, kept an eye out for any sudden, slithering movements. "Anyway, it's nice. That you're tidy. Did you learn that in the military?"

In the act of getting a coffee mug from an upper cabinet, he paused. "I never told you I was in the service."

"Everyone knows. Small town. No secrets." Though seeing him now, he seemed a far cry from a spit-shined soldier. "Do you miss it? Being a Marine?"

He looked at her as if she'd just slapped his face and called his mother ugly. "I was a Ranger. In the Army."

"Ranger. That's Special Forces, right?"

He grunted.

So charming.

"I'm sorry," she said, "I always get them confused. Is it one grunt for yes, and two for no?"

No smile. No glint of humor in those green eyes. Nothing. He simply watched the coffeemaker as if it held the answers to life's most pressing questions. Since he refused to notice what a fetching image she made, she straightened. She needed a few more sessions at the yoga studio before she could hold the arched pose for any length of time, especially after a twelve-hour shift in the E.R.

Covering her mouth with the back of her hand, she yawned so hard her eyes watered. A shift that was quickly catching up with her.

She wandered into the living room. His apartment was small, maybe half the size of her own, with a view of the empty armory building next door and the Dumpster in the alley.

She continued her exploration, trailing her fingers over the back of a checked high-back chair when he stepped into the doorway. He leaned against the doorjamb, the angle causing his stomach muscles to clench, the ridges clearly defined. Steam rose from the mug in his hand as he sipped his coffee, his biceps rounding with the movement.

Now that was somebody who knew how to pose.

She felt his gaze on her, steady and searching, as she crossed the room, so she put a bit of sway into her walk, and wished there was more to see, to pretend to study, but the man put the minimal in minimalist. Other than the ugly chair, the only furnishings in the room were a small, flat-screen TV on top of a scarred wooden end table and a lumpy floral couch. No knickknacks. No decorative pillows or throws. No pictures or personal effects at all.

She glanced down the small hallway. The door to the right was shut—bathroom?—the other, at the end of the hall, open far enough to give her a glimpse of his bed, the covers rumpled, the pillow still indented from his head.

She imagined him getting out of that bed, tugging his jeans on, cursing and muttering about people interrupting his precious sleep.

Was the bed still warm from his body? Were his sheets soft or crisp? Did his scent linger on the pillow?

She crossed to stand in front of him. Funny how now that he looked at her, she felt more vulnerable, exposed, though he was the one only half-dressed. She had no idea what to do, what to say to get him to cooperate with her. That was the problem with not making plans. No road map. She needed one. Her sense of direction sucked.

"Uh…I'm…uh…thinking of getting a tattoo," she said.

He raked his gaze over her, from the top of her extremely smooth hair to the tips of her ridiculously high heels. "That so?"

Did he have to sound condescending? So disbelieving?

"That's so." She edged closer, breathed in the rich scent of coffee, the spiciness of his soap, surprised by how pleasant she found the combination. "Did they hurt?" she continued, her tone husky. Breathless.

He shrugged. Lifted the mug to his mouth again, almost clipping her on the chin.

She wanted to swipe it out of his hand, throw the damn thing against the wall. Couldn't he see she was flirting with him? The least he could do was reciprocate, especially when she was so out of her element.

Hard not to be when he was the epitome of physical perfection. She should have known he'd look like some freaking underwear model.

While she was too tall. Too thin. With small breasts and more angles than curves.

She'd have to make sure they kept the lights off when it came time to get naked.

When he lowered his arm, she touched the tip of the sword on his biceps. Traced her fingertip up the sharp line to the flame. His skin was warm. Softer than she'd expected.

"What does this one mean?" When he didn't answer, she tried a teasing smile, one that would bring out her dimple—and hopefully loosen him up a bit. "Or did you just think it was pretty?"

His body went rigid. "In some cultures it symbolizes judgment."

"Judgment," she whispered almost to herself. "I would have thought you'd choose a different emblem, something more…antiestablishment. Skull and crossbones or a hand with the middle finger sticking up."

"What are you doing?"

His question startled her, the low timbre of his voice causing gooseflesh to prick her arms.

She licked her lips. His eyes, following the movement, narrowed to slits. "Wha—what do you mean?"

He looked pointedly at her hand still on his arm, her fingers caressing the smoothness of his skin as if of their own will.

Her first instinct was to leap back, to put as much distance between them as possible. But that would defeat the purpose of her visit, wouldn't it? She could do this.

She'd come too far to back down now.

Charlotte flattened her palm against his biceps, and he tensed, the muscle flexing momentarily before relaxing. "I'm touching you," she said softly, smoothing her hand up his arm and settling it on his shoulder.

Oh, please don't let my palms start sweating. Not now.

"Why are you touching me?"

Seriously? You'd think it was the first time the man had been hit on by a woman. Jeez. "Because I want to."

Determined, and more than a little terrified, she laid her other hand on his opposite shoulder and held his gaze, annoyed and deflated when his remained steady. She wanted to fluster him, for him feel a fraction of the nerves, of the crazy energy, she felt whenever they were together.

Thanks to her high heels, it was easy, incredibly easy, to link her hands behind his neck and tug his head down. Her heart pounded painfully. Good Lord she hoped she didn't have a coronary. Not now, not when his mouth was inches from her own, his breath mingling with hers.

She brushed a soft kiss across his mouth. Leaned back, her stomach in knots. But Kane didn't jerk as if she'd tossed acid in his face, didn't push her away as if she were some leper come to spread her disease. Didn't treat her as if she were unattractive. Unwanted.

As James had when she'd kissed him.

Kane simply watched her. Patient, curious and waiting for her next move.

Emboldened, she stepped closer until their thighs touched, her breasts pressing against his chest, his warmth seeping through the silk of her shirt. She wished he would take the initiative, would sweep her up in his arms and carry her to his bed. That he'd take control and show her how this was done.

He didn't move.

She should kiss him again, a real kiss, one with tongue, but she was frozen, unable to move. Unable to think. There was something about the way he looked at her that made her want to curl into herself, to slink away. But she wasn't a quitter. The only way to get what you wanted was to go after it.

And what she wanted was Kane.

"Take me to bed," she told him, albeit a bit shakily. "Now."

WHY HIM?

Kane sighed, the movement causing his shoulders to rise and fall, which in turn caused Red's breasts to brush against his chest. She didn't have a lot going on in that department, but she had enough for his body to notice.

Hell.

Reaching behind his neck, he tugged her hands apart, then set her away from him. "Sorry, Red. Not interested."

He went into the kitchen, but not before seeing the hurt, the embarrassment, cross her face.

Not his problem, he told himself, pouring more coffee into his cup. It wasn't up to him to soothe or coddle her. She'd come here, had come to him. He hadn't asked for her attention or her clumsy attempts at seduction.

She stomped after him, the embodiment of a woman scorned, complete with narrowed eyes and red splotches coloring her cheeks. She'd come to him and obviously wasn't in a hurry to leave.

"What do you mean you're not interested?" she

asked, sounding incredulous. Disbelieving. "You're a man. I'm a woman."

Sipping his coffee, he looked her up and down. Her hair, red as a clown's wig and stick-straight, fell past her shoulders. Heavy makeup hid the freckles on her nose and upper cheeks. She'd done something to her eyes, had lined them in thick black, used dark shadow on the lids then coated her pale lashes with what looked to be several layers of mascara. Her lips were a glossy pink.

She looked like a kid who'd gotten into her mother's makeup.

"Just what I meant," he said. "Not interested."

Maybe he'd been a little bit interested a few minutes ago. She was right about one thing; he was a man. And she had been plastered against him. Not that skinny women with bad attitudes did much for him, but her hands had been soft on his arm, her fingers warm. And, he had to admit, she smelled good, really good, her perfume subtle and sweet. A contrast to her do-me heels and the permanent scowl she wore around him.

Practically vibrating with fury, she slapped her hands on her hips, the move tugging her shirt open and giving him a glimpse of smooth, creamy skin and the edge of a lacy black bra.

His body stirred. It was that damn man thing again.

"Oh, no. You are not doing this to me. Do you have any idea how long it took me to straighten my

hair?" she asked, jabbing at her head hard enough to
drill her finger right into her brain. "I can't breathe,
my feet hurt and I paid one hundred dollars for this
stupid push-up bra."

He let his gaze drop to her chest for one long, lazy
moment. When he raised his eyes back to hers, she
swallowed visibly. He smirked. "You might want to
get your money back."

She blanched before color rushed into her cheeks.
She opened her mouth, no doubt to lay him flat, but
then she shut her eyes and inhaled deeply, which, ad-
mittedly, did some interesting things to those small
breasts.

On second thought, maybe that bra had been a
good investment.

She opened her eyes, the glint in the light blue
depths warning him he may have made a misstep.

Wouldn't be his first.

She stormed up to him, all painted-on jeans, long
legs and bad humor. "We are going to have sex, you
hear me?" To punctuate her statement, she undid the
top button of her shirt.

Kane paused in the middle of taking another sip
of coffee. Raised an eyebrow. It was a bluff, that single button. It had to be. She didn't have the guts to
undo another one.

He hoped.

"Right here," she continued, proving him wrong
by yanking another one free. "Right now." And an-

other. "So stop pretending to be noble and take what is being offered to you."

She dragged her shirt off her arms and threw it on the ground like a football player spiking the ball after a touchdown. Held his gaze, her breathing ragged, her chest rising and falling rapidly, her pale skin fairly glowing in his dimly lit kitchen.

His body responded to the sight of the soft curve of her breasts, her flat stomach and the ever-so-slight indentation of her narrow waist, and he considered, seriously considered, doing just that. Whether it was due to her being half-naked, his recent sexual dry spell or simply his resistance being down didn't matter. In that moment, he wanted her. It pissed him off, this sudden, vicious need to have her.

Again and again and again.

That's what his father would have done. What Kane had been brought up to do. Take what was so easily offered, so carelessly given. He'd been born into a wealthy family. A powerful one. Raised to believe he was better than others by virtue of his last name and his father's financial worth.

Throw in his looks, and there had never been a shortage of available females ready and willing to do whatever it took to make Kane happy. To get his attention, to be on his arm—or in his bed.

There was a time when he wouldn't have cared that Red was his employee's sister, that they barely knew each other. That she didn't want him so much as she

wanted to use him. He would have used her, too, then
set her aside without another thought or care.

He liked to think he wasn't that big of a prick
anymore.

"Seriously?" Red asked through gritted teeth, her
arms splayed as if to point out she was, indeed, par-
tially naked and offering herself to him. "This is
something you have to think about?"

"No," he told her in all honesty as he set his mug
down. "I don't have to think about it at all."

He closed the distance between them, noted how
she started to step back before catching herself. She
lifted her chin as if facing the grim reaper head-on.

Kane moved closer, stopping shy of actually touching her. "You want me, Red?"

Her eyes widened. She licked her lips. "Yes," she
said, holding his gaze, all stoic and brave, her pale
skin beckoning him to touch, the pulse beating rapidly at the base of her throat enticing him to taste.
Her scent wrapped around him, making him want
something he had no business wanting, something he
never would have even considered before she barged
into his apartment and stripped off her shirt.

"You want me to touch you?" he asked, his voice
rough, his caress whisper-soft as he slowly trailed
his fingertips up her arms.

A blush started at the base of her throat, bloomed
in her cheeks. He wanted to press his lips to the side
of her neck, to feel the warmth of that color wash-

ing over her skin. She swallowed hard, then nodded once, a quick jerk of her head.

He'd known she was irritable, temperamental and overbearing. He never would have guessed she was also a liar.

He settled his hands on her shoulders, kept his touch light. Impersonal. "You want to have sex with me? You want me to make you come? Because that's what I'd do if you were in my bed. I'd strip you bare," he murmured, for some reason envisioning doing just that. In intimate detail. Scowling, he forced the image from his head. "I'd touch you everywhere with my hands, my lips." He leaned in, put his mouth close to her ear. "My tongue."

Gasping, she reared back, her spine hitting the counter with a sharp thud. She pressed herself against it as if that alone could stop his words, could stop him from coming closer.

It couldn't. Wouldn't. Not yet. Not until he'd made his point and made it well.

"Or maybe you don't want something as ordinary as sex in a bed," he continued quietly. Relentlessly. "Something as mundane as soft touches and reverent kisses."

He nudged one thigh between her legs, ignored how she stiffened, her hands going to his chest. She didn't push him away, stubborn thing that she was. But her fingers trembled against him.

"I…" Her nails dug into his skin. She cleared her throat. "A bed is…fine."

"You didn't come here for a tame experience. We could do it here, on the floor or the table. Or maybe you'd like it against this counter, hard and fast. Your legs wrapped around my waist." His voice dropped, grew husky. "Me buried deep inside of you."

She flinched, but it wasn't enough, not when she hadn't pushed him away yet, hadn't tried to cover herself. Hadn't slapped him, called him a few choice names and stormed off. Not when, for a moment, she'd reduced him to the man he used to be.

"I'd make you feel good," he promised, tracing lazy circles just below her collarbone. She shivered. "You wouldn't care that it was me on top of you. I could make you forget your name." He paused, laid his palm flat above her breast, felt her heart beating, too hard, too fast. "I could make you forget him. At least for a little while."

She opened her mouth, but he shook his head before she could deny what they both knew was true.

"I could do all of that," he continued. "If I wanted to." He stepped back, the move not as easy to do as he would have liked. One more thing he blamed on her. "I don't."

Her fingers curled, scraping his skin before she slowly lowered her arms. "You...what?"

"I don't want to." He kept his voice flat. Cool. Honest. "I don't want *you*."

Her throat working, she hunched her shoulders, curling into herself and staring at him like a puppy he'd drop-kicked. Guilt and regret nudged him. Told him he could have been more sympathetic. Kinder. Except he'd learned to reserve his sympathy for those who truly deserved it.

And that kindness would only be used against him.

Besides, this wasn't his fault. It was hers.

All hers.

She yanked on her shirt. "You don't want me? Fine. Great." Her head bent, her hair hiding her face, she buttoned it. "But let me tell you something, buddy, you're the one missing out here. Not me."

That was better, so much better than the disappointment that had been in her eyes a moment ago. The hurt.

"Someday," he promised, "you'll thank me for this."

Her head whipped up, her eyes narrowing. "And someday you'll kick your own ass for passing up the opportunity to be with me."

Lifting her pointy chin and haughty nose, she swept past him, regal as a queen.

Because he worried she might be right, because she'd come here and stirred up this unwanted hunger for her, he snatched her arm. Whirled her around to face him. "Should I be honored that someone of your high moral standing offered herself to me?" he asked, his voice silky despite the tightness of his jaw. "Grateful to help you prove you're over some other guy?"

"Yes...I mean...no. I mean...I..." She tugged her

arm and he let go. She stepped back, her top teeth worrying her lower lip. But she held his gaze. "This isn't about anyone but you and me. I'm here because I...I'm attracted to you."

There it was. The truth. Part of it, anyway, said in a rush. A guilty secret.

An attraction that was purely physical. If she ignored it long enough, the flash of heat between them would eventually flicker and fade. When presented with a bright, burning flame, the best thing, the smart thing, was to keep your hands to yourself.

She wanted to touch it, to feel its burn. A good girl taking a walk on the wild side. Rebelling against the endless repetition of her tidy life and daily routine, the expectations of others and her own boredom.

"You're here," he said, "because you thought getting laid would make you feel better."

Her shoulders snapped back. But then, that seemed to be her natural stance—rigid. Uptight. Condescending. "You don't know anything about me."

He knew the last time she was at his bar, she and Sadie had fought about James Montesano, a local carpenter. That their argument had disrupted Kane's night and upset Sadie enough that she'd ducked out of work three hours before the end of her shift.

"I know you want to piss off your sister. Find some other way than throwing yourself at a guy."

Charlotte's hands balled into fists. "This has nothing to do with Sadie."

"Bullshit. You think sleeping with me will prove you're over him? That you don't care he chose Sadie over you? All you're doing is embarrassing yourself."

Her eyes welled. Her lower lip trembled.

Panic squeezed his spine. Had his palms sweating. He had no use for tears or the women who used them to get what they wanted. Women like his mother.

"Swallow those back," he growled. "Or I swear to God I'll toss your skinny ass out the window."

"I wouldn't cry over you," she said with a deep sniff. "I wouldn't waste one single tear. You're not worth it."

She had that right. "Good to hear."

"You...you're..."

"Could you spit out whatever you're choking on so I can get back to my bed?"

"You're an ass. A bastard. A—"

Someone knocked on the door.

Red, her mouth open, her eyes wide, leaped behind the chair, half crouching behind it. "Who's that?" she whispered.

"Sorry but my X-ray vision is on the fritz." He stepped toward the door.

"No," she gasped, grabbing his hand. "For God's sake, don't answer it."

More knocking, rapid in succession and annoying as hell.

"If I don't," he ground out, pulling free, "I can't get rid of them."

For the second time that morning, he opened the door.

And for the second time that morning, found an unwelcome visitor.

"I'm sorry," Sadie Nixon blurted, her blond hair a wild mass around her face, dark circles under her eyes. "Did I wake you?"

"I run a bar that doesn't shut down until 2:00 a.m. What do you think?"

"I'm sorry," she repeated, sounding as if she was about to burst into tears any second. Christ, but this was not his morning. "I didn't know where else to go."

He raised his eyebrows at the suitcase she held. "I hear the Holiday Inn off the highway has affordable rates."

He started to shut the door, but she blocked it with her foot. "Please," Sadie said, much nicer than Red ever spoke to him. "Just for a night or two."

Have her bunk with him for a few nights? No way. He didn't get involved in personal problems, didn't get personally involved with the people he worked with.

Or, in this case, the people who worked for him.

"You don't want to come in here," he said.

"I do. I really do."

Maybe the only way to get rid of her—of both of them—was to let Sadie in.

Scratching his stomach, he stepped aside. "Don't say I didn't warn you."

"Thanks," she said, brushing past him. "I promise not to—"

"You have *got* to be kidding."

Sadie slowly turned, her eyes about popping out of her head when she saw her sister. "What are you doing here? Where did you get those clothes? I didn't realize Nordstrom had a tart department." She whirled on Kane. "And you. You should be ashamed of yourself. She's just a child!"

"I probably should be," he agreed. Would be if he'd gone through with some of the more lewd thoughts he'd had concerning Red. "But I'm not."

He had more than his fair share of sins, but this wasn't one of them.

Red stalked over to her sister, towering over the curvy blonde. "How dare you? I'm a grown woman, damn it."

Sadie sniffed. "Then I suggest you act like one."

"I don't need to stand here and listen to this." With a toss of her hair, Red snatched up her purse. "You're in my way," she told Sadie, who blocked her exit.

"You're not going anywhere until you tell me what, exactly, you're doing here."

"I'm not telling you anything. Now move. Or I swear, I will move you."

Sadie narrowed her eyes. "I'd like to see you try."

"And I'd like to see the backs of both of you as you leave me in peace so I can get some more sleep," Kane said.

"Blame her—" Red jabbed a finger at Sadie.

He yawned. Rolled his shoulders back, then took them each by the upper arm and tugged them out into the hallway. He stepped inside his apartment and faced them. "Let's not cast blame."

He shut and locked the door, the soft click echoing in the stunned silence.

Stunned, blessed silence.

He walked to his room. He might not have been as gentle as he could have been with Red, but he'd done the right thing. Which wasn't something that came often or, to be honest, easily. Mostly because he couldn't care less about what other people thought was right. But, yeah, for once he'd made the morally acceptable choice.

Give him a freaking medal.

He kicked off his jeans and padded naked to the bed. Lying down, he linked his hands behind his head and stared at the ceiling. He blew out a heavy breath. Shut his eyes, but could still feel the warmth of Red's fingers on his skin. Could still smell her. She'd invaded his apartment and now her ghost was sticking around.

Women. They never knew when to leave a man alone.

He rolled off the bed, yanked the window open, then flopped onto his stomach. All the cool breeze did was blow around her phantom scent so he pulled the pillow over his head. He tossed and turned for what seemed like hours, the memory of Charlotte standing before him in nothing but jeans and a bra imprinting itself in his mind. When he finally, gratefully, fell asleep, he dreamed of her. Of her long legs, bright hair and wary eyes.

And when he woke, hard and aching for her, he could have sworn he still tasted the whisper of her kiss on his lips.

CHAPTER TWO

Seven months later

Behind the bar, Kane wiped his hands on the towel he kept in his back pocket. Julie Moffat, law student by day and kick-ass waitress by night, wove her way through the crowd at O'Riley's, a tray of cosmos in her raised hand. She delivered the drinks to a table of coeds celebrating a twenty-first birthday, said something to the girls then nodded toward the corner where two dudes raised their beers in a toast. By the time the girls smiled their thanks to the guys, Julie was back at the bar.

"I need four margaritas," she told Sadie, "two regular, one of those no salt. One strawberry, the other pomegranate, both blended. And four shots of Cuervo."

Sadie, already pouring tequila into the blender, raised her eyebrows. "Sympathizing, celebrating or just loosening inhibitions?"

"They're celebrating," Julie said with a nod toward the four middle-aged women at a booth by the dartboard. "The blonde in the mom jeans got some big promotion, finally getting out from under the ass-hat supervisor she's had to deal with for the past five years."

"Good triumphs over evil." Sadie raised the bottle in a toast before setting it on the counter. "I love when that happens."

Kane handed a customer two bottles of Corona, a lime quarter wedged in each one. "Give the ladies that round on the house," he told Julie.

"Will do." And with that, she and her asymmetrical dark hair and neck tattoo were off again.

Sadie poured herself a glass of ginger ale. "While I have your attention—"

"You don't have my attention." He pointedly took in her cheetah-print dress, the snug material hugging her curves. "But PETA called. They'd like to talk to you about that outfit."

"Oh, ha-ha. Such wit. Ease your mind, my little animal advocate. No cheetahs were injured during the making of this dress."

"Maybe not, but you've blinded half the people in here with those tights."

She glanced down at the neon pink covering her legs. Grinned. "Just trying to bring a little bit of brightness to this dreary place. Unfortunately, I won't be able to do so next weekend as I need it off. That's the whole weekend—two days. Two. Don't try to schedule me for Saturday night and then claim you thought I meant only Friday."

"You don't seem to get how this works," he said. "I'm the boss. I write the paychecks. I make the rules."

And holy shit, but he had sounded just like his father.

"Yes, yes," Sadie agreed pushing her fluffy blond hair from her shoulder. "You're the big boss man. You have all the power in this relationship while I am just an employee, et cetera and so forth."

"Glad you finally see things my way."

"And as your employee, I'm giving you advance notice that I will be unable to work next weekend."

"No."

"You don't seem to get how this works," she said, throwing his words back at him with a sunny grin that made his left eye twitch. "I'm not asking for permission. I'm telling you I'm not working next weekend. James and I are going out of town."

Sadie and James had become an official couple not long after Kane kicked Sadie and Charlotte out of his apartment last fall. They lived together. Why did they have to go out of town?

"You have to work." He kept his tone calm. No sense losing his temper or his control. Though dealing with Sadie Nixon would be enough to make the most patient man lose his cool. "I already gave Mary Susan the weekend off so she could drive down to see her granddaughter in some school play."

Sadie patted his arm, all faux conciliatory, as if

the headache he'd developed wasn't entirely her fault. "You'll figure something out."

"Do I have any other choice?"

Frowning, she pursed her mouth as if she seriously considered his question. "You could always close the bar. Hey, you could take a little vacation yourself. You haven't had a day off since I started working here."

He finished his water, tossed the empty bottle into the recycling bin. "You take enough days off for both of us."

"So fire me."

It was one of her favorite rejoinders, one she used mostly because she knew damn well he had no intention of doing it. He hated having anyone read him so clearly. If people knew you too well, they had the power to use that knowledge against you.

"Don't think I'm not considering it."

She laughed loudly, the sound somehow rising above the bar's din. Several people—mostly men because, hey, pretty blonde in a tight, low-cut dress—glanced their way. "Oh, you slay me. You really do."

"What's so funny?" Bryce Gow, a heavyset elderly man with red cheeks and a bulbous nose, asked as he hefted himself onto a stool.

Sadie fixed his usual—rum and Coke—and set it on the bar, then leaned forward to tip her head conspiratorially toward Bryce. "Kane said he's going to fire me," she told the retired electrician.

Bryce's expression brightened, but that could've

been due to the fact that Sadie's pose gave him an excellent view of her cleavage. "Fired shmired." He sipped his drink, then patted Sadie's hand. "Quit this dump—"

"Funny how this being a dump hasn't stopped you from parking yourself on that stool every Saturday night for the past one hundred years," Kane said.

Bryce, eighty if he was a day, and a regular long before Kane had ever set foot inside O'Riley's—hell, before Kane, or even his father, had been born— glared, then turned back to Sadie. "You can work for my grandson," he told her. "He's a good boy. Respectful of his elders and his paying customers."

Kane pulled yet another beer. "Last week you said he was lazy, ungrateful and running the company you'd built into the ground. You called him an idiot who'd touched one live wire too many and fried his brain."

Bryce lowered his eyebrows. "At least he's smart enough to appreciate good employees."

"I am undervalued and underappreciated," Sadie agreed with a sigh that was pure heartfelt drama. "I would quit in a heartbeat, but if I wasn't around, poor Kane would miss me—"

"Poor Kane?" he mumbled, seriously considering sticking her head under the beer tap and giving her a good dousing. "Jesus Christ."

She batted her eyelashes at him. "And I'd hate to see a grown man as pretty as him cry."

"You're a pain in the ass."

"So I've been told," she said cheerfully. She blew him a kiss. "You know you adore me."

The worst part? It was true.

"I'm heading to the back of the bar," he said. "Give you and that big head of yours more room."

He really should fire her, he thought, as he made his way to the other end of the bar. She was flighty and unreliable, showed up for most of her shifts late, and took too many breaks when she was working.

She was also a great bartender, cheerful and chatty, always ready with a joke, a compliment or a sympathetic ear.

As much as he hated to admit it, he liked her. Hell, if he believed men and women could be friends without sex getting in the way, he might just say she was the closest thing he'd had to a friend in years.

If she ever suspected, she'd never let him hear the end of it.

"Slow night," Sadie commented, joining him.

"Not too bad," he said. "The birthday ladies alone are making us a lot of money."

"Only because every guy under the age of fifty keeps buying them drinks. Men. Always so hopeful they'll get lucky."

"It's what gets us through each day. Any of them getting pushy?"

"If they do, Julie will let you know."

He expected that. Was glad his employees knew to come to him if there was a problem. He kept an eye out for everyone in his place. Took care of them.

He'd been in Shady Grove less than a year and already he was turning into a damned Boy Scout.

For another thirty minutes, Kane filled drink orders, yakking with those who wanted to chat, leaving the ones who didn't alone with their thoughts and alcohol. The song on the jukebox ended and the familiar opening riff of Nirvana's "Smells Like Teen Spirit"—a Saturday night mainstay at O'Riley's, along with Guns n' Roses' "Sweet Child o' Mine" and Bon Jovi's "Livin' on a Prayer"—started.

It was a good song. A classic. At one time it had been one of Kane's favorites.

Until he'd seen people dance to it.

It wasn't a tune made for smooth moves, but that didn't stop a small portion of his customers. All that twitching and hopping and head-banging—most of the time simultaneously—could put off even the most die-hard Nirvana fan.

Averting his gaze from the dance floor, he opened a bottle of water and took a long drink. Scanned his domain from his position behind the bar. The booths along the back wall were filled, as were a few of the tables, late diners finishing their meals or enjoying a nightcap before heading home. The in-between stage of the evening meant those who'd come in for good food at reasonable prices mixed and mingled with the drinking crowd.

Shady Grove was a long way from Houston, but if there was one thing Kane had learned it was that people—whether at a honky-tonk stomping their cowboy boots to classic Hank Williams or in an exclusive club shaking their designer-clad asses to the latest techno hit—were the same everywhere. When Saturday night rolled around, they wanted a good time. To forget their problems, lose their inhibitions and seek out the mystical happy place where their pain magically disappeared, their checkbook wasn't overdrawn and their boss/spouse/parent/kid wasn't such a douche bag.

Only to wake up Sunday morning hungover and right back where they'd started.

Nothing sucked the life out of a good time like the real world. But, for a few hours he gave them a reprieve from their lives. That the reprieve came with copious amounts of alcohol caused him some guilt. Not so much he seriously considered turning O'Riley's into a coffee shop or bookstore, but enough that he wanted it to be more than a bar where the locals got hammered every weekend.

He'd come up with the idea of serving meals. Full dinners instead of bar fare—though they offered burgers, wings and a variety of vegetables coated in thick batter and deep-fried.

Turning O'Riley's into as much restaurant as bar had been a good idea, a smart one. An idea that had increased his business's revenue over 30 percent since the fall. He wasn't about the bottom line—that was his old man's thing—but he couldn't deny the sense of pride that came with being successful.

O'Riley's was in the black, and it was all because of him.

Not that it had been a struggling business to begin with. When Kane had first stepped into O'Riley's, it had a solid customer base, a good reputation and income enough for Gordon, the previous owner, and his one employee.

Now Kane did enough business for him to be more than generous with his six employees and still have money left over.

He should use it to buy some new chairs, maybe have the floors redone or renovate the kitchen. After all, this was his place. Every shot glass, every bottle of whiskey, every damn thing, from the beer taps to the utility bills to dealing with pain-in-the-ass customers who couldn't hold their drinks or their tempers, was his problem. He knew these people, the men and women—young, old and in between—who came here night after night, weekend after weekend. He was a business owner, a member of the Shady Grove Chamber of Commerce for Christ's sake.

In a short time, he'd somehow become enmeshed in this small town, a part of it.

He could see himself here next year. And the year after that. His roots digging deeper and deeper into the Pennsylvania ground, his ties to this community, to these people, growing tighter and tighter.

Cold touched the back of his neck. His stomach got queasy.

He'd tried ignoring the signs, had pushed aside the

sense of unease, which had dogged him for weeks, riding his back like a deranged monkey, screeching, tugging his hair and slapping him upside the head. A man could only escape the truth for so long.

It was time to move on.

He'd given it a good run, he told himself, twisting the lid onto his water bottle and setting it aside to take an order from a fortysomething-year-old guy in khakis and a button-down shirt. He drew a beer for Button-Down, exchanged it for money and added the small tip to the wide-mouth jar under the counter.

Buying this place had been an impulsive move, born of instinct and perhaps heredity. He'd seen an opportunity to take a business and build it up, make it bigger, better and more profitable.

And if that opportunity just happened to be in some small town where no one knew him or his family, far away from Houston and his past? All the better.

O'Riley's was doing well, better than he'd expected. Despite his best intentions, he'd taken after his father after all. At least in one area: making money.

But staying in one place too long was never a good idea. It made a man comfortable. Complacent. Careless.

Better to stay one step ahead. Always.

First thing Monday morning, he'd call a real estate agent, see about getting the building appraised. Start thinking about where he wanted to go next. Maybe he'd head north this time. It didn't matter where he ended up, Maine or Greenland or somewhere in between. As long as he kept moving.

IT'D TAKEN A WHILE, but Charlotte was back on the horse.

Her sneakers squeaked on the gray floor as she walked down the main hallway of Shady Grove Memorial's E.R. The baby with a high fever in room 3 cried, his scream heartbreaking and eardrum-piercing. Two middle-aged men—brothers by the resemblance between them—spoke quietly outside room 5, their faces drawn in worry.

Char approached the nurses' station. Okay, so technically there was no horse to speak of, but figuratively she was there, sitting tall in the saddle, ready to gallop after her dreams.

And to think, she'd almost talked herself into believing she'd made a mistake, a big one, in going after what she'd wanted. In planning, scheduling and goal-setting. That she could float along, living the rest of her life taking each moment as it came all willy-nilly without a thought or care about her future.

Oh, she'd tried to do exactly that. Hard not to want to try something different after you've been rejected by the man you'd planned on marrying. Throw in a second rejection, this time by a man the complete opposite of what you were looking for, and any woman would question herself, her choices. So she'd gone in the opposite direction of anything and everything she'd ever done.

She'd stuck with it for as long as she could, shoving aside her dreams and goals and letting life happen. She'd gone to the grocery store without a list, didn't note appointments in her phone's calendar and spent her weekends zoned out in front of the TV, ignoring the work needing done around her new house. For six long months she'd been laid-back, spontaneous and impractical.

It had been torture. Pure, unadulterated torture.

Until one gloomy Wednesday morning last month when, on her way to the store to buy milk after discovering the empty carton in her fridge, her car had run out of gas. Waiting for her mother to come get her, good sense returned. Once back at home, she'd immediately listed her one-month, six-month and yearlong goals, cleaned and organized her refrigerator, and balanced her checkbook and, just like that, all was right in the world again.

Sitting back and waiting didn't make things happen. It took planning. Control. Discipline. With those three things—traits she had in spades, thank you very much—anything was possible. Any goal achievable.

She walked around the high counter of the nurses' station, plugged in her laptop and printed out her patient's discharge papers. She'd been foolish, idiotic even, to try to be something she wasn't. Someone she wasn't.

Someone like her sister.

It'd taken time, but luckily she had come to her senses, Char thought as she gathered the papers and scanned them to make sure the information was correct. There was no way she could blithely toss aside all her dreams and the future she wanted.

Her mistake wasn't in believing in that future, in working toward it. No, her mistake was choosing the wrong man to share it with. Yes, technically James fit the bill when it came to the type of man she wanted to marry. He was successful and smart, handsome and kind.

It was his kindness that had done it. He'd been so sweet to her when she'd been a gawky teenager, too tall, too thin and way too awkward around the boys her own age. James had assured her those boys were blind and stupid not to notice the wonder and awesomeness that was Charlotte Ellison, and they would, one day, line up for the chance to be with her.

Alas, no lines had ever formed, but she had eventually blossomed—her mother's word for Char's miraculous transformation from a skinny, flat-chested, geeky teenager to a fashionably thin, small-chested, personable college coed.

Ah, the miracle of those latent hormones finally kicking in. She'd developed curves—slight as they were—and, more importantly, confidence. James had been right that hot, sunny Memorial Day, the day she fell and fell hard for him. The day she got it into her head he was the only man for her.

How ridiculous.

She'd developed a crush. Well, honestly, what teenage girl wouldn't when an older, darkly handsome guy smiled at her? Laughed at her jokes? Paid attention to her?

So, mistake number one? Confusing a childhood crush with true love.

Mistake number two? Not realizing the object of her affection was already in love with her sister.

Of course, it was incredibly clear in hindsight. James had always been head-over-heels for Sadie, even when they'd been just friends.

Stupid hindsight. It could have shown up a bit earlier and saved Charlotte a ton of humiliation.

Taking the papers, she went into room 1. After going over the discharge instructions for five-year-old Dallas Morrow with his mother, Char led them through the maze of hallways to the exit. Heading to the break room where she could hopefully—oh, please, please, please—have time for a quick bite to eat, or at least another cup of coffee, she turned the corner and ran into a solid body.

Strong hands gripped her upper arms, steadying her. "Hey there, gorgeous. Fancy bumping into you here."

At the husky, somewhat familiar male tone, prickles of anticipation, of excitement, tightened her skin. Breathless, her heart racing, she lifted her head. "Oh. Leo. Hi."

Leo Montesano, all six-plus feet of tall, dark and

dazzling, raised his eyebrows as he stepped back. "Ouch. No need to sound so disappointed."

Maybe she had sounded less than enthusiastic about running into him. Poor guy probably didn't know what to do with a female who didn't fall at his feet.

She smiled, both to ease her initial reaction and because, well, it wouldn't hurt to try her flirting skills on him. God knew she needed the practice. "Don't be ridiculous. What woman could be disappointed to see you?"

It went against human nature. Shaggy dark hair with just the right amount of wave fell in artful disarray around a face designed to make women thank the Lord for one of His greatest works. Brown, soulful eyes, a sharp jaw, full lips and a Roman nose completed what was, all in all, a mighty pretty package. Throw in an abundance of charm, good humor and the fact that as a firefighter he saved lives for a living, and he was the very definition of Fantasy Man.

Then again, with his perfect, muscular body—honestly, he had to spend a good portion of his day in the gym—he could be dog-ugly and dumb as dirt, and women would still write poetic odes about his broad shoulders, bulging biceps and top-notch rear.

He made a humming sound of disbelief. "Nice recovery attempt, but I saw your face. It's like you were expecting Brad Pitt and instead, you got stuck with me."

"Yes, that would be quite the letdown."

His lips quirked. Clearly the man knew what he looked like. "Who is it?"

"Who is what?" she asked over her shoulder as she walked into the empty break room.

Leo followed, leaned against the door frame. "The guy you're tossing me over for. It hurts. Really. If you're not careful, you're going to break my heart."

Pouring coffee into her favorite mug, she snorted. Oh, yeah, he was full of charm. And bull. "I highly doubt it."

He grinned, and she could've sworn she heard every female within a mile radius—along with a few angels up in heaven—sigh in pleasure. "Don't underestimate yourself."

She didn't.

But she was smart enough to know her limits. She'd learned her lesson with Kane. She'd tried out for the big leagues when she would have been better off staying on the bench. Kane and Leo were cut from the same cloth: too sexy, too enigmatic and way too experienced for the likes of little ol' her.

"Did you come in just to boost my ego?" she asked, adding cream to her coffee and pulling out a protein bar from her lunch in the fridge. "Or have your Saturday nights become so boring you've resorted to hanging out at the E.R. instead of bars?"

"Hey, now, I don't just wear this because the ladies love it," he said, gesturing to his dark firefighter uniform. "I'm on the clock. We brought in an elderly man with chest pains. The new doc is looking at him."

"Dr. Louk?" she asked, proud she sounded casual and barely curious.

Leo lifted a shoulder, not giving her any info about the new physician, such as which room he'd taken the patient to so she could oh-so-casually walk past. After she'd checked her hair and makeup, of course.

"You hear about James and Sadie taking off next weekend?" Leo asked.

Nodding, Char unwrapped the bar, bit into it and wanted to spit the chalky, faux-chocolate thing right back out. "Sadie's really looking forward to it," she said around her mouthful.

She swallowed. Considered taking another bite, but no one should ever be that hungry.

"You think it's a good idea?"

Char tucked the bar into the pocket of her scrubs. "They're going to a bed-and-breakfast outside of DC. Not traveling to some politically unstable hot spot overseas."

"No, I mean..." He stepped farther into the room and looked around. She looked, too, but the room was still empty. "Them getting married."

Charlotte went absolutely still. She laid a hand over her chest to make sure her heart still beat. "Sadie and James are eloping? Oh, she is so dead. The only question is, who'll kill her first? Your mom or mine?"

"They're not eloping. James would never do something that spontaneous."

"Then what—"

"He's going to propose to her."

"Did he tell you?" Char asked, for some reason matching Leo's scandalized whisper with one of her own.

He nodded. "Last night."

Well, what do you know? James was going to ask Sadie to marry him.

It stung. Just a little. Enough to remind Char that not long ago, she'd dreamed of James getting down on bended knee in front of her. But mostly she was happy for her sister. Really, truly happy.

She and Sadie had made up. It hadn't been easy or quick, but they were once again as close as they had been before their horrible fight. Closer—both figuratively and literally—now that Sadie lived in Shady Grove instead of traipsing around the country. It was impossible to stay mad at Sadie and, as much as it pained Char to admit it, she had, perhaps, gone a bit overboard with her crush on James.

"That's so great," Charlotte said, her smile widening as she imagined her sister's surprise. Her happiness.

"Yeah. Maybe."

"You don't think they should get married?"

"I just don't see why they want to rush into anything."

"They're both thirty-three and have known each other since they were kids. I'd hardly call that rushing."

Leo's radio went off and he checked it as he said, "You ask me, it's always too soon to commit to being with one person the rest of your life."

"That's about the sweetest thing I've ever heard," Charlotte faux-gushed. "I hadn't realized you had such a deep, emotional side. You're just a big romantic, aren't you?"

He sent her another grin, this one more devastating than the last. Seriously, if she was made of weaker stuff, she might be swooning about now. "I have plenty of emotions," he assured her. "And I'm all for commitment—for other people. Me? I like to have options. Lots and lots of options." He sent her a sharp salute. "See ya later, gorgeous."

Thank God she hadn't fallen for him, Char thought as Leo left. It'd been bad enough making that mistake with someone like James, a good guy who'd let her down as gently as possible. Sure, Leo would've been kind. He wasn't a jerk. Just careless with the hearts he held in the palm of his hand.

But women who fell for men like him—men who kept their options open, their bed partners varied and a tight grip on their single status—were only asking for heartbreak.

And she liked her heart in one piece, thanks all the same.

After rinsing out her coffee cup, she went out to triage, picked up a folder and opened it.

"Hello, Charlotte."

The papers fell from her suddenly clumsy fingers. She picked them up, swallowed, then turned. "Hello, Doctor."

She winced. Shoot. What was supposed to be a friendly, casual greeting had been more of a squeak.

"Please," he said with an easy grin. "Call me Justin."

Some doctors—mostly of the younger generation—preferred to be addressed by their given names, though she'd never do so in front of a patient.

"All right. Justin." And that was just a bit too dreamy. If she wasn't careful, he'd think she was one of the many, many nurses—along with a few female doctors and one gay anesthesiologist—who were infatuated with him.

Okay, so she *was* infatuated. She was living and breathing, wasn't she? And he looked like a young Nathan Fillion, had a runner's long, lean body and spoke with the New England accent of a Kennedy. He was also an excellent doctor, passionate about helping people and dedicated to his profession. His patients loved him. His coworkers liked and respected him.

He'd moved to Shady Grove after his residency in Philly so he could be closer to his older sister and her family in Pittsburgh. He'd quickly become a part of the community, volunteering his time at the local free clinic, sitting on the boards of several charitable organizations.

He was everything, absolutely everything, she'd ever wanted in a husband. They were going to make such a perfect couple.

She hoped it didn't take him too long before he figured that out as well.

"Dr. Louk," Regina, the triage nurse, said from behind the counter—not sounding the least bit mouse-ish, damn her, "I made some of those oatmeal cookies you like so much." She leaned forward, grinned conspiratorially. "I hid a dozen just for you in the cabinet above the microwave."

Char had to cough to hide a snort. Cookies. Rookie mistake. She'd made cookies for James and it hadn't done her any good.

"Thank you," Justin said, as polite as always. "I'd love one, but I'll have to leave the rest in the break room." He glanced at Char. "I'm training for a half marathon and I've never been good at resisting temptation."

Ducking her head to scan the chart of the ten-year-old girl who'd come in with stomach pains—and to possibly hide a small, satisfied smile—Char walked away. If she were a better person, she'd feel bad for her coworker. And while she liked Regina, and didn't wish her any ill will, she couldn't deny how happy she was the good doctor was going to stay far away from the pretty brunette's cookies.

Even better, she'd learned something new about Justin. He, too, was a runner.

Could they be any more perfect for each other?

"Charlotte," Justin called as he caught up with her. "I wanted to thank you again for recommending a real estate agent."

"You're welcome. How's the house hunting going?"

He gave a rueful shake of his head. "Not well. I'm looking for something smaller than what she's shown me so far."

"When she looks at you, she probably sees little dollar signs floating around your head." He stared at her blankly. "Because you're a doctor," Char explained. "She might be hoping you have money to burn and want something huge and obnoxious with a big enough commission for her to retire on."

He nodded sagely. "I wondered why she was so insistent on showing me that six-bedroom mansion on the outskirts of town. I guess I'm going to have to break it to her that until I've paid off my college—and med school—loans, I won't be able to afford anything bigger than a one-story, two-bedroom house."

He'd put himself through both college and med school, another point in his favor. No, she hadn't done the same, but it didn't mean she couldn't appreciate a man who was financially prudent.

Besides, if her parents hadn't paid her tuition, she wouldn't have been able to afford the down payment on her house.

Charlotte stopped outside exam room 8. "It's

tough," she said, nodding in what she hoped was a commiserative way and not in a way that made her look as if she was having a seizure. "I recently went through it when I bought my house. Luckily, I found a great place over on River Road."

"River Road…by the big steel bridge?"

Shady Grove, nestled along the winding Monongahela River, had two main bridges separating the west and east sides of town; a steel one north of the highway, and an ornate wooden structure near Washington Square park. "It's about a mile from it, yes."

He nodded at Dr. Saleh as she walked by. "That seems like a nice area."

"It is. I love it. It's not too far from the hospital, but the houses are spread out so there's plenty of room for nice-sized yards." Even if buying her house had eaten into her savings. But oh, well. Some things, such as sticking to her five-year plan, were worth a little sacrifice.

She was still on track. Even if some of the players in her game had changed.

And this player didn't seem as clueless as James had been. Yay for her. While having a simple conversation at work didn't quite compare to Justin actively pursuing her, he had initiated said conversation. He was also smiling at her. Interested in what she had to say.

Possibly even interested in her.

"If I see any houses in my neighborhood," she said, "I'll be sure to let you know."

His smile widened. "I'd appreciate it."

Appreciated it, but not enough for him to give her his cell phone number so she could get a hold of him easily.

For once, why couldn't a man she found attractive take the lead instead of leaving it up to her to do everything? If she was better at flirting, this wouldn't be so difficult. She'd drop a few hints and let Justin take it from there. But she'd never developed the art of the come-on, had always felt fake and foolish trying to be coquettish and seductive.

Proof of which was when she'd tried using her feminine wiles—as they were—on sexy Kane Bartasavich.

"Good luck with the house hunting," she said, keeping her friendly, but not too friendly, smile in place, and her tone light. She knocked on the patient's door, then went in, proud of herself for a job well done.

She hadn't pushed. Hadn't made the same mistakes she had with James, trying to rush a relationship. The old Charlotte would have tried to set up a date and time for her to show him the neighborhood, offering to cook him a homemade meal afterward.

But the new and improved Charlotte knew better. This time she was going to rein in her impatience and take things slow. Let things grow organically between her and the man she wanted.

Though she wasn't above using a bit of fertilizer if need be.

She still had her plan: to be married by the time she was twenty-seven, start having kids when she turned thirty and raise those adorable children in her house by the river.

No, the plan hadn't changed, but she'd had to adjust certain areas of it. James wasn't the man for her. They hadn't had enough in common, not nearly enough for a lifetime of marital bliss. She'd wondered about it all those months ago, had worried over it, but had brushed aside her concerns about their stilted conversations, the long, drawn-out pauses where neither seemed to know what to say. The dreaded discussions about the weather.

Whereas she and Justin were well-suited. He understood the demands of the medical profession, the long hours, difficult cases and how stressful it was caring for the ill. How hard it was to lose a patient.

She and Justin were meant to be together. Of that she was certain.

CHAPTER THREE

KANE LOCKED THE back door to O'Riley's, pulled on the handle to be sure it was secure. A light spring rain dotted his hair and shoulders, the sky an inky black. He breathed in the cool, damp air, but it did nothing to soothe the edginess inside him.

A couple blocks away, a car revved its engine before the sound faded and all turned silent again. When he'd lived in Houston, his night would be in full swing at 3:00 a.m. He'd take whatever party he'd started in the clubs back to the apartment his old man kept in the city, but rarely used. Outside, sirens would blare, alarms would sound. Inside, he'd do whatever it took to forget how much he hated his life.

How much he hated himself.

Three in the morning in Afghanistan meant being hyperalert to every sound, every slight movement, as adrenaline rushed through his body. The occasional shout or, on more than a few occasions, the *pop*, *pop*, *pop* of automatic gunfire, shattering the night. Or else it meant spending the night in the barracks, stuck in the halfway point between sleep and wakefulness. Always fitful. Always on edge.

It'd taken him months after leaving the service

before he could sleep for more than a few hours at a time. Longer before he'd become accustomed to 3:00 a.m. in Shady Grove. The quiet. The absolute stillness.

The peace.

It was that sense of calm that was getting to him, threatening to drive him crazy. There was something inside him, a restlessness he'd never outgrown, pushing him to keep moving. Job to job. Town to town. Woman to woman.

Afraid to stop.

Palming his keys, he turned the corner of the building and stepped into the alley. Slowing, he frowned. Apprehension tightened his spine. His scalp prickled with unease. The instincts he'd developed as a wet-behind-the-ears recruit in boot camp, the ones he'd honed during his eight years of active duty, kicked in. Call it a premonition, intuition or good old paranoia, but he knew he was being followed. Watched.

So much for the whole peace thing.

His muscles tensed. His grip tightened and the sharp edges of the keys dug into his palm as he glanced around. The light above the door leading to his apartment didn't do more than illuminate the entrance and throw shadows on the pavement. Kane did a slow turn.

Nothing.

Blowing out a breath, he forced his fingers open. He was getting paranoid. Small-town living. It got the best of people. Wherever he ended up next would have to have cars and bright lights and tall buildings. And people. Plenty of them.

It was easier to lose yourself in a crowd.

Mreeow.

A yellow cat darted out from behind the garbage cans. Kane didn't jump—but it was close. The cat took off across the parking lot, its tail down, ass swinging side to side as if its back legs were unable to keep up with its front ones.

As if it was trying to outrun itself.

Kane knew the feeling.

He tipped his head back and shut his eyes as the rain cooled his face. Inhaled to the count of five, then exhaled until his lungs were empty and his head light.

But the hunger inside him remained. The need, not quite as desperate as it had once been, a constant presence, a reminder of what he'd almost lost. It was nights like these where he was most vulnerable. Times when he was alone with his thoughts. His memories. When the monster inside him reared its head, demanding to be fed no matter the cost. No matter who got hurt.

Kane ground his back teeth together until his jaw ached. It was the middle of the night and he'd just spent nine straight hours on his feet followed by another hour of setting chairs onto the tables and scrubbing the bar's floor and bathrooms. Exhaustion tugged at the outer edges of his consciousness, reminding him it'd been over twenty-four hours since he slept. He should go inside, drag his sorry ass and weary body up the stairs to his apartment, then into bed.

But he'd been here before, too many times to count. The setting might change—different town, different apartment and bed—but the plot remained the same. He'd spend hours tossing and turning while the sneaky, hypnotic voice of his past whispered in his head, testing his willpower. Tempting him into giving up. Into giving in to his body's demands, just this once.

He whirled around, and with long, determined strides crossed to the small garage in the corner of the parking lot. He unlocked the side door. Inside, he pressed the automatic opener, then swung his leg over the seat of his bike while the garage door lifted. No, sleep wouldn't come tonight. Rest never came. Not for him.

He started the motor, revving the engine a few times before shooting out into the street, not bothering to lock up behind him. The wind blew his hair back. Rain stung his cheeks and eyes. At the corner, he barely slowed, then took a hard right, his rear wheel swerving for a moment on the wet pavement, much as the cat's back end had done.

Unlike the stray, Kane had learned he couldn't outrun himself or his past. But for a few hours, he could outrun his demons.

"HELLO?" ESTELLE MONROE called as she poked her head into the doorway. "Anyone here?" She waited a beat. Then two. "Hello?"

Silence.

She frowned. She didn't even want to think about why he wasn't home, safe and snug in his bed in the middle of the night. A man who looked like Kane, with his rough edges and bad-boy attitude, never lacked for female companionship.

Her mother had warned her years ago that if Estelle was going to love Kane, she couldn't be jealous of his flings, the time and attention he gave other women. She had to learn to share him.

And console herself with the fact that he always, always came back to Estelle.

With an inner shrug, she walked into the dark apartment, slipping her key into the front pocket of her jeans.

She felt a little bit like Goldilocks.

She even had the blond hair. Well, Goldilocks minus the breaking and entering, running into angry bears and eating porridge, of course.

She'd never had porridge but it did not sound very tasty.

Hefting her backpack onto her arm, she took a cautious step only to hear Kane's stern voice in her head.

Lock the damn door.

Even in her imagination, he was a grouch. That man needed more laughter in his life. For Christ-

mas this year, she was so getting him the entire set
of *Friends* DVDs.

She flipped the lock, then pulled out her phone
and used its light to guide her around a tall-backed
chair to the squat lamp on a table next to it. She
turned it on.

And wished she hadn't.

Por dios...

Because it couldn't hurt, she crossed herself, too,
since it seemed to go with the prayer and all. Or,
at least, she gave a close approximation of the way
she'd seen her best friend—*ex-best friend*—Pilar
do it. If ever there was a good time for genuflect-
ing, this was it.

Bare walls, ratty carpet and god-awful furniture
he'd probably bought secondhand, though she'd explained to him time and time again it wasn't sani-
tary. The apartment itself was tiny, a living room
that opened into a kitchen and a short hallway. The
man lived like a hermit or something. There were
no decorations anywhere, no pictures on the wall
of her or the rest of his family. Lord knew he didn't
have any friends to take snapshots of. Nothing even
matched, for Pete's sake.

Well, she decided, lifting her pack—and her
chin—higher as she headed toward the hall, she'd
just have to stick it out. The alternative was simply unacceptable. She skirted a particularly disgust-
ing-looking stain on the floor. Honestly, though, she
should get hazard pay.

It took her only a moment to find his bedroom. She probably should take a shower. But his bed looked so inviting with its heavy blanket and soft pillows. More importantly, it looked clean. Something she could achieve herself tomorrow.

She quickly changed into her oversize Texans jersey and slid beneath the covers. Her phone buzzed. Mouth tight, she checked the message.

I'm so sorry!!! Please call me!!!

Message number thirty-six. And those were just the ones Pilar had sent since Estelle landed in Pittsburgh's airport a few hours ago. Pitiful.

With a flourish, and a great deal of glee, Estelle deleted the message and tossed the phone onto the other pillow. Pilar obviously didn't understand that Estelle was not going to forgive her. Ever. There weren't enough exclamation points, sad-faced emojis and sobbing voice-mail messages in the world to make up for what she'd done.

A betrayal like that was unforgivable.

She inhaled sharply, the sound loud and mournful in the silence. What if…what if her mom thought the same thing about *her?*

Queasiness turned her stomach. A nasty, sick taste rose up in her throat. Coated her mouth.

Breathing through her nose, she shook her head. No. They were two totally different things. Pilar had gone behind Estelle's back with her secret texts and phone calls to Chandler, making sure she was there to keep him company when Estelle was busy.

All Estelle had done was be nice to Adam, her mom's fiancé. Yes, she'd flirted, but it hadn't meant anything. Surely her mom would understand that. She and Estelle were best friends, Mama always said so. There was nothing, *nothing* Estelle could do that would make Meryl stop wanting her. Stop loving her.

Estelle snuggled down until the blanket was up to her chin and said a prayer.

Just in case.

CHAR LOOKED UP from the computer at the nurses' station to see Leo—back for the third time tonight, lucky her—push a gurney into room 4, his hair and clothes wet. She caught sight of the patient's muddy, damp jeans and worn biker boots, the length of the legs, the size of the boots telling her their latest guest was a man.

She turned her attention back to the screen. Frowned when a cool breeze caressed the back of her neck. She rubbed at the spot but the tingling sensation remained. Looking up again, she tipped her head to the side, narrowed her eyes thoughtfully. There was something familiar about those legs, those boots. She knew him, she realized, walking around the high counter.

Then again, she knew most of her patients. All part of living in the same small town she'd grown up in. It was a blessing, being able to help those she cared for.

It was a curse when they were beyond help. When all she could do was offer comfort, try to ease their pain. Hold their hand while they slipped away. Then comfort the loved ones they'd left behind.

This guy didn't seem to be in that situation. No codes had been called. Thank God.

"What do we have?" she asked Leo as he stepped out of the room. She'd been with a patient and had missed the EMT report given while they'd been en route to the hospital.

Jocelyn Deems, a fellow RN, brushed past them with a wave. She would take the patient's information, get him registered into the computer system and determine the priority of the patient's treatment based on the severity of his injuries.

"Male, age thirty-four," Leo said, flipping through his book of notes. "Single vehicular accident on Songbird Lane. Patient took a corner too fast and lost control of his motorcycle. A passerby called it in, said the patient was on the side of the road, unresponsive. When we got there, he was conscious and had managed to sit up on his own. Suffered contusions and abrasions, possible concussion, rib injuries, as well as a likely fracture of right arm."

Char winced. "Ouch." She tried to look over his shoulder at his notes. "Intoxicated?"

"No, thanks," Leo said with a grin. "I'm on the clock."

"Ha-ha. I meant the patient."

"My best guess based on years of experience and, of course, my infinite wisdom would be no." Though a blood test would tell them for sure. Leo flipped his book shut. He had a thing about people reading his notes before he'd transcribed them into an official report. "So you won't have to deal with a drunk puking all over your clean exam room."

She blanched. "It was reflex, okay?"

His grin turned absolutely wicked. "Sure. Some people just can't handle certain smells. Or sounds. Or stomach contents being—"

"I get it," she said. "Jeez, you lose your cool one time and you never hear the end of it."

Most cases she handled without a problem. Blood, even copious amounts squirting from one of the main arteries? Keep pressure on it. Broken bone sticking through the skin? Make the patient as comfortable as possible and send them up to X-Ray. Mangled flesh, infected cuts, snotty noses, puss-oozing polyps? No problem.

But no matter how hard she tried, her stomach rebelled each and every time a patient puked. Oh, she did her job. Made sure the patient was taken care of, called janitorial to clean up the mess.

Then she'd head to the nearest bathroom and promptly lose whatever she had in her stomach.

It was annoying. Interfered with her doing her job. But mostly, it was humiliating.

"Nurse!"

At the sharp bark, Char jumped and whirled around. She saw Dr. Stockdale—with her linebacker's build and coarse gray hair pulled back in a severe bun—bearing down on her and Leo. The physician's high-stepping, arm-pumping walk clearly said, *I move at this incredible speed because I am superior to you in every way.*

A belief she never let the people who worked with her forget.

"You need to give her your best De Niro," Leo whispered out of the side of his mouth.

Char didn't take her eyes off the older lady. Kept her own voice low. "I think by this time in her life she has plenty of money of her own."

He laughed. "Not dinero. De. Niro. As in Robert. You know. *You talkin' to me?*"

Char snorted out a laugh, then quickly schooled her features into a calm, expectant expression. "I bet she'd just love that."

Dr. Stockdale got closer and closer, making it pretty darn obvious she was, indeed, talking to Charlotte. Char leaned back, realized what she was doing and that it could be construed as intimidation, and straightened. "Yes, Doctor?" she asked, all pleasant and professional.

Ha. Take that, you old biddy.

Dr. Stockdale, clearly not grasping the concept of personal space, didn't stop until the toes of her ugly brown pumps bumped Char's sneakers. "Why hasn't my patient been taken up for a CT scan?"

"And which patient would that be?" Char asked, sounding quite reasonable. Easy enough to do when compared with the doctor's strident tone.

Dr. Stockdale waved her hand vaguely in the direction of the west hallway. "My patient in room 9."

"I'm not actually the nurse for that patient," Char said. "But I'd be happy to find out who is and they can check on the delay for you."

"Oh, never mind," Dr. Stockdale snapped, already whirling around, the hem of her mid-calf-length skirt hitting Char's legs. "I'll do it myself." She searched the empty hallway and, despite there being no other people around, bellowed, "Nurse!" as she stormed off.

"I'm not sure which one is worse," Leo said. "Her or Hamilton."

Dr. Nathan Hamilton's resignation from the hospital—due to an icky and completely perverted incident involving a consenting twenty-two-year-old certified nursing assistant, three silk ties and a few chairs from the X-ray wing's waiting room—had led to Dr. Stockdale being hired.

It still ticked Charlotte off. Not that Hamilton had quit—she thanked God for that. But that, despite the numerous complaints filed against him, he hadn't been fired.

"You only say that because Dr. Hamilton—" also known as Hands-On Hamilton, as in he-got-his-hands-on-everyone "—didn't try to grope you on a regular basis," Charlotte told Leo.

"Don't be too sure about that."

Her eyebrows rose. "Oh, really? Do tell."

"Sorry," he said as his partner, Forrest Young,

stepped up to them. "I don't spill sordid details with a woman unless she buys me dinner first."

"You want to know something about this joker?" Forrest asked her, wrapping his arm around Leo's neck. Forrest, as homely as Leo was handsome, was a favorite among the E.R. staff due to his laid-back disposition and sense of humor. "You just ask me." He grinned and squeezed Leo's neck, causing Leo's head to bob. "I know all his secrets."

"I'll keep that in mind," she told him as Jocelyn came out of the room. Leo untangled himself from Forrest's grip and they left with a wave. Char turned to her coworker.

"He's all yours," Jocelyn said. "Though I wish I didn't have to pick up Michael from the sitter's." She nodded toward the room. "That is one seriously yummy man."

As if to make her words more believable, Jocelyn gave an exaggerated shiver of delight that had everything, breasts and ample hips especially, shimmying. Four inches shorter than Char, her friend was curvy with dark hair, red lips and nails, and a penchant for bad boys and one-night stands.

She also had a three-year-old son she adored who wasn't feeling well, forcing Jocelyn to leave work early.

"You said that about the appendectomy two weeks ago, remember? The one with the porno mustache?"

"I'm telling you, under that furry thing was a handsome man. And did you see his six-pack?"

It would have been unprofessional to point out she'd seen pretty much every inch of him. "I think I'll stick with clean-shaven men just the same."

"He—" Jocelyn jerked her thumb at the door behind Char "—has that stubbly thing going on. Plus I saw ink. You know how much I love tattoos on a man. If you're lucky, maybe you'll get to see his body art up close and personal."

"There's not much personal about helping a patient get undressed or examining them."

"Please," Jocelyn said, handing Char the patient's chart, "it's the only reason I busted my very cute butt at nursing school."

Smiling, Char shook her head and knocked on the door as Jocelyn flipped her hair and sauntered off, the very cute butt she was so proud of wiggling.

Char was still smiling as she opened the door, scanning the patient's chart. Her smile slid away when she read the name at the top of the form, written in Jocelyn's neat handwriting.

No. It couldn't be.

"If it isn't Little Red," a husky, male voice said. Her head snapped up as Kane's gaze drifted lazily over her, from the top of her hair to her sensible shoes. She had a feeling if he could have, he would have raised one eyebrow in scorn. As it was, both brows were lowered, probably due to pain. "Cute PJs."

She strangled the doorknob. Pretended it was his neck. Kept her lips pressed tightly together. It was better than informing him of the difference between sleepwear and her favorite scrubs— purple pants, lighter purple long-sleeved tee under a floral top.

She squeezed her eyes shut, but when she opened them, Kane remained. No figment of her imagination, no hallucination brought on by a strong resemblance and bad lighting. He was here.

He was also her patient. Hers to take care of.

Fan-freaking-tastic.

Damn it. She should have known it was him from the way she'd reacted to the sight of his legs. It was as if every time she was around him, her body went haywire. Hot. Then cold. Then hot again.

And that was just from getting a glance at his legs and feet. His feet, for God's sake.

He shifted. Winced and blew out a breath from between his teeth. "Speechless?"

Maybe it was the pain she saw in his eyes, the way he went white with it. Or maybe it was the decidedly missing mocking tone from his voice. Or, she thought as she took in his appearance, it could be his torn clothes and the many bloody gashes on his person. Whatever it was, she snapped out of her reverie. She had a job to do and she'd lick the bottom of his stupid, scarred boots before she'd let him get to her. Even for a moment.

Besides, it wasn't as if she could load him off onto another nurse. Well, she could, but she never shirked her duty. And if she asked someone else to take him on, they'd want to know why. She wasn't prepared to give that answer. Ever.

She crossed to stand next to his bed. "Actually, I was just lamenting about how, of all the ERs in all this great land of ours, you had to walk into mine." She pursed her lips, somehow knowing he'd hate it if she showed him too much compassion. That he'd mistake any sympathy for pity. "Then again, you didn't technically walk in." Because she figured it would annoy him, she added air quotes to the last two words.

Opening her laptop, she cleared her throat. Set the computer on the stand and plugged it in.

"Let's get some information," she said, bringing up the file Jocelyn had started. "What happened?"

"Didn't you talk with those EMT guys?"

"Yes, but—"

"Then you know what happened."

Couldn't he cooperate at all? She pushed aside her irritation and glanced up at him. His face was a sickly color now—the pain must be getting to him. She softened a bit. She hated seeing anyone suffer. She'd get him something as soon as possible.

The EMTs had taped a piece of gauze to a cut on the side of his right eye, the flesh around it already turning interesting shades of yellow and green. His hair was disheveled, his shirt wet and torn, his jeans ripped, his right arm bent at an interesting and far-from-natural angle.

"Motorcycle accident," she said, typing the words into the computer.

He shut his eyes and gingerly laid his head back. "A deer ran out in front of me. It was either lay the bike down or fly over the handlebars."

"Guess you made the right decision."

The police department would do whatever it was they did to ascertain if he'd been speeding or driving recklessly.

"Right before the accident," she said, "were you light-headed or dizzy?"

"No."

"Sick to your stomach?"

He snorted and she had no idea whether that was an affirmation or not.

"Were you drinking tonight?"

"Just water."

"What about recreational drugs?"

Now he opened his eyes, pinned her with an unreadable look. "What about them?"

Something told her to tread carefully here. It was always a sensitive subject, but one she needed to address. Too bad most people were less than forthright about their bad habits, especially the ones that were illegal. She kept her voice matter-of-fact, her expression clear and nonjudgmental. "Were you impaired in any way?"

The fingers of his left hand clenched. "I don't drink. I don't do drugs." His mouth thinned, but she wasn't sure if it was due to physical discomfort or the topic of conversation. "I went for a ride after work. The roads were wet. A deer ran out into the road and I lost control. End of story."

She picked up the electronic ear thermometer. "The EMTs' notes said you weren't wearing a helmet." Yes, her tone made it clear she was judging him. Bad enough he drove a powerful vehicle that could reach great speeds. The least he could do was protect his head. "You're lucky you weren't more seriously injured."

Or killed.

"Worried about me, Red?"

Taking his temperature, she rolled her eyes, caught herself mid-roll and pretended to be checking out a very interesting speck on the ceiling. "It's part of my job to be concerned about any and all of my patients."

"And here I thought I held a special place in your heart. With what happened between us and all."

His voice was low. Husky. It seemed to vibrate right into her chest.

Neat trick, that.

Straightening slowly, as if her inner voice wasn't screaming at her to leap back and run like mad, she gave him her haughtiest look, the one she reserved for unruly, rude or pain-in-the-rear patients.

He definitely qualified for the latter.

"Did you injure your left arm?" she asked, her cool tone daring him to make another comment about the night she'd gone to his apartment.

In answer, he held it out. She gently wrapped the

blood pressure cuff around his upper arm, unwound the stethoscope from her neck and inserted the ear tips. After taking his blood pressure, she removed the cuff and checked his pulse. Typed all three figures into his file.

"Any allergies to medications?" she asked. He shook his head. "What about tape? Latex? Iodine?"

"No."

"Are you currently taking any medications?"

He shook his head then winced.

She opened a drawer and pulled out tubing. "I'm going to get your IV started, get you something for the pain. Could you straighten your left arm for me?" she asked, pulling on sterile gloves.

She tightly tied a thick rubber band around his forearm just under his elbow, found the vein she wanted to use on the back of his hand, then disinfected the area. While it dried, she peeled open the catheter.

"You ever do this before?" Kane asked, his tone wary enough to make her glance at him.

He was staring at the catheter in her hand with what could only be described as trepidation. What was that about? She'd had plenty of people—young, old and in between—who were terrified of needles, more that weren't thrilled about them, but could handle a shot or IV being inserted as long as they didn't watch it piercing their skin. But Kane had tattoos. Several intricate, rather large ones, which would have taken hours upon hours to complete.

That's when it hit her, the realization swift and producing a giddy sort of triumph. He wasn't afraid of needles.

He was afraid of her.

CHAPTER FOUR

"YOU LOOK HAPPY," Kane grumbled, not liking the small smile playing on Red's mouth.

She made a humming sound, pure contentment and satisfaction. "Do I? Must be because I'm loving my job at the moment."

"Loving that you get to poke at me a few dozen times. Literally. With a very sharp object."

"Don't worry. I'll be gentle."

But her grin, just this side of mean, said otherwise.

He shouldn't think it looked good on her.

He shifted. Pain stabbed his ribs, shot up his side. He held his breath, kept his face expressionless, but that didn't seem to stop eagle eye from noticing. She didn't frown—her usual expression around him—but there was no ignoring the concern in her eyes.

"You okay?" she asked.

She was doing her job, and that was all he wanted from her.

He exhaled carefully. Slowly. Inhaled the same way. "You didn't answer my question."

Just as he didn't answer hers.

She noticed but didn't call him on it.

"What question?" she asked, poking and prod-

ding the back of his hand again with her finger, the
sharp point of the needle closer to his skin than he
would have liked.

He didn't mind needles, could handle pain just
fine. Though he'd rather avoid it if possible. Mostly
he didn't like the idea of her using him as a pincush-
ion. Not when he was having a hard enough time
keeping himself together. Acting calm and collected
when all he wanted was to jump off the bed and
get as far from this place, with its institutionalized
smells and windowless walls, as possible. Before he
completely lost it.

"Have you done this before?"

She raised her head, blinked at him as innocently
as a newborn babe. "Once or twice. I'm getting really good at it, too." Leaning forward, she lowered
her voice, her blue eyes wide. "With my last patient,
it took me only six or seven tries to get it right."

She was messing with him. She had to be.

He hoped.

Before he could find out, someone knocked at the
door, and Charlotte excused herself—like the polite
little nurse she probably was with every other patient—to see who was there.

A reprieve. He was smart enough to be thankful.

Then again, the more she stabbed at him, the longer his mind was occupied and he didn't have to
think about anything else. Such as how much it hurt
just to breathe. Hell, he'd gladly forgo the process
altogether if it wasn't an instinctual, and necessary,

act to remain alive. How pain swamped him with every movement, no matter how slight or how slowly done, making his stomach turn. How the mother of all headaches pounded at the base of his skull, blurring his eyesight and making him want nothing more than to go home, down a few shots of whiskey and slip into a dreamless, painless sleep.

Too bad he'd given up drinking.

But the physical discomfort was nothing compared to the memories.

The familiar sights and sounds of the hospital threatened to drag him back to the past. Reminding him of the accident that had almost cost him his life.

That had almost taken away the most precious thing in his world.

And it had been all his fault.

"Sorry about that," Red said as she returned to his side. "Okay, here we go." She bent over his hand and that's when he realized her hair was different. Short, like a pixie, the red strands loose and waving slightly. "Slight pinch," she murmured, inserting the needle into his vein.

He barely felt it.

And he'd let her rip off his good arm and beat him over the head with it before he admitted it.

She taped the port to his hand then gave it a gentle pat. "You were very brave," she told him soberly. But her eyes gleamed. "Want a lollipop?"

She smiled. A real smile, one that reached her eyes and made a dimple in her left cheek form. A sudden, vicious craving swept through him, a hunger for something sweet.

Something like skinny, small-chested Charlotte Ellison.

He must have hit his head harder than he thought.

In answer to her smart-ass question, he scowled. But that only made his head hurt more, so he stopped.

As if sensing she'd won the point, she tossed the packaging from the IV into the trash. "I'm going to let you rest. If you need anything before I get back, just press your call button."

She was leaving. He should be glad. Was glad. He could use some quiet. Some peace.

But the quiet gave him too much time to think. To remember. And peace had always been beyond his reach.

"You cut your hair."

He winced at how accusing he sounded. As if he gave a shit about it. She could shave it all off and it wouldn't matter to him.

Turning to face him, she lifted a hand toward her head only to curl her fingers into her palm and slowly lower it. "Months ago," she said as if this was old, old news and he had no reason to be bringing it up.

"Months, huh? Well, I haven't seen you at O'Riley's for a while," he said. "Must be how I missed it."

She raised both eyebrows. "I hadn't realized you'd been looking for me."

He hadn't. But he had thought of her once or twice. Dreamed of her more often than he'd liked.

And that pissed him off but good.

"Just noticed after your little visit to my apartment you've kept your distance," he said. "No need to be embarrassed, Red. You're far from the first woman to throw herself at me. You weren't even the last."

She flushed, color washing over her cheeks, a pretty pink that made her look flustered and as tasty as the lollipop she'd offered him. "How comforting. Now I can sleep peacefully as I've thought of nothing but you and that night since it happened."

It was as if she didn't really mean it. "You don't have to avoid O'Riley's. No need to hide from me, Red."

"I'm not hiding," she said, humor lacing her tone. "I've been a tad too busy to hang out at bars."

"Getting your hair cut."

She gave him that grin again, the one that had her dimple winking. "Yes. Along with a few other things, such as working, moving into and decorating my new house. And of course, working some more to pay for said house."

"Aren't you a little young to buy a house?"

"That seems to be the consensus. But please—" she held a hand out in the universal stop sign "—spare me the wisdom of your advanced years—"

"Advanced years?" he muttered, his eyes narrowing.

"I've already heard it all from my parents, Sadie, coworkers and friends. Even the loan manager at the bank acted like she wanted to pat me on the head when I signed the papers for what promised to be a long and healthy mortgage. So you see," she continued with that same grin, that same amused tone, "as much as it may shock you—and bruise what appears to be your very big ego—I haven't been avoiding you. I haven't, actually, given you much thought at all."

Obviously knowing the strength of getting the last word, she walked out of the room leaving him with his thoughts, his memories and his past sins.

KANE JERKED AWAKE, his body lurching to a sitting position. His heart raced, his chest throbbed, a cold sweat coated his skin. The remnants of his nightmare clung to his consciousness, blurring the lines between dream and reality. His throat was dry, sore, as if he'd been yelling. Screaming, like in the dream.

He covered his face with his good hand, gulped in air. The IV tugged sharply. His lungs burned, the stabbing pain almost doubling him over. Bringing with it a slow, dawning awareness. Relief.

He wasn't a terrified twenty-year-old being wheeled into St. Luke's hospital in Houston, a neck brace holding him immobile, his own injuries forcing him to lie still, leaving him to stare up at the bright lights as they raced him down the hall.

He was a grown man in a dimly lit room at Shady Grove Memorial, his arm in a sling. An hour ago they'd reset and casted his arm. They'd cut off his shirt, stripped him of his pants and checked every square inch of his person for injuries, then put him in a pair of lime-green scrubs. He'd been poked and prodded, had his blood drawn and his chest and arm X-rayed. He'd answered questions about his medical history and given his statement to the cop taking the accident report.

The panic, the fear, the coppery taste of blood filling his mouth, the frantic screams, were all part of a dream. A memory.

One he relived, over and over again.

As he should. After all, the memories deserved to be kept alive, nurtured so they didn't fade. What better way to pay homage to the moment that had, in the weird, circular way karma had of doing things, saved his life?

Made him a better man.

Someone knocked twice on the door. "Good news," Charlotte said cheerily as she walked into the room like a freaking ray of sunshine. "Dr. Louk is on his way."

"What?" Kane asked, his voice hoarse.

She glanced at him, her eyebrows raised. "Dr. Louk. The attending physician who did your initial exam? He's on his way to do your sutures. You'll be out of here soon."

Kane lifted his good hand, touched trembling fingers to the bandage on his forehead, then scrubbed his palm over his face. He reached for the cup of water on the table next to his bed, but misjudged the distance, knocking it over.

"Oops," Charlotte said, pulling several paper towels from the dispenser on the wall above the sink.

She lightly brushed his hand away when he went to straighten the cup. Mopping up the mess with one hand, she poured more water with the other. Tossed the towels into the trash and gave him the cup.

His hand shook. Water sloshed over the edge, splattered his arm and the leg of his jeans.

Without a word, Charlotte covered his hand with hers, helped him lift the cup to his mouth. He drank deeply.

"Thanks." His voice was gruff, and warmth crawled up the back of his neck.

She shrugged. "The meds leave some people unsteady. No big deal."

Meds they'd given him through his IV. He didn't want to take them, didn't want to need them, but he knew he did.

He hated that she was seeing him so vulnerable. So out of sorts and messed up.

She laid a sterile pad on a rolling metal tray. "I know it's been a long night. How are you holding up?"

"I'm fine."

Standing close enough so her sweet scent—the same scent that had lingered in his apartment for days after her failed seduction attempt—wrapped around him like a cloud, she studied him. Trying to see inside his head, no doubt. Gauging his mood, his words, to see if they were the truth.

"You don't look fine." Her voice gentled, and he hated that almost as much as the sympathy in her eyes. She set her hand on his shoulder, her touch light, her fingers warm. "Are you having pain?"

He wanted, more than he could admit even to himself, for her to keep her hand there. To reach up and link his fingers with hers, to hold on to something real. Something to ground him in the here and now, to yank him out of his past.

In the guise of sitting up, he shifted and her hand dropped back to her side. "I've had worse."

"Oh. Well, good. Not good you've had worse pain," she rushed on, a blush staining her cheeks. "But that it's not that bad now."

He'd embarrassed her. Flustered her. He hadn't meant to. He didn't care about the pain, he just wanted out of the hospital.

Before he lost what little control he had left.

The medicine they were pumping into him made his head heavy, his thoughts blurry—like when he'd spent most of his time wasted, wanting nothing more than the next high. The room, the sights and smells of the hospital, the sound of doctors being paged, of codes being called, tortured him with memories.

The only time he could breathe, could forget for a few minutes where he was, could pretend his past wasn't pressing down on him, was when Red came in the room.

She was a distraction, he assured himself. That was all. A way for him to forget the pain. Yes, she was interesting and intelligent and, he supposed, attractive in a unique way. But that wasn't why she occupied his thoughts. Focusing on her was a way to keep his control.

She looked so naive. Innocent. It was partly the freckles, he thought, taking in her profile as she laid out the instruments needed for his stitches. Hard to come across as mature and tough when it looked as if God himself had sprinkled cuteness across your nose and upper cheeks. Or maybe it was her hair. No adult should have hair that bright.

But, he had to admit, the particular shade of orangey-red suited her, went with the pale creaminess of her skin, the new super-short cut accentuating the sharp angle of her jaw, the shape of her eyes.

She was in her element here, surrounded by the sick and injured, the constant noise and odd smells. Gone was the awkward, slightly gawky girl he'd first met at his bar when he'd pissed her off by asking to see her ID. There was no sign of the angry woman who, a few weeks later, had accused her older sister of stealing her one true love, or the nervous, desperate woman who'd come to his apartment. Here she was confident and in control. In charge.

It suited her.

Someone knocked and the doctor, the one who looked like some actor Kane couldn't quite put a name to, came in.

"How are we doing, Mr. Bartasavich?" Dr. Movie-

Star asked in nasally, flat tones that should be illegal in the good old U.S. of A.

"If I had to guess," Kane said, tired enough to let out his own accent, "I'd say you're doing a hell of a lot better than me at the moment."

Washing his hands, the doctor grinned at Kane over his shoulder. "I'd have to agree with you."

Charlotte took the bandage off Kane's cut and cleaned the cut, then the doctor gave him a shot to numb the area. Kane almost asked to forgo that step. The sting would give him something else to focus on, something other than the panic trying to wash over him.

But he wasn't a masochist. Just completely messed up.

"We'll give it a few minutes to work," the doctor said while Char cleaned up once again.

They left. He almost called Char back, almost said something else like his inane comment about her hair to keep her in the room with him. It was easier when she was with him, all bright and capable and whip-smart. But once she left, it was as if she took all the air in the room with her. His heart rate increased. The memories threatened, there, at the edge of his mind, pushing, pushing, pushing to be let loose.

He stared at the TV mounted on the wall, the images of an old movie flashing by, the sound muted. Concentrated on nothing more than his next careful breath. Inhaling, he filled his lungs, his ribs pinching, and counted to five. Exhaled for another five. Again. And again.

Finally, they returned. "All right," the doctor said, putting on the gloves Red handed him. "Let's get this done so you can go home."

He could do this. He *could* do this. But his stomach turned. His throat tightened.

The doctor put in the first stitch. Other than a slight tugging, Kane didn't feel anything, but anxiety settled in his chest, growing and growing, pushing even the shallowest breath from his lungs.

Bile rose. He swallowed it down and stared at a spot above the doctor's head. Tried to forget.

"You okay?"

Red's voice, calm and concerned. He couldn't speak, though, and nodding while someone stitched his skin together didn't seem like the best idea.

She moved to the other side of the bed, brushed her fingers against his forearm. "It's okay," she said softly. "You're doing great."

And she covered his hand with hers.

He jolted. Met her eyes.

The doctor said something in a sharp tone, but Kane didn't catch it. Couldn't. The blood was rushing in his ears, a roar of sound drowning out everything else. Until Red spoke, barely above a murmur, but to him her voice was clear, the low, soothing tones easing the ache in his chest.

"Try to stay still." She sent him a small smile. Gave his fingers a squeeze. "Only a few more."

Moving was not an option. He was frozen, held immobile by her light touch, the feel of her cool fingers on the back of his hand, the power of her gaze on his. He should pull away. Let her know in no uncertain terms he didn't want her assurance. Didn't need her comfort.

He sure as hell didn't deserve it.

But he was weak. So weak he turned his hand, linked his fingers with hers and held on tight.

THERE WAS SOMETHING wrong with Kane.

Something other than the injuries he'd sustained, Charlotte amended. Something—dare she say?—deeper. Emotional or psychological or a combination of both. Something that had him clutching her hand as if the link between them, the very basic, instinctive need for human contact—skin-to-skin—was the only real thing in his life. The only thing keeping him grounded.

Keeping him safe.

She would have shaken her head if she hadn't been afraid to break the eye contact between them. Keeping him safe? Some sort of deep, emotional issue? Please. Her imagination was running wild.

There was nothing deep or emotional about Kane. He was hard, caustic and cynical. Thinking there was more to him was ridiculous. Thinking he needed her to protect him from a few stitches, to save him from whatever had produced the haunted look in his eyes, bordered on delusional.

And she was too smart, too careful and way too afraid of making another grand mistake to let delusions ruin her life again.

But that didn't stop her from murmuring nonsense to him, careful to keep her voice soft, her tone calm as she repeated how great he was doing, that it'd all be over in a few minutes and he just needed to hang in there. She was there for him.

Time slowed. She had no idea how long they stayed that way, eyes locked, hands clasped. All sound seemed to dissipate so even her own words disappeared, though she kept up the mindless chatter. Her entire world narrowed so the only thing she saw was Kane. Color slowly seeped back into his face. His gaze sharpened, came back into focus. His hand warmed against hers, his palm rough, his fingers twitching with every pull of the thread. He inhaled, quick and shallow.

"You're okay." She kept her voice quiet, her own breathing deep and even in the hopes he'd follow suit. "You're okay."

"Last two stitches," Justin said, his low tone mimicking her own.

She stood, but Kane didn't let go. She patted his hand. "It's all right now. Dr. Louk is done, but he needs my help." For a moment, she was afraid Kane didn't hear or understand what she was saying. But then he slowly, reluctantly, slid his hand from hers.

Wiping her tingling palm down the front of her thigh, she crossed to the hand sanitizer on the wall, cleaned her hands, then walked around the bed, all the while hyperaware of Kane's intense gaze on her. She held the scissors out for Justin, hating the unsteadiness of her hands, of her heart. The way her mind raced with questions, with concerns. She wanted to get to the bottom of Kane's behavior, wanted to ask him what had brought it on, what she could do to help him.

She must be a complete idiot.

Because no matter what had come over Kane, the last thing she needed was to try to fix him.

One of the most difficult lessons she'd had to learn as a nurse was no matter how hard she tried, no matter her education or experience, no matter how skillful the physicians, how quick the first responders, they couldn't save everyone.

Some people were beyond help.

And she was done fighting lost causes.

Justin tied off the last stitch, cut the thread and studied his handiwork. He gave a short, satisfied nod at the row of neat, tiny stitches. Stood. "All done."

Thank God.

Charlotte blocked the sound of his very nice voice giving Kane instructions on caring for the stitches. As she cleaned up, she avoided any and all eye contact with Kane.

Hey, she'd already slipped there for a moment, thinking he was some troubled, tormented man wanting only to escape the mysterious pain dogging his heels.

Wanting only to heal him.

She snorted softly. Realizing the room had gone silent, she lifted her head. Her face warmed. Oops. Guess her snort hadn't been quite as soft as she'd hoped. Both men stared at her. She coughed gently. Cleared her throat, then smiled at no one in particular. "I'll get the discharge papers."

By the time the papers had printed, she was calmer. Clearheaded. It had been a long night, after all. In less than fifteen minutes, her twelve-hour shift would end. She'd go home, get something to eat, maybe veg out in front of the TV for an hour and then get some much-needed sleep.

She'd stop thinking about hard-eyed Kane Bartasavich. Stop worrying about him.

She watched Justin come out of Kane's room. She'd get back to thinking about her future husband.

"Very good work in there, Doctor," she called to him.

Humble, wonderful man that he was, he grinned shyly as he joined her. "Thank you. But I doubt things would have gone as smoothly as they did if you hadn't kept the patient so calm." He paused, used his fingertip to move a paper clip on the desk from side to side. "Are you two...close?"

"Who?" Realization dawned and she laughed, the sound more horror-filled than amused. "Me and Kane? No."

"You held his hand."

Her eyes narrowed. Was that an accusing tone she heard? "He needed me. I would have done the same for anyone."

"Right. Of course. Sorry. It was just… I thought…" He shook his head, a blush climbing his neck. "I thought maybe you and he were…friends."

Except the way he said it made it clear he thought she and Kane were more than that. Could he be… Was he…jealous? And if he was, shouldn't she be thrilled instead of irritated?

"Well, we're not. Friends, that is." She doubted someone like Kane even had friends. "He's my sister's boss, but he and I barely know each other."

"Has your sister ever mentioned his problems with PTSD?"

"You think Kane is suffering from post-traumatic stress disorder?" Was it even possible when he acted so emotionless all the time?

"If I had to guess," Justin said reluctantly, making it clear he did not like something as nebulous as guesswork, "then I'd have to say yes. The hospital where I did my residency had an affiliation with a local VA hospital and Mr. Bartasavich is displaying several signs similar to what I saw during my shifts there."

"Sadie never said anything about it," Charlotte said, staring at Kane's door as if she could somehow see him through the wood. See if he was okay.

"Then again, I doubt he'd mention it. He was in the service, though. He served in Afghanistan."

Though anyone could suffer from PTSD, not just veterans.

"There's nothing in his history," Justin said, pointing to the computer screen where he'd pulled up Kane's medical records. Shrugging, he closed out the program. "Maybe I'm wrong."

He pulled the next chart in the rotation. Charlotte wanted to snatch it from his hands, toss it aside. Wanted to demand he dig a little deeper into Kane's past, figure out what had happened to him. But Justin was already on to the next case. As she should be, would be, once she got Kane discharged. It wasn't up to her to get to the bottom of his problems.

His demons weren't any of her concern.

CHAPTER FIVE

"You're all set," she said as she entered his room. Kane sat on the side of the bed, his booted feet on the floor. How he pulled his boots on, she had no idea. Must have been a painful experience. He looked much better, though; his face had color again, some of it bruising, but still... "Dr. Louk did a great job with the stitches." They didn't have a plastic surgeon on staff, but luckily, Justin did excellent work. "I doubt you'll even have much of a scar."

Kane just glanced at her, a flick of his cool green eyes saying she couldn't possibly bore him more.

So they were back to that, huh?

"Then again," she said, her smile more of a gritting of teeth, "you probably don't care about a scar as it would make the poor, simpering ladies swoon over your pretty face even harder than they do now."

"You gonna swoon over me, Red?" he asked in an odd, low tone.

Or maybe it was her reaction to it, to his question, that was odd, the way her stomach tumbled. Her pulse skittered.

"Sorry. My supervisor frowns on us swooning

while on duty." She held out a paper for him to sign. "Here are the rest of your discharge papers."

She cleaned her hands and put on gloves. Removing his IV, she went over everything he was and was not allowed to do, in order to let his ribs heal. She explained about setting up an appointment with the orthopedic surgeon to have his arm X-rayed a week from now, repeated Justin's instructions for how to care for his stitches…and realized he wasn't listening to a dang thing she said.

She set her hands on her hips. "Did you catch all of that?"

"Do this," he said wearily, "don't do that, and a lot of blah, blah, blah."

Really. Why did she bother? "So succinct. Though in the medical profession we prefer to use yada, yada, yada."

His lips twitched. "As long as we're on the same page."

They weren't. How could they be when he refused to even open the book? But she wasn't about to argue with him. She'd had her fair share of stubborn patients, and she had gone over everything. In detail. Whether he chose to follow the doctor's instructions wasn't up to her.

"Here's your script for pain meds," she said, handing it and a prescription bottle to him, "along with enough to get you through until tomorrow when you can fill it at the pharmacy."

He eyed both warily. "Are they necessary?"

Since he still hadn't taken them, she tucked them into a small plastic bag. "That would depend on your level of pain now, wouldn't it? Don't take them on an empty stomach and don't take more than two in the same dosing period. If, by Monday, you're still in pain that's over a five on a scale of one to ten, call your primary care physician about getting a higher dose or new prescription."

Still, he hadn't moved. She shook the bag so the pills rattled and he finally took them.

He stood and she quickly stepped back, but when his face went white with pain, his lips pressed together, she reached out. Steadied him.

"Okay?" she asked.

He nodded. Seemed to have some heavy internal debate before exhaling heavily. "Thanks."

She couldn't help it. She grinned. "Wow. So polite. Those pain meds really are miracle workers."

If possible, his expression got tighter. Darker.

What had she said?

Before she could decide whether or not to ask—or apologize, which for some crazy reason she felt the need to do—he brushed past her, his steps slow and measured, his left arm wrapped around his ribs as if holding them in place.

"Hold on," she said, hurrying past him. "I'll get you a wheelchair."

He pinned her with his flat gaze. "You're kidding."

"I don't kid about the hospital being liable if you fall flat on your face before reaching the exit."

"Your concern is touching."

"Hey, I'm very concerned."

"About lawsuits."

She nodded. "About lawsuits."

"I don't need a wheelchair."

As if to prove it, he skirted around her, opened the door and walked out.

She debated for all of ten seconds whether or not to just let him go, but in the end, her basic humanity won out.

Stupid humanity.

Catching up with him was easy enough since he'd gotten only a few feet, and now stood glancing around as if unsure which way to go.

"This way," she told him, gesturing to the right.

They walked side by side down the brightly lit corridor, the harsh lighting only proving how truly horrible Kane looked. They turned left, then left again. She hit the big red button to open the automatic swinging doors and stepped out into the cool early morning with him.

She lifted a hand to the EMTs getting in the ambulance. Behind them, a car pulled in and a young mother holding a crying, red-faced toddler got out and hurried inside. "Where's your ride?" Char asked, the breeze ruffling the ends of her hair.

"I'm walking. See ya, Red."

And damn if he didn't start doing just that. For a moment, she simply stared, her mouth hanging open like a fish washed up on shore. Finally, she snapped out of her stupor—brought on by a long shift, lack of sleep and dealing with more than one bozo. The King Bozo was now making his way toward the road.

She jogged over to him and carefully caught his good arm, stopping him before he could cross the street. "Whoa, whoa, whoa. You can't walk home."

"Neither of my legs are broken so I'm pretty sure I can."

"Yes, but…but…"

"For Christ's sake," he said, irritated and grumpy, as if she was the one being a major pain in the butt. "Spit it out."

"It's at least two miles," she said, somehow able to keep the snap out of her voice. It helped to remind herself that he, too, was exhausted plus he'd been in a motorcycle accident.

It helped, but not enough for her to forget his default mode was jerk-wad.

"You'll be lucky to get there before the sun comes up," she continued.

"Then I'd better get going."

"Oh, for God's sake…" The man took stubbornness to whole new heights. "Don't you have someone you could call? What about Sadie?"

"I'm not getting one of my employees out of bed on a Sunday morning, especially after she worked until 2:00 a.m. last night."

"Why not? I'm sure she'd be—"

"No."

"So call someone else to give you a ride home."

"There's no one to call."

She laughed, the sound dying when she realized he was serious. "Oh, come on, now. Everybody has at least one person they can call, one person they can count on to have their back."

She had several. Her parents and Sadie of course, but also her cousin Harper. Jenn, her ex-roommate, a couple of girlfriends from college and high school, and even one or two coworkers.

Kane didn't answer, though, and that, in and of itself, was all she needed to know.

He'd lived in Shady Grove for what...a year? A little less? And he still hadn't made any friends, didn't feel close enough to the people he did know to impose on them. Didn't have anyone he could call to let them know he'd been hurt, to sit in the waiting room worrying while he was being examined and X-rayed. No one to keep him company, to lift his spirits while he was stuck in a hospital bed for hours. No one to take him home, then check in on him every day to make sure he was all right.

He didn't have anyone.

She had a feeling, a weird premonition his lack of social circle was somehow going to become her problem. Possibly even her undoing.

No. That was silly. This had nothing to do with her and everything to do with his being aloof and unlikable.

"The sooner you let go of me," Kane said, his words slurring slightly, "the sooner I can get home."

Her hold on him tightened. She shifted her weight to the left. Then back to the right. Tried like mad to keep the words forming in her throat from bubbling out. She clenched her teeth together. Reminded herself, rather sternly, she was in no way, shape or form, responsible for making sure Kane got home safely. She didn't even like him, for goodness' sake. Why on earth would she even consider going out of her way for him?

Because he's your patient. Because he's hurting. Because he has no one else.

The first two reasons rolled off her back. The third, however, stuck.

"Come on," she groused.

"Where are we going?" He sounded merely curious and didn't resist when she tugged him back toward the hospital. He must be worse off than she thought. Or else those pain meds were making him more amenable.

"I'm clocking out." They stepped up to the emergency room doors, walked through after they swished open. "And then I'm taking you home."

SHE WAS LIKE some incredibly annoying, stubborn, fiery-haired guardian angel, Kane thought, as he and Red climbed the stairs to his apartment. She hovered at his side, one hand behind his back, close enough that every once in a while, her fingers brushed his shirt, the other under his good arm. As if she and the force of her will alone were enough to stop him, to catch him, should he decide that falling off his bike wasn't enough for the day and he'd like to take a tumble down the stairs, too.

She wasn't any happier to be here playing the role of saving grace than he was to have her. Yet she'd still insisted on seeing him home, despite his best efforts to dissuade her.

Not that he'd tried very hard. Not when the alternative meant his walking two miles.

He may not want her help, but he wasn't stupid enough to cut off his nose to spite his face.

Each step caused pain to shoot up his side, as if someone thought it would be fun to stab him repeatedly and often with a thick needle. Every inch of his body hurt. His legs felt as if they weighed two hundred pounds each. His muscles trembled.

Kane refused to let any of it show. No easy task, but if Red sensed any weakness in him, if he gave even the slightest hint he was unable to take care of himself, she'd never leave.

He wanted her gone. Needed her gone. He hated that she was seeing him at his weakest—and he didn't mean physically. When the doctor had done his stitches, there had been concern in her eyes. Pity. Kane had let his guard down, hadn't been able to hide the panic clawing at him. Had clutched at her as if he was freaking Leonardo what's-his-name, freshly dumped from the Titanic, and she was sexy Kate Winslet, his only hope for salvation.

Too bad Kane was way beyond saving.

Halfway up the stairs, he paused. Pretended it was so he could scratch an itch near his stitches, but was really so he could catch his breath. Damn it, he'd forgotten how painful cracked ribs were.

He started climbing again and Red was right there with him, watching him like a blue-eyed hawk. Back at the hospital parking lot, she'd asked if he needed help getting into her car. He hadn't responded, just sent her a hard look guaranteed to let her know he could get into the damn car on his own. She'd rolled her eyes, but had kept her mouth shut while he'd struggled to lower himself into the passenger seat.

She hadn't spoken since.

He wondered if he could get lucky enough for that to stick for the rest of their time together. Their hopefully brief time together. Or, better yet, for the rest of their lives?

A man could dream.

Finally, they reached his door. Sweat coated his skin, his breathing ragged. He lifted his left arm slowly, wiped the dampness from his forehead with the back of his wrist.

"Aren't you going to open it?" Red asked in her exasperated, impatient tone. As if dealing with him pushed her right to the edge of insanity.

"I've got it from here." Because she probably wouldn't leave until he'd displayed the correct amount of gratitude, he added a gruff, "Thanks for the ride."

"What kind of person would I be if I didn't see you safely inside?"

"The kind I don't want around?"

"It's shocking, really, you don't have any friends. I mean, you're so charming and gracious and all."

Friends. Christ. That was the last thing he needed. Relationships. People with expectations of him. Wanting more from him than he could give.

He'd left his jeans in the hospital, but had remembered to take his wallet and keys and put them into the pockets of his borrowed scrubs. Mouth tight, well aware Charlotte watched his every move, he gingerly reached across his body, tried to slide his left hand into the right front pocket.

He hissed out a breath. Shit.

Dropping his arm, he sent her a narrow look. "Don't. Say. It."

She held up her hands. "Say what?"

And that innocent tone wouldn't fool a deaf man. "Anything."

She mimed a zipper being pulled across her mouth. If only.

Then she stood there. Silent, yes, but also not making a move to help him.

"Could you get the damn key?" he snapped.

She raised her eyebrows.

"Please," he ground out from between his clenched teeth.

"How can I refuse after you asked so nicely?" She stepped forward only to pause as if just realizing where she had to put her hand. How close she had to get to him. "I swear to God, if you make one snide comment or a sleazy innuendo, I will poke you in the ribs. Hard."

Holding her gaze, he brought his left hand up, mimicked her zipping motion.

She ducked her head, but hesitated again, her teeth worrying her lower lip.

Then, resolute thing she was, she inhaled and slipped the tips of her fingers into his pocket. With a sound of frustration that sounded oddly sexual to him, she stepped closer, dipping her hand farther into the pocket. If his entire body didn't hurt like a son of a bitch, he might be able to appreciate the feel of her knuckles pressing against his hip, how the warmth from her hand seemed to seep through the fabric to brand his skin.

Her fingers curled around the key and she dragged it out. Raising her head, her hair brushing against his chin, she stepped back, a blush staining her cheeks. Then, before he could snatch the key from her, she turned, unlocked the door and let herself into his apartment.

"Well?" she asked, setting the key on the table. "You coming in or not?"

Stepping inside, he left the door open, hoping she'd get the hint. "Do you barge uninvited into other people's apartments or am I just special?"

"I'm here in a professional capacity."

She shut the door.

He tipped his head back. "I'm in hell."

"Not yet," she said, way too cheerfully for his taste or peace of mind. "But give it time. I'm sure you'll end up there eventually."

He crossed the room and gingerly lowered himself onto the couch. "What are you doing now?" he grumbled while she banged around in his kitchen.

She opened a cabinet, wrinkled her nose at the contents then closed it again. Opened another one. "Getting you something to eat. Don't you have any soup?"

"I'm not hungry." He sounded like a spoiled ten-year-old, but he was tired and his entire body hurt. "I'm just going to go to bed."

As soon as he could stand up again.

Obviously giving up on finding what she was looking for, she opened the fridge, pulled out a stick of butter and the block of cheddar cheese. "You need to eat. You're due for another dose of your pain meds and there's less chance of you getting sick to your stomach if it's not empty."

He'd lied. He really was hungry. Maybe that was why he didn't argue anymore. Then again, arguing with any female was pointless. With this one, it seemed especially so.

He watched as she sliced cheese, then layered it onto a piece of bread. Her movements were quick and efficient, as if she couldn't wait to be done so she could hurry and collect her good-deed medal. Watching her wasn't a hardship, though. She was thin, yes, but his initial view of her as being all lines and angles was off base, he thought, his gaze taking in the slight indentation of her waist, the slope of her hips. Her legs were long, and he couldn't help but wonder what she'd look like in a skirt. A really short one.

He liked the image. Too much. Before he did something incredibly stupid like start seriously considering ways to charm Red into his bed, he shut his eyes. Drifted in and out of sleep until she set a plate on the table in front of him.

He opened his eyes, saw a grilled-cheese sandwich, cut into two neat triangles, along with a glass of water.

She shook a pain pill into her palm, held it out for him.

He looked at it then up at her face. "If I'd known the E.R. staff made house calls, I would've requested the brunette who took my medical history."

Red blushed. She did that a lot and easily. Must be her fair skin. Every flush showed. If he touched her now, cupped her face in his hand, he bet her skin would be soft and incredibly warm.

But when she spoke, her words were cool. "I'll be sure to let Jocelyn know you're interested."

"No need." She'd already given him her number. He'd tossed it in the trash can.

Charlotte waved her hand in front of his face. "Are you going to take this? Or do you need me to crush it up into some applesauce for you?"

Sitting up was a struggle, but he managed. He bit

into his sandwich. Chewed and swallowed. "I don't need it."

"You might not think you need it right this minute, but you should take it every four hours. They're not as effective if you take them after you start hurting again."

Hurting again? He hadn't stopped since he'd come to on the side of the road.

"I don't want to get hooked on them."

He fisted his good hand in his lap. Damn it, he hadn't meant to say that. Had never wanted anyone, least of all Red here, to know he'd been an addict. But he was so terrified of becoming dependent on anything again he'd gladly offer up what was left of his pride if it meant staying clean.

At least she didn't laugh. But she did smile, one of those patient, condescending grins medical professionals were so good at. "You won't become addicted—"

"You don't know that." He kept his gaze on the second half of his sandwich. "A few years ago I had...I had a...problem. With drugs and alcohol."

If you called being drunk and high more often than sober a problem.

"Oh," she said softly, not giving him any hint as to what she thought of his confession.

She sat on the table, her knees brushing his. He didn't look at her. Couldn't. Told himself it was because he didn't want to see her judgment of him, but he wondered, worried, if there was more to it than that. As if he cared what she thought about him.

"There are resources available locally." She laid her fingertips on the back of his right hand below his cast. He stared at that, the sight of her long pale fingers with the neatly shaped nails on his hand. Was mesmerized by it. "Alcoholics Anonymous for one. I can get you the infor—"

"I'm not much of a joiner." Because he liked the compassion in her tone, the feel of her skin against his way too much, he smirked. Pulled away from her touch. "I'm clean now. I just want to be careful."

Didn't want to take any chances when it came to his sobriety. Not when he'd fought so long and hard to achieve it. He had people depending on him to stay strong.

She nodded, her fingers curling on her thigh. "I don't think you need to worry about becoming dependent on the pain pills, especially after only a few doses. But if it'll ease your mind, I can look into getting you a new prescription. There are other medications you can take, ones that people with a history of…of…"

He leaned back, exhausted and more than ready for this entire shitty experience to be over. "You can say it, Red. Drug abuse. I was an addict."

His past, the mistakes he'd made, the person he'd been, didn't embarrass him.

It shamed him.

But it should give her a clear picture of what he'd

been. Prove to her once and for all he wasn't worthy of her time, her concern.

Her mouth turned down slightly at the corners. Funny how that move, too, brought out the hint of her dimple. "Medications that people with a history of addiction can safely take."

She stressed the word *addiction* as if to prove she wasn't scared of it. Or him.

Once again she held out her palm, showing him the pill. He stared at it. Hated that he wanted it so badly, wanted nothing more than to slide into the oblivion only drugs and sleep could provide.

His fingernails dug into his palm, a bone-deep fear keeping him from reaching for the small pill.

"Kane," Red said, all compassion and patience, "have you had counseling?"

One side of his mouth kicked up. "From the time I was ten until I turned eighteen."

Her eyes widened, her mouth parted. "Actually, I meant if you've had it specifically for your experiences in the military."

"We're all given a mental health review when we're discharged."

She scooted even closer, her knee pressing against his. "But it's been a few years since you were discharged. Maybe talking to someone now will help you deal with your memories."

Women. They all thought talking solved any problem. Some things were better left unsaid. "I'm good."

"Obviously you're not." Her tone was soft, the

hand she laid on his knee warm. His thigh muscles tensed. "There's nothing to be ashamed of. Many soldiers turn to drugs and alcohol to deal with the effects of PTSD."

"I didn't start using because of PTSD or because of my time in the Rangers." It was one of the things he was most proud of, that he'd managed to stay clean after his discharge.

"But you had an episode. When you got your stitches," she added, as if he needed reminding of how he'd lost control.

"I didn't have an episode." Whatever the hell that meant. "I just don't like hospitals."

Too bad he hadn't realized exactly how much he hated them until he'd been stuck there.

"Are you sure?" she asked. "Because Dr. Louk has worked with veterans and he said you displayed symptoms—"

"For Christ's sake," he grumbled, "do you ever let anything go?"

She bristled. Slid her hand from his leg and crossed her arms. "Not when it's important."

"This isn't." *He* wasn't important. Not enough for her to worry about. But he'd hurt her feelings; it was clear by the pout in her bottom lip, the lowering of her eyebrows.

Damn it, he was the injured party here—literally. So why should he feel bad about not wanting to share every tiny piece of himself with her? He'd already humiliated himself in front of her in the E.R. Had just admitted his greatest secret to her. He didn't owe her anything else.

Wouldn't owe her anything else if she hadn't held his hand while he'd gotten his stitches. If she hadn't insisted on bringing him home and then made him a sandwich. If she hadn't accepted his admission about being an ex-junkie without batting an eye.

Damn her.

"What happened back at the E.R…" he began, but then had to stop and search for the right words. Confession might be good for the soul, but it was hell on the pride. "The reason I…acted that way…wasn't from a flashback or memory of the war. I was in a car accident when I was twenty, a bad one, and I guess being in the hospital brought it all back."

Some of the rigidness left her shoulders. Her mouth relaxed. "You don't have to tell me about it if you don't want to."

"I know. Which is why I'm not going to." He had a right to keep certain things to himself. "There's a bottle of pain reliever in the cabinet above the microwave. I'll take a couple of those."

She got the bottle from the kitchen, shook two into her palm. "I wish you would have said something about your past in the E.R. We would have made sure to give you a non-narcotic."

"I don't like sharing my history with people."

"Yet you told me."

"Yes. I told you." He held out his hand.

She stared at it, then lifted her gaze to his face trying, he knew, to see his thoughts. Judging if she could trust him or not.

But that's not what this was about. This was about him letting her know he trusted her.

In this, at least.

Finally, Charlotte laid the pills in his palm, the tips of her fingers trailing against his skin. He swallowed the medicine with a long drink of water.

"Now," she said, wrapping her fingers around his left arm and tugging, "we can get you into bed."

He didn't move. "You offered to get me into bed once before." He settled his head back against the couch and shut his eyes. Going to bed sounded great. Except the part about actually getting up and walking all the way to his bedroom. "Remember?"

"Hard to forget when you keep reminding me. But you're in no shape to do me or any other woman any good in bed right now."

She sounded so certain. Amused. She was right. He was in no shape to take a woman to bed. But it pinched his ego just the same.

He opened his eyes to find her leaning over him, close enough for him to count those freckles adorning her nose and upper cheeks. Their gazes locked. The air between them stilled. Heated. And damn himself for wanting to close the distance between them. For wanting to capture that smart-ass mouth of hers with his.

He didn't so much as blink, barely breathed, afraid if he moved even the slightest bit, he'd do just that. "Want to bet?"

CHAPTER SIX

Kane's words washed over her, his voice low and husky. Sexy. She couldn't think. Her body was warm, her thoughts hazy. His words buzzed in her head, indecipherable. Incomprehensible.

Want to bet?

Her brain clicked into gear again and she jerked back, as if he'd decided to show her how wrong her assumption of his prowess was. Luckily, he hadn't moved.

Unfortunately, he hadn't moved.

She was still close to him, too close, her knees pressed against his, one hand still holding his arm, the other sinking into the cushion by his hip.

His gaze dropped lazily to her mouth. "Or maybe you want to see for yourself?"

See for her—

Realization dawned. Her palms grew damp. Her scalp prickled. Oh, dear God.

She leaped to her feet and practically hurdled the table, her knee catching the pointed corner with a dull thud. She inhaled sharply, tears springing to her eyes. Turning, she pretended to rearrange his empty plate with the water glass. His gaze burned a hole in the spot between her shoulder blades.

She shut her eyes and took a moment to catch her breath, to calm her racing heart.

Holy spit, even banged up, bruised and mildly concussed, sex appeal rolled off the man as if he were producing the stuff to sell wholesale. Oh, she'd dodged a bullet when he'd turned her down all those months ago. More like she'd dodged a big, bad, lethal cannonball that had the potential to rip her world apart. Sleeping with Kane Bartasavich would have been one of those mistakes in life you never forgot.

Or got over.

"Not interested in taking that bet?" he asked in a husky tone, a hint of an accent, Southern, maybe, slipping into his voice.

Giving him the not-in-a-million-years-or-even-if-you-had-a-million-dollars look she'd seen Jocelyn use both at work and when they'd gone out clubbing, Charlotte straightened. "I'm not much of a gambler. I prefer a sure thing over some nebulous big payoff. Besides," she couldn't help but point out, "you're not interested in me. Remember?"

"Maybe I've changed my mind."

Did his voice have to be so deep? So compelling with that previously unnoticed twang? Did he have to be so damned seductive in that *wrong for her, but oh so tempting* way?

For a moment, one brief, delicious second, she imagined what it would be like if he were being truthful and sincere. What it would be like to be wanted by a man like him.

No doubt it would be flattering. Thrilling.

And out-and-out terrifying.

"Nothing's changed," she told him, needing to believe it herself, if only for her own peace of mind. "You're tired and, if I had to guess, feeling a little loopy from the pain meds. Don't worry, after a few hours of sleep, you'll go back to thinking I'm completely unattractive."

"I never said you were unattractive," he mumbled, his words slurring, his eyes drifting closed.

Giving her an opportunity to make a face at him. No, he hadn't said that. There was no need, not when he'd made his feelings for her perfectly clear. It wasn't like he needed to whap her upside the head with a bat to let her know she did nothing for him.

His shoulders relaxed, his expression softening as he sank into the couch cushions. Well, guess he was comfy. And really, she'd already gone above and beyond the call of duty as it were. He'd been fed and given his medication. There wasn't much else she could do for him. She should go home, get some sleep herself…after she cleaned up his kitchen.

Call it a character flaw, but she couldn't, in good conscience, leave the man dirty dishes to deal with. She'd have nightmares of her mother finding out and scalding her ears with one of her lectures on the right thing to do and the horrors of waking up to find plates with dried-on food stacked in the sink.

A few minutes later, she was washing the plate and glass he'd used, along with the few dirty items left in the sink. When she was done, she wiped off the counters. After laying the dishcloth on the sink, she wiped her wet fingers on her pants, then picked up the prescription bottle she'd left on the table. She opened it. Two pills were left. Justin had given Kane only enough to get him through until he could fill his prescription at the pharmacy—which didn't open until noon on Sundays.

She nibbled her lower lip, stared at the bottle.

I was an addict.

It explained quite a bit. Why he was so hard. So cynical. What had he survived? Had he grown up on the streets, struggling to get by, and turned to drugs and alcohol to forget his horrible circumstances? Was he neglected? Abused? Or had he started using while he was in the service, a way to forget the things he'd seen? The things he'd had to do while protecting his country, his fellow soldiers?

What demons was he fighting?

She squeezed the bottle so hard she was surprised she didn't dent it. No, she didn't think a few pills were going to push Kane back into addiction, but he'd been worried about it. Worried enough he'd opened up to her, admitting something that obviously bothered him.

He'd trusted her when she said he'd be okay.

She put the cap back on the bottle, then slipped it into the pocket of her tunic and called the E.R. Justin was off duty so she spoke with Dr. Fitton about getting a new prescription faxed in. Char would call the pharmacy later and ask them to deliver it so Kane wouldn't have to worry about going out.

She brushed her hands together then, because she totally deserved it, gave herself a nice little pat on the back for a job well done.

When she returned to the living room, she found Kane sound asleep, still sitting up on the couch, his head back, his mouth open.

Sleep didn't soften his appearance much, though he didn't come across quite as imposing as when those cool green eyes of his were opened and focused on her. She stepped closer, weighing her options. He was home and he was fine, his belly fed, his pain meds in him. She could go, leave him to rest, even if that rest meant he'd wake with a stiff neck.

Or she could wake him, help him to his bedroom, pull off his boots, remove the scratchy, too-tight scrub top and tuck him safely into bed.

She imagined it, as clearly as if she'd done it dozens of times before. She'd slide his shirt up, her knuckles grazing the flat planes of his stomach while he watched her out of hooded eyes, that damn smirk of his playing on his mouth. Then he'd say something, something inflammatory or just plain antagonistic, something guaranteed to tick her off.

Since neither leaving nor helping him into bed suited her, she'd go with a happy medium. A compromise, one that would enable her to help him and keep her pride. Win, win.

She leaned over him. Paused. Okay, so maybe he did look softer in sleep, his expression relaxed, the bruising stark against the paleness of his skin. His hair was mussed, a lock of it falling over his forehead. She smoothed it back, marveled at how it could be so soft, his skin so warm when he was so cold. So hard. Maybe that was why she gently combed her fingers through his hair, once…twice. Or maybe she'd simply lost her mind and, along with it, her good sense. Because when she glanced at his face, she found him watching her.

She held her breath, waited for his smart comment, the sharp bite of his tongue. And almost swallowed her own when he did finally speak.

"You didn't leave." His voice was heavy with fatigue. With wonder and, if she wasn't mistaken, gratitude.

"No." She slowly pulled her hand away. Tried to smile in a purely professional manner as if she hadn't been caught fondling his hair while he slept, like some perverted nurse in a horror film. "I didn't leave. I thought I'd help you get more comfortable first."

Yes, that was it. She was concerned only with his comfort, which was why she was sighing and mooning over his hair—his disheveled, badly-in-need-of-a-cut hair, for God's sake.

"Here," she added, wrapping her arm around his shoulder and pulling him forward. "Let's get you stretched out a bit, then you can go nighty-night and I can go home."

She grabbed a square pillow from the ugly chair and set it against the couch's armrest. Kneeling in front of him, she untied his boots and tugged them off, well aware of his eyes on her. She liked it better, liked him better, when he was asleep. She set the boots aside and straightened. She wanted to leave him that way, she really, really did, but his shirt was too small and not very warm.

Crap.

"Can you stand?" she asked.

"Don't wanna," he murmured.

Poor guy must be exhausted. "Okay," she said, eyeing him like a general studying a battle plan. "We'll do this with you sitting."

She took off his sling then reached around him and gently slid the hem of his shirt up. He was remarkably compliant, lifting his good arm without a word, letting her pull the shirt over his head and then down the arm with the cast.

Yep, those tattoos were still there, along with some bruising on his right side and an ugly scrape above his hip.

"Your turn," he said with a crooked, not-quite-with-it grin.

"Yeah, that's not going to happen." She dropped the shirt to the floor, then riffled through the laundry basket by the table.

She found a worn sweatshirt, the cuffs frayed,

the material thin and soft from repeated washings. She hesitantly brought it to her nose. Sniffed. Clean. Great. She pulled it over his head.

"You took your shirt off the last time you were here," he said when his face was visible again.

"True. But all of my clothes are staying on this visit."

He looked comically disappointed. "I liked your last visit better."

"You must." She helped his arms into the sleeves. "You keep talking about it."

"It was a memorable experience." He slid his finger up her arm, eliciting goose bumps and a weird sense of longing inside her. "I'll never forget how you looked standing in my kitchen in your jeans and bra."

She wanted to slap his hand away, had to remind herself he was injured and under the influence of pain meds. But still, he had a lot of nerve saying that. Hadn't he humiliated her enough that morning? "Please. You can barely remember my name, let alone what I look like."

"I remember your name." He settled his hand on her hip, slipped the very tips of his fingers under the hems of her tunic and the T-shirt beneath. "Charlotte."

She shivered at the combination of his nails lightly scraping her skin and the sound of him saying her name slowly, drawing it out as if tasting it on his tongue. Savoring it.

"I remember everything about that morning," he

continued softly as if talking to himself. Confusing her even more with his quiet words, his thumb now rubbing the slope of her waist. "Standing there in your black, lacy bra, your skin so smooth and pale. Your hair like a sunset, all bright and flaming. I wish I could forget. I want to forget. But I can't." His fingers tensed, pressing into skin. He tilted his head back, held her gaze. "I dream of you, Red."

Oh. My. God.

Her breath shuddered out. A flush crept up her body from her toes to her scalp, leaving all sorts of interesting and dangerous tingles in its wake. Only to be doused by a wave of sanity, of cold, calculating reason.

He couldn't forget her? He dreamed about her?

What the hell was she supposed to think about that? How was she supposed to act? Flattered? Grateful? Oh, he was good. Excellent at drawing a woman in, making her believe every word he uttered and begging for more. But she wouldn't beg. Not any man. Not ever again.

Did he think she was so lonely, so needy she'd fall all over him because of a few pretty words? The only reason he was even saying any of those things was because he was hurt and, thanks to the pain meds working their way through his bloodstream, not in complete control of himself.

He didn't want her. Not really.

Shoving his hand away, she smirked. And hoped it was as sharp, as condescending, as the ones he always gave her. "Then I guess I was right when I said you'd be kicking your own ass for not taking me up on my offer."

He stared at his hand as if wondering why it wasn't still on her person. "I guess you were."

"Well, now you can be stuck in your misery," she told him as she helped him put his good arm into the sleeve of the sweatshirt, her moves ruthlessly controlled. "While I revel in knowing I was right."

He closed his eyes. Sighed. "You're a cold one, aren't you, Red?"

Cold? Her? Please. She was as sweet and good-natured as they came, damn it.

"What I am," she said, tugging his shirt down, then tucking her hands behind her back so she wouldn't smooth his hair, "is smart." Smart enough to learn her lesson the first time. "You sure you don't want me to help you to your bed?" She held up a hand. "And before you answer, let me make it clear that is not an invitation to join you."

"I'm good here."

She wasn't about to argue with him over where he slept. "Can you lie down on your own?"

He nodded and eased back, resting his head on the pillow. She helped lift his legs onto the couch. He put both hands on his flat stomach and she balled up another shirt from the laundry, carefully wedged it under his cast between the back of the couch and his side.

She straightened. Turned.

His good hand shot out, grabbed her wrist, his eyes closed, his voice low and rough. "Stay with me."

She tried to tug free, but it was no use. "I have to go."

She was tired, closing in on exhausted, and that exhaustion was playing tricks on her mind. Had her thinking maybe Kane wasn't an arrogant ass. That there was more to him than his good looks and bad attitude, both of which drew women to him like suicidal moths to a bonfire.

He really was dangerous. And she was a girl used to playing it safe.

"You'll be okay," she assured him. Still, he held on tight, reminding her of how he'd clung to her while he'd gotten his stitches. She crouched next to his side, gentled her tone. "I'm going to get you a blanket. I'll be right back."

"Promise," he murmured, his eyes staring into hers as if knowing she prided herself on never breaking her word. "Promise you'll stay."

He needed her. She wasn't sure whether to sigh, scream or run like hell. Knew there was only one thing for her to do. Stay.

"I promise."

His fingers loosened enough for her to slip free of his grip. His breathing relaxed.

Now she was stuck.

Staying meant she was in very real danger of losing her sanity, her peace of mind. Shaking her head, she hurried to the bedroom. She'd get a blanket, tuck him in all nice and snug, then curl up on the chair. Hopefully, he'd only be out an hour or two. Once he woke up, he'd realize he was fine on his own and let her go on her merry way.

She thought about his reaction to being in the hospital, his admission to being an addict, how he'd seemed so ashamed and lost. So...damaged.

Okay, so he obviously needed someone. But that didn't mean she had to volunteer. She wasn't looking to be anyone's crutch.

Besides, some people were beyond help. Kane Bartasavich being at the top of that particular list.

Her resolve firmly in hand, she slapped on the light to his bedroom.

And wasn't sure who was more shocked. Her.

Or the gorgeous blonde in Kane's bed.

ESTELLE JACKKNIFED INTO a sitting position, her fingers brushing a thin blanket and not the fluffy down of her white comforter. Her heart pounded, her pulse mimicking it at the corner of her jaw. Blinking at the horrible, painfully bright light, she glanced around, frantic to see ugly beige walls and some sort of ancient brown carpet.

Where were the clean lines of her room, the white tree she'd painted on the black wall, the black-and-white photos of her friends and narrow planks of the wood floor? Where was her stuff, her clothes and jewelry, the self-portraits she'd done; stark, penciled sketches showing herself at five, eight, eleven and fourteen? Where was the photo of her parents, the only one of them together, taken at her dance recital four years ago?

"Uh…good morning," a female voice said. "And who might you be?"

For a moment, in that no-man's-land between wakefulness and sleep, Estelle thought Meryl stood in the doorway. Except her mother had never sounded so wary.

Plus, she didn't often ask who Estelle was.

Frowning, Estelle pressed the heels of her hands against her eyes. Reality kicked in as it often did, hard and swift, followed quickly by clarity. She lowered her arms, focused on the tall, thin redhead across the room. Of course that wasn't her beautiful blonde mother, with her perfectly applied makeup, expensive clothes and toned, perpetually tanned body standing there.

Her mother was far, far away. Was probably at this moment lying on the Saint Tropez beach, her string bikini showcasing her recently upgraded breasts, and the results of a no carb, no sugar, no flour, no fun diet and the two hours spent sweating with her personal trainer six days a week.

Her mother hadn't come for her. She probably didn't even know Estelle was gone.

She was in Kane's run-down apartment. In his bedroom.

"Are you going to answer me?" that same voice asked. "Or do I need to call the police?"

Estelle blinked, realized her mouth was open—which was so unattractive. She snapped her lips shut. "The police? Why on earth would you do that?"

The redheaded amazon in the doorway looked at her as if she was a brainless idiot just because she was blonde, built and beautiful. People always underestimated her, just because she was as lovely as her mother.

But her brains? Those she got from her dad.

"I should call the police," the redhead said slowly, "because you broke in here."

"Hardly. I used my key."

"Okay, well how about I call them because you could be a stalker or a psychopath."

A psychopath? Harsh. "That's not very nice," she said as she struggled to kick the covers off. She stood and held her hands out as if to indicate her very sane, very perfectly normal self. "Do I look like a psychopath? And for the record, I have never stalked anyone. No matter what Michael Langworthy said."

"Tell me the truth," the redhead said quietly, as if they were in church. Or trying to gossip in study hall. "Are you…are you sleeping with Kane?"

Estelle reared back, her face scrunched up. "Eww. Eww! No. God." She shuddered. Maybe she should be worried this chick was the psycho. "Eww. I just threw up in my mouth."

The redhead pressed her fingers against her temples as if she had a headache. A lot of people did that when Estelle spoke with them. "Then why are you in his bed at 7:00 a.m. looking so…" She indicated Estelle's bare legs, waved vaguely at her head. "Disheveled?"

Estelle tucked her hair behind her ears, knowing it was the best she could do without a brush or a hair band. "Uh, I'm disheveled because you woke me up."

Duh.

"Okay. Well, good. That's good. And it means I wasn't completely wrong to start thinking Kane isn't a total ass."

Estelle rolled her eyes. "Of course he's not a *total* ass. Don't get me wrong, he has his moments. Like last year when all I wanted for Christmas was to go to Cancún with my friends and he was like, completely unreasonable just because Terrance had one underage citation and—"

"Why would Kane care if you went to Cancún?"

"I know, right? He didn't care when I went to Paris, which is like, even farther away. But that was okay because it was a school trip. And there was the time Granddad wanted to buy me a horse—"

"No, no. I mean why, specifically, would Kane care, or have a say in where you go or what you do?"

Estelle frowned, her feelings hurt. She didn't expect Kane to blab about her to everyone he met, but you'd think he could tell the women he slept with she existed.

"He has a say," Estelle told her, "because he's my dad."

CHAPTER SEVEN

THE REDHEAD DIDN'T look so good. All the color—
and there hadn't been much to begin with—drained
from her face, making her freckles stand out even
more. Her eyes were unblinking, and she was breathing funny, like an invisible noose was tightening
around her neck.

"Are you okay?" Estelle asked, approaching her
slowly. Great, if she broke her dad's latest…what-
ever…he'd never let her move in with him. "Can I
get you something? Some water?"

Finally, the redhead blinked. "Kane's your dad?"

Hadn't she just said that? You'd think her dad
could pick someone a little brighter. And closer to
his own age. "Yes. I'm Estelle Monroe," she said,
her mama's lessons on manners firmly ingrained.
She sent the redhead a small, polite smile and held
out her hand.

"Monroe?" the redhead asked, giving Estelle's
hand a firm shake. "Not Bartasavich?"

Estelle kept right on smiling. "That's right. And
you are?"

"Charlotte Ellison."

"Have you and my dad been...seeing...each other long?"

Seeing...sleeping with. Same thing when it came to her dad. He didn't do relationships, not even casual ones. He barely had a relationship with her and she was pretty certain she was his favorite person in the whole world.

Charlotte was cute, like one of those fairies in the picture books Meryl used to read to Estelle when she was little. She hadn't known her dad liked cute.

To each their own.

"We're not... Oh, that's right," Charlotte murmured, looking worried. "You don't know. About the accident."

"Accident?" Estelle asked sharply. "What accident?"

"Your father was in a motorcycle accident last night. He's okay," Charlotte added quickly, probably because for a moment there, Estelle felt ready to pass out.

Crossing her arms, she dug her nails into her biceps. It hurt. This was real. Not a nightmare. But Charlotte had said Kane was okay. She took in Charlotte's scrubs. "Are you his doctor?"

"I'm a nurse. I took care of Kane at the E.R. tonight."

"Is that where he is?" Estelle asked, already searching the room for her jeans. Spying them on the floor next to her backpack, she swept them up and tugged them on. "Can you take me there?"

"He was discharged. He's home now."

"He's home?" Then he couldn't be that hurt. Please, please, God, don't let him be that hurt. "He's here?"

"Whoa." Charlotte grabbed Estelle's forearm, stopping her before she made it to the hallway. "Slow down."

Estelle stiffened. "Let go of me," she said through numb lips, her voice strangled and weak when she'd meant to sound strong. Brave.

Like she should have been brave with Adam.

Charlotte held both hands up in an exaggerated motion, as if to show she was harmless. "I just didn't want you running out there, making a lot of noise. He's sleeping."

That made sense. What didn't make sense was Charlotte being here in the first place. A horrible, tragic thought occurred to her. "His injuries are severe, aren't they? They're so bad there was nothing else you could do for him at the hospital so you sent him to die in his dumpy apartment surrounded by his crappy things."

"Wow, that was quiet the leap in logic," Charlotte said, her lips twitching. "I brought him home because he couldn't drive himself, but he was discharged with a clean bill of health. Well, clean with the exceptions of a broken arm, cracked ribs, stitches and mild concussion."

Each listed injury was like a punch in the stomach. Her poor dad. "If you're trying to reassure me, you're doing a really terrible job."

"He's going to be fine. Honestly."

"Can I see him? I'll be quiet."

"Sure. I'm going to get a blanket for him, but you can go on out. I'll warn you, though," she said over her shoulder as she crossed to the bed, "he's pretty banged up and not looking his best."

A moment later, Estelle stared down at her dad. Didn't look his best? That was like saying Channing Tatum was a little bit good-looking. Her throat tightened, her nose stung. But her dad would hate her crying over him like he was in a casket or something, so she bit her lower lip hard. Fought back the tears.

His face was sickly pale, an ugly bruise forming on his right eye. The skin above his eyebrow was red from the row of black stitches. His right arm was in a cast, the fingers sticking out from it puffy.

Charlotte joined her and laid the blanket that had been on the bed over Kane. He didn't stir, not even when she touched her fingertips to the back of his right hand where the plaster ended.

"He looks like he's in a coma or something," Estelle whispered.

"That's the miracle of today's pharmaceuticals. The pain pill he took causes drowsiness, plus he's been through quite a lot. He needs his rest."

Nibbling on her thumbnail, she nodded. "That makes sense." She fought a yawn, and lost. "Since he's so out of it, I guess I'll go back to bed, too. What time does your shift end?"

"Shift? At the hospital? It ended an hour ago when I brought your dad home."

"No, I mean, your shift here." When Charlotte looked at her in total confusion—another expression Estelle was used to getting—Estelle added, "Aren't you my dad's private nurse?"

"No," CHARLOTTE SAID on a short laugh. "I'm not your dad's private anything. He's more than capable of taking care of himself."

Stay with me.

She pressed her lips together until they turned numb. He hadn't meant that. It was the drugs talking.

Still, she'd promised…

"But someone is coming over, right?" Estelle asked. "To, like, help him if he needs it, to take care of the cooking and cleaning and stuff?"

"Kane could definitely hire someone to assist him with everyday tasks if he feels that's necessary. Though he won't be able to until Monday."

It was a good idea. One Char should have thought of and brought up to Kane herself. And she would have.

If he didn't constantly frustrate, annoy and, yes, surprise her.

"Now that you're here," she continued, "I guess he won't have to."

"What do you mean?"

Char almost laughed again, but swallowed it back when she realized the girl was serious. Serious and seriously clueless. "I mean you can wash the dishes, do the laundry and light housework—"

Estelle giggled. "I don't think so. After all, I'm a Bartasavich."

"I thought you said your last name was Monroe?"

Estelle waved that away with one perfectly manicured hand, her short nails painted a dark blue. "Bartasaviches don't wash dishes or scrub floors."

Well, well, well. Seemed Kane's daughter here was a princess of the highest caliber.

If she really was Kane's daughter.

Char had been so shocked when Estelle had claimed that title, she hadn't questioned it. She couldn't help but do so now. What proof did she have, anyway, other than the teenager's word?

Charlotte studied her, trying to find Kane in Estelle's fine features. No luck.

But even with her long golden hair a tangled mess and dark makeup smudged under her brown eyes, Estelle had the type of angelic beauty that eluded most mere mortals.

Just like Kane.

Except Char would bet money Estelle was more devil than angel.

Just like Kane.

But that didn't mean they were related.

"Does Kane know you're here?" Charlotte asked.

Estelle rolled her eyes. But she also shifted and twisted a lock of hair around her finger. "Of course."

"Really?" And Char sounded exactly like her own mother when Irene hadn't believed a word coming out of a teenage Charlotte's mouth. "Then why didn't he mention it? Not once while he was in the E.R. or when we got back here did he say anything about you being in town."

"He was probably in so much pain, he forgot. Plus," she added, in a tone most people only used when shouting *Eureka,* "he's always been horrible with dates. He probably thinks I'm not coming until next weekend."

"Hmm. Probably."

Char wasn't buying it for a moment.

Kane stirred and shifted. Winced.

Charlotte motioned for Estelle to follow her into the kitchen.

"Ugh," Estelle said when she joined Char by the microwave. "It's even uglier in here."

Char couldn't argue with that. "Why do I get the feeling you're hiding something?"

"God. Suspicious, much?" Estelle brought her hair forward over her shoulder, started combing her fingers through it. "Do you want to know what I think?"

"I can barely contain my curiosity," Charlotte said, meaning it. She didn't believe everything that came out of Estelle's mouth, but that didn't mean she didn't find the teen's tidbits fascinating. And wildly entertaining.

"I think you're trying to divert attention from the real question here. Which is—why are you here?"

"I told you—"

"Yes, but why did you bring him home? Or is that some small-town thing where nurses drive patients home? Because that's just weird."

"That would be weird, except Kane and I know each other. My sister works for him at the bar."

"So you're friends."

Barely. "Yes. Plus, I felt bad for him."

She had, she insisted to herself as guilt poked her, incessant and irritating. Okay, so maybe part of her, a small, tiny part, had hoped that by helping him, she'd get to feel—and this wasn't easy to admit—superior.

Or better yet, he'd feel indebted to her. Grateful.

Shame filled her, effectively shoving that guilt far, far away.

Time to look at this rationally. She had an unconscious man in the living room, his could-be daughter in the kitchen and the promise she'd made to stay echoing in her head.

"Why don't you go back to bed," she told Estelle, "try to get some more sleep. When Kane wakes up, we can figure out what he wants to do about bringing someone in to help around here while his injuries heal."

"We? So you're staying, too?"

A sigh rippled through Char, shuddering out before she could stop it. "I'm staying."

KANE AWOKE WITH a groan as pain shot up his side. His dry mouth, pounding head and queasy stomach all reminded him of the many mornings—or afternoons—after a bender, his brain fuzzy, memories of the night before hazy. Or worse, nonexistent.

Fear coated his throat. Had he fallen off the wagon? He shifted onto his back, felt something heavy on his arm. Using what seemed like a Herculean effort, he lifted his head, saw the cast decorating his right arm. It all came back to him in a painful flash.

The pressure of staying in one place too long had gotten to him. He brought his good arm up, covered his eyes. And he, being the idiot he was, had thought a good way of dealing with that pressure was to drive his motorcycle like a bat out of hell on wet, slick roads.

Not his finest hour.

He shoved the blanket that was covering him to the floor. The blanket that was usually on his bed. Charlotte must have done that, must have made sure he was all snug and warm. He remembered her bringing him home, his confession about being a former addict, but then things got hazy.

He just hoped he didn't say or do anything else that was going to come back and bite him in the ass.

He rolled over and, ignoring the ache in his side, pushed up into a sitting position, the cast weighing heavily without his sling. Breathing hurt as much as it did last night, if not more, the fingers of his right arm were stiff and swollen, the stitches in his face stung and itched.

All letting him know he was still alive.

Whoop-de-freaking-doo.

Not that he had a death wish or anything. Being alive was all well and good, especially since he had work to do. The bar needed to be restocked, inventory taken and paperwork handled. Tomorrow, he'd contact a real estate agent about putting O'Riley's up for sale.

He'd been looking for a sign, something to let him know it was time to move on. Last night had taken care of that. He didn't need to hit his head twice before he got the message.

Standing, he shut his eyes against a wave of dizziness. When he opened them again, he caught a bright flash of color from the corner of his eye.

A bright flash of red.

He pressed his forefinger and thumb against his closed eyes but when he dropped his hand and opened them again, the image was still here.

Charlotte Ellison, curled up in his chair, fast asleep.

He'd thought he was in hell last night when she'd refused to leave him alone. What had she said? Something about him getting to the fiery depths eventually.

Eventually was here.

He frowned at Charlotte. Her legs were bent, the side of her head leaning against the back of the chair at an awkward angle guaranteed to give her a sore neck. Her shoes were lined up next to the chair leg, her arms crossed.

She'd stayed.

Something niggled at the edge of his brain, remnants of a conversation between them, but the images were vague, the words unclear. He needed coffee, a shower and copious amounts of over-the-counter pain medication.

Not necessarily in that order.

He dragged the blanket behind him as he crossed to the chair. Stared at Charlotte for a moment. She didn't look peaceful, not with her mouth open and her neck bent that way, but she did look sort of sweet with the faint color in her cheeks, her expression soft.

There'd been a time when he'd been big for sweets. For anything and everything that was decadent, sinful or just plain bad for him.

Thank God those days were over.

He covered her, the simple task hampered by his injuries, but he managed to get the blanket spread over her legs. The other corner was stuck on the edge of the cushion. Crouching slowly, he winced at the pain in his side, then pulled the blanket free and tugged it over her arms.

He glanced up and found her staring at him.

"Hi."

Her voice was soft. Husky. Her breath warm as it washed over his face.

Speech was beyond him so he nodded in greeting.

Told himself to ease back, but his body didn't seem to be listening to his brain.

"What are you doing?" she whispered.

"You looked cold…" The rest was self-evident so he lifted his left shoulder, only able to achieve an inch or so of height, but she got the idea.

She uncrossed her arms and rubbed the edge of the blanket between her forefinger and thumb. "You covered me?" Her voice was still soft, as if she was in that halfway point between wake and sleep and didn't want to ruin a good dream. "That was nice of you."

And she smiled at him, a sleepy half smile that was somehow wistful and sexy at the same time. Something caught in his chest, like a hand squeezing the air from his lungs. A craving for her dug in with sharp claws, taking hold of his willpower. His good sense.

Before he could regain either, he leaned forward and pressed his mouth to hers.

She gasped, the sound rushing through him like a windstorm, blowing everything out of his mind except the taste of her. Her hands flew to his chest, but she didn't push him away. Not yet. So he kissed her again, slowly, carefully, doing his damnedest to coax a response from her. Her shoulders relaxed; her body lost its stiffness.

And she kissed him back, hesitantly. Sweetly.

Sweet, that was what she was, despite her smart mouth and cocky attitude. Too goddamn sweet for the likes of him with her big heart and willingness to help others. To help him. He'd end the kiss, end this madness…

In a minute. Or two.

Her hands slid up, one curving over his good shoulder, settling there lightly, the other tangling in his hair. He cupped her cheek with his left hand, the tips of his fingers pressing into the back of her long neck, his thumb on her jawline. He deepened the kiss, flicking his tongue over the right corner of her mouth. Then the left.

And went suddenly, viciously hard when she did the same to him.

A low, desperate sound ripped from his throat as he jerked her to him and kissed her harder, deeper, his tongue sweeping inside her mouth. Her hand tightened, tugging at his hair, the sharp bite only adding to his hunger. The beast inside him, the one he'd long ago caged, reared up, snarling and snapping, demanding to be fed.

He wanted to devour Charlotte. To take whatever she gave until his pain was gone, until he stopped yearning for something—alcohol, drugs, or those prescription pills that were close by—to take the edge off.

This, he thought, rising up so he was pressed against Charlotte's slight curves, her breasts brushing his chest, this would work. Being with Charlotte, surrounded by her scent, accepted by her body, moving inside her, would take away his pain. At least for a little while.

But when they were done? When the sweat had dried, when their hearts no longer raced and their bodies' desires were satiated? He'd still feel empty inside.

Worse, he was afraid that so would she.

He pushed to his feet. Pain rocketed through him, turned his stomach, had him swaying. Before he could even catch his breath, Charlotte was next to him, a steady, solid presence at his side, one hand at his lower back, the other under his good arm.

"Why don't you sit down," she said in her soothing nurse's tone as she led him toward the chair.

He shook his head. Afraid to open his mouth in case the whimper trying to work its way up his throat should get out. He stared at her. He was an idiot. An asshole for taking advantage of her like that, kissing her that way when she'd barely even been awake.

"Why the hell did you stay here?"

He winced. That hadn't been what he'd wanted to say. What he'd meant to say.

I'm sorry.

Two simple words. Simple to everyone but a Bartasavich. But those words hadn't come out. Only a low growl of accusation.

"I'm still here," she said slowly, as if he should already know her answer, "because you asked me to stay with you."

His head snapped back as if he'd been punched. "What?"

"You wanted to know why I stayed. It was because you asked me to."

He stilled, his shoulders going rigid. "I asked?"

"Yes."

"I asked you to stay."

"You seem confused, so let me make this as clear as possible. I wanted to leave, but you asked me not to, so I didn't."

A memory, faint as a wisp of smoke, floated through his brain.

Stay with me.

His voice. His words.

Hell.

"You could have left after I fell asleep," he grumbled.

"After you begged me not to?" Eyes wide, she shook her head. "What kind of person would that make me?"

"Begged?" Pinching the bridge of his nose, he muttered one word—a very succinct curse—under his breath. Dropped his hand and glared at her. "I need coffee."

Except when he got into the kitchen, he realized there was no way he'd be able to get the grounds from the upper cabinet without either passing out or crying like a baby.

Shit.

"You should have a sling on," Charlotte said as she walked into the room.

Straightening, he faced her. "I can't even get the coffee down. I doubt I'm up for turning a triangle into a sling."

She glanced from him to the upper cupboard to the material in her hand. Sighed. "Don't move."

Tossing the thin material over her shoulder, she opened the cupboard door, then rose onto her toes to reach the bag of coffee on the upper shelf.

It was far from a seductive pose, but he couldn't tear his eyes from her. His blood stirred. An image, crystal clear and unwanted, slammed into him. One of her stretched out in his bed, her short hair mussed, her blue eyes dark and heavy-lidded. In his imagination, she continued to smile at him, reach for him, her long, lean body covered only by a sheet. Her pale skin his to touch. To taste.

In reality, she lowered back to her heels and tossed the bag of coffee onto the counter, then took the material and laid one long pointed end over his left shoulder. "Lift your arm."

"You told me not to move," he reminded her.

She made a frustrated sound again, as she had when she'd been forced to dig into his pocket for his key. It yanked his mind back to his daydream, and he wondered what he'd have to do to her to elicit that enticing rumble in a sexual way.

He doubted he'd ever find out.

Shouldn't want to find out, he reminded himself, as Charlotte gently raised his broken arm and laid it across his chest, pinning the material in place. Wanting someone, something so much, was dangerous. It made you weak. Took away your control.

Hadn't he proved that already? First by asking her to stay. Then by kissing her.

Now, by wanting to kiss her again.

With quick, deft movements, she brought up the other end of the fabric, tied the points together at the side of his neck. Stepped back. "That should do until you get a regular sling."

Before he could make a mental note to do so that afternoon, she was filling the coffeepot at the sink. He didn't bother pointing out that he preferred using distilled water; he just opened the bag of coffee and measured out grounds into a filter. A few minutes later, the air filled with the scent of brewing coffee.

Since Charlotte seemed content to remain silent for the time being, Kane gladly followed suit. Never let it be said he ever did anything to encourage a woman to rip him a new one.

That he deserved to be ripped into was beside the point.

Less than ten minutes later, he was taking the first fortifying sip of coffee when she broke the silence.

"Want to tell me what that was all about?" she asked, pouring herself a cup.

He sipped again, prayed the caffeine did its work quickly. "Care to be more specific?"

She blushed and dropped her gaze. He didn't think she'd actually call him on it, on the kiss or his reaction to it. But then she lifted her chin and met his eyes.

And he knew he was screwed.

"You kissed me," she said, as if daring him to dispute that.

"I remember." He was afraid it was going to take him some time to forget.

"Why?"

Now he raised his eyebrows. Did he really need to spell that out? "The usual reasons, I suppose."

Her color deepened, but she forged ahead. He could almost admire that about her. "No, I mean what was it? Gratitude? Pity? Good old-fashioned curiosity?"

He pressed his lips together. "No."

"No?" she asked when he remained silent. "That's it, just no?"

What else did she want from him? He hadn't kissed her out of gratitude or pity. He'd kissed her because he'd wanted to. It was as simple—and as complicated—as that.

He'd kissed her because he couldn't *not* kiss her.

He'd spent so many years taking, taking, taking. Whether it was women, drugs and alcohol or something he could purchase with his old man's platinum card, if Kane wanted it, he got it. Until he'd hit rock bottom and realized nothing—not the best sex or latest designer drug or high-priced clothes—would ever be able to fill the emptiness inside him. He'd gotten clean, and had spent the past fourteen years able to withstand any temptation.

Until today. Until Charlotte.

Damn her.

"No," he repeated, angry with her for proving to be more enticing than he'd originally given her credit for. Pissed at himself for being so weak. For wanting to blame her for that weakness. "It wasn't any of those things. It was a mistake."

His. But hopefully it would be the last one he'd make around her.

CHAPTER EIGHT

IT WAS A MISTAKE.

Charlotte wanted to throw her coffee at him. But it was still hot and she'd hate to see him burned. Still, the man pushed her buttons. No doubt on purpose.

"So you mistakenly kissed me?" she asked, unsure why she felt the need for clarification when so far, all of his answers to her questions only left her more confused and embarrassed. "How, exactly, does that work? Because it seems to me, you leaning forward and placing your mouth directly on mine was a deliberate action."

Deliberate. Slow and sensual. God. Her lips still tingled, and she'd bet if she ran her tongue over them, she'd still taste him. She took a quick swallow of coffee.

"The action was deliberate," he finally said. "The mistake was in thinking it was a good idea."

That didn't clear things up at all. Men. The last time she'd kissed him—sort of—hadn't gone well, either. Then there had been the lip-lock she'd put on James when she'd been trying to convince him they were meant to be together.

If she wasn't careful, and didn't have a deep well

of self-confidence, she just might get a kissing inferiority complex.

"Of course it wasn't a good idea," she said, shooting for haughty, but coming across as just bitchy. A woman scorned and all that. "Please do me a favor and the next time you think about kissing me, don't."

"Don't think about it?"

Now he was messing with her. "Don't kiss me."

He nodded as though he was completely on board with that idea. "No problem."

No problem? *Not* kissing her was no problem?

Jerk.

His lips twitched as if fighting a smile. He'd better keep fighting or so help her, she might resort to violence. He cleared his throat. "I'm curious about one thing...."

She wasn't going to ask. She wasn't going to ask. She was not going to...

Oh, who was she kidding? "What's that?"

His gaze pinned her to the spot. "Why you kissed me back."

Her face flamed. How could she not kiss him back when he was so good at it? She'd never been kissed like that before, as if every thought he had, every minuscule part of his being, was focused on her.

As if he wanted her, bedhead, shapeless scrubs and all.

"I was still half-asleep." It wasn't quite a lie. More like a half-truth. "I wasn't completely sure what I was doing. Plus," she hurried on before he could say something else guaranteed to make her feel like even more of an idiot, "I was surprised you'd kiss me. What with your daughter sleeping down the hall and all."

Pouring more coffee into his mug, he jerked, had the hot liquid puddling on the counter before making a mad dash for the edge and dripping over the side. "What?"

His face was white, but she didn't think it was from his injuries.

"You didn't know," Char said. She shook her head. "She told me you were expecting her."

"She's here?" He looked around, expecting the teenager to materialize out of thin air. "Estelle is in Shady Grove?"

Char almost felt sorry for him, he seemed so shocked. So out of his element. "She's in your bedroom."

He slammed the pot down and hurried out of the kitchen. Charlotte tossed a few paper towels over the mess on the counter before easily catching up with him at the end of the hall.

"Estelle." Using the flat of his hand, he pounded on the door. "Open up." He juggled the knob—locked—before knocking again, this time with the side of his fist. He whirled on Charlotte. "You saw her? Spoke to her?"

"Yes and yes." She frowned at him. "You don't look so good. Why don't we go back to the living—"

"Estelle," he called again, turning back to the door.

Amazing how angry he could sound when he barely raised his voice. If she was Estelle, she'd be mighty worried about now. "If you don't open this door by the time I count to three, I'm going to kick it in. One…"

"Do you really think threats are the best way to go?" Char asked. "She's not a toddler."

"This doesn't concern you," he told Char tightly. "Two…"

"True, but I feel I have a certain vested interest, what with me making sure you survived the night and all. I'd like to make sure your daughter survives the morning."

"I only beat her on alternating Tuesdays," he said drily. He raised his voice. "But I might add in a Sunday whipping if she doesn't get her butt out here. Thr—"

The door opened. "Good morn…" Estelle's eyes widened and the serene—probably practiced—smile on her face slid away. She swallowed. Her lower lip quivered on a soft sob. "Oh, Daddy!"

And she threw herself into Kane's arms.

With a grimace and a grunt that sounded as if he'd been tackled by a 300-pound linebacker, Kane stepped back before regaining his balance. Estelle clung to him, her arms around his neck, her face buried in his good shoulder.

He lifted his arm and wrapped it around Estelle's waist. Sighed the heartfelt, resigned sigh of fathers of teenage girls everywhere and kissed the top of her head.

He was obviously in pain. Just as it was obvious he wasn't going to do anything about it. Such as tell Estelle to stop squeezing him like a boa constrictor.

Charlotte tugged on Estelle's elbow. She didn't so much as lift her head. "How about we ease off a bit?" Char asked, then gentled her voice. "Honey, you're hurting him."

Estelle loosened her hold enough that Kane was able to extricate himself. "I'm sorry," Estelle cried softly. "It's just…" She raised her head, her eyes swimming in tears. "You look so awful!"

"You saw him earlier this morning," Char reminded her.

"I know." Estelle sniffed. "But he looks worse now."

"Well, that is true. What?" Char asked when Kane glared at her. "It is."

He turned his scowl on his daughter—his daughter. Char could hardly believe it. But the proof stood before her in an oversize jersey and bare feet. And she didn't have to worry about Kane following through on his threat to beat the girl, either. The way he looked at Estelle, as if she was a precious gift he'd been given and had no idea what to do with, told Char as much.

"What are you doing here?" Kane asked Estelle.

She chewed on her thumbnail. "Maybe you should sit down."

"What did you do now?"

"Nothing. God. I just meant you know—" She gestured at his broken arm. "Because of your injuries and everything. I want you to be comfortable."

"I'd be more comfortable if you were back in Houston where you belong."

"Dad-dee," she said with an eye roll and a toss of her snarled hair before she brushed past him and padded down the hallway.

Kane went after her as fast as his healing body would let him. Char couldn't help but follow along.

"Don't you have any flavored creamer?" Estelle asked, sticking her head in the fridge, which made her jersey ride dangerously high.

"Use milk," Kane said. "And put some pants on."

Another eye roll, this one accompanied by the slamming of the refrigerator door. "Milk?" she asked, as if he'd suggested she put a drop or two of arsenic in her morning cup of joe. "Yuck. You know I like flavored creamer."

"I do know that," he said as he gingerly lowered himself to the couch. "What I didn't know was that you'd be in my apartment this morning." He turned to Char. "You knew she was here."

"Hey, don't start growling at me. She told me you were expecting her. Plus she has her own key."

"Daddy always gives me a key to his place," Estelle said, having relented and poured a good amount of milk into her coffee. She sipped it. Made a face. "This is the first time I've used one, though."

"Really?" Char sat on the opposite edge of the couch. It was her day off and she had tons to do, not to mention she could use another hour or so of sleep, but this entire scene was fascinating. And way too interesting to walk away from. "Why is that?"

They both ignored her.

"I'm not going to ask again," Kane told his daughter. "What are you doing here?"

"I had to come," she said, flopping onto the chair and tucking her legs underneath her. "If I had to stay at that bitch Pilar's house one more day, I'd die. I'd seriously die!"

"Who's Pilar?" Char asked.

"She's Estelle's best friend," Kane said.

Estelle crossed her arms. "Not anymore, she's not."

Kane's lips pinched. "You two had a fight?"

"A fight? I wouldn't waste my precious time fighting with her. If she wants Chandler so badly, she can have him."

"Your best friend stole your boyfriend?" Char asked. "That's low." She reached over and patted Estelle's knee. "I don't blame you for leaving her place."

Estelle leaned forward. "I know, right? I mean, I was going to break up with him anyway—all he ever wanted to talk about was baseball. So boring. And then I find out he and Pilar have been, like, hooking up behind my back!"

At the mention of his daughter's ex-best friend and ex-boyfriend hooking up, Kane turned green. "No hooking up for you," he ordered roughly. He jabbed his finger at Estelle. "Not ever."

Her innocent expression was a work of art. It was as if the heavens had opened up and holy light shone down on the teenager's head. "Of course not, Daddy."

Char glanced between daughter and father. Couldn't help but grin. She should be horrified to find out these secrets about people she barely knew. Not eating up every word and wondering what they'd be serving for dessert.

After Kane kissed her, she'd thought for sure she'd never get over her confusion and, yes, her disappointment that he'd ended said kiss rather…abruptly. Despite his confession last night, how he'd asked her to stay, she'd still considered him hard and rough and dangerous. Their kiss only proved how dangerous. But somehow, witnessing him in this new light—this new, amazing paternal light—made him seem less of a rogue-seducer-slash-breaker-of-female-hearts and more vulnerable.

She wished she knew what to do with all this new-found insight.

"This is so much fun," she was surprised to hear herself admit. She shouldn't take such enjoyment from his discomfort. But boy, oh, boy, she did. "I'm glad I stayed."

Kane obviously didn't agree. He stood—albeit painfully and slowly—then tugged Charlotte up by her elbow. "Time for you to go."

"Daddy," Estelle cried, leaping to her feet. "That is, like, completely rude."

"Charlotte's used to me being rude," he told her. "Now toss her those shoes so she can be on her way."

"This is exactly the reason you don't have any friends," Estelle told him as she handed Char her sneakers.

Char grabbed her purse from the end table, having no reason to stay—having many reasons to go—but reluctant nonetheless. "She's right."

"She's always right," Kane muttered. "Just ask her. Or her mother."

"Goodbye, Estelle," Char called over her shoulder as Kane led her to the door. "It was nice meeting you."

"You, too."

Kane opened the door, but Char just slung her purse over her shoulder, then pulled on her shoes. "You sure you don't want me to stick around?" she asked. "I think Estelle and I have bonded. And now, in the way of women everywhere, we'll probably be BFFs before the day is through."

He sent a beseeching look at the heavens. "Just kill me now."

"Not sure you're looking in the right direction for that request." Her shoes on, she straightened. And was practically pushed out the door. She stood there for a moment, frozen in time, her mouth open. When he started shutting the door, she slapped her hand against it. "You know, just when I start to think you're not as big of a jerk as I initially thought, you do or say something to prove me right. I mean wrong." She waved a hand in dismissal, irritated with herself for not making sense. Wanting to blame him for that as well. "Oh, you know what I mean."

He didn't respond. Just shut the door in her face. The ass.

And to think, she'd actually wanted to stay so she could learn more about his relationship with his daughter. Their history. What Estelle was doing in Shady Grove.

She'd wanted to learn more about him.

If he was an ass, then she was a fool.

She turned on her heel and stomped down the stairs, resolved to forget every moment of their time together and move on with her life.

"START FROM THE beginning," Kane said.

Estelle ducked her head to scoop up a bite of vegetable omelet—and, okay, to hide an eye roll. "Can I at least eat before you start interrogating me?"

They'd just gotten served and she really was starving. After Dad kicked Charlotte out, he'd demanded—yet again—to know what Estelle was doing there. As if she could get into the whole story without proper nourishment.

Especially as she was making up said story on the spot.

She'd told him there was no way she could get into all the details without some breakfast first.

And, since all her dad had was an almost-empty box of generic corn flakes and stale white bread, he'd brought her to Wix's Diner. It was a dump, but not as bad as some of the dives he took her to when he visited her in Houston.

At least the silverware was clean. She shoveled in another bite of omelet. And the food was good. Best of all, they had lattes. Not real ones. Just the kind you got from one of those machines, like at the convenience store. But at this point, begging couldn't make her choosy.

Or something like that.

"Estelle," her dad said in the deep, serious tone he used when he was trying to intimidate her. "I know you're smart enough to figure out how to eat and talk at the same time."

God, did he have to be so grumpy? Even on his best days, he was never exactly cheerful, and yeah, he had the whole "I'm recovering from a motor vehicle accident" thing going on, but please.

He didn't have to be such an old grouch.

"You're mad I'm here." She set down her fork, worked a good amount of vibration and pitifulness into her voice. "You could at least pretend you're happy to see me."

He sighed. Looked tired. And way older than usual. "Of course I'm happy—"

"You don't want me." She added a loud sniff, which had several other diners turning their heads her way. Managed some moisture in her eyes, though try as she might, she couldn't get a single tear to fall. "You wish I was never born!"

He didn't so much as blink. Didn't seem to care about the attention they were attracting, just set down his coffee and leaned forward. "Knock it off or I'm putting you on the first plane back to Houston."

He meant it, too. Her dad never said anything he didn't mean. And he always, always followed through, always did what he said he was going to do.

It was so annoying.

Not that she was afraid of him—even if he was totally scary-looking. Especially now with his too-long hair, bruised face and grim expression.

"I already told you," she said, spreading jelly on a piece of toast. "I couldn't stay at Pilar's so I came here. It's not like I could go back to my house or anything, since you and Mama banned me from my own home."

"No one's banned from anything. Your mother and I decided it'd be best if you stayed with someone while she and Allan were in France."

"Adam," Estelle corrected. "And Mama didn't decide that. You did."

She'd almost had her mother convinced to let Estelle stay home alone while Meryl and Adam enjoyed a romantic getaway. Instead, Meryl had to "run it by Kane" who'd given it the big veto.

He never wanted Estelle to have any freedom. Or any fun.

"Your mother and I decided—together—that it'd be best for you to stay with someone while she's away."

Yeah. Someone. Just not him.

She shrugged. Bit into her toast. "I *am* staying with someone. I'm staying with you."

He could at least pretend to be okay with it.

"If you were upset with Pilar, you should have gone to Clarice's house. Or Gwen's."

"Nana's still wintering in Santa Barbara," she said of Meryl's mother. "And you don't even stay with your mom when you come to Houston. Why would you want to torture me by making me stay with her for two whole weeks?"

Torture it would be, too. Grandma Gwen was nothing if not uptight, abrasive and bossy.

"My point," he said, though his lips barely moved, "is you should have called your mother to find somewhere else for you to stay. In Houston. Instead of flying halfway across the country by yourself, without permission or even letting anyone know. What if something happened to you?"

"Nothing happened. I'm not six, Daddy. I've flown by myself before. And I didn't want to stay in Houston. I missed you." She stuck out her lower lip. Too bad pouting didn't have any effect on her dad. "I haven't seen you in, like, forever."

Oh, he visited her often, at least four times a year. Usually. But he'd been so caught up in this new bar he owned, he hadn't been back to Houston since last spring.

He exhaled, his expression softening. "I missed you, too, brat."

She grinned. "Then I can stay with you until Mom gets back?"

She'd never stayed with him before. He always came to her.

"You can stay," he said, not sounding too happy about it. He stood and pulled out his phone. "If your mother agrees."

Estelle kept right on smiling as he excused himself to call Meryl. It wasn't until he pushed through the diner's front doors that she slumped back into her seat.

Please, please let Meryl agree. There was no reason she shouldn't. Then again, Meryl always cautioned Estelle not to ask too much from Kane, not to expect too much.

But shouldn't she have some expectations? Such as him stepping up when Estelle needed him?

When Estelle discovered those texts from Chandler on Pilar's phone yesterday morning, it had hit her that this was her opportunity to escape Houston without her mom becoming suspicious. Then, in a few days, when Estelle told her parents she wanted to stay with Kane permanently, they wouldn't ask too many questions.

She swallowed, but it still felt as if there was something stuck in her throat, so she gulped her lukewarm latte. Stay here in Shady Grove permanently. Or, at least until she turned eighteen and went to college.

Chewing on her thumbnail, she watched out the large window as her dad paced the length of the sidewalk in front of the building, the phone to his ear. It wasn't that she didn't love her dad. She did. It was just that she was going to miss Houston and her friends.

She was really going to miss her mother.

A tickle formed in the back of her throat. She had to stay strong. To remember she was doing this *for* her mother.

"You done with that?"

At the deep voice, Estelle twitched in surprise and glanced up. Frowned at the dark-haired guy standing next to the table.

"Excuse me?" she asked. Done with what? Her thumbnail? Her little inner whine-fest?

"Your food. Are you done with your plate and stuff?"

"Oh. Yes." She straightened and set her silverware on her plate. "Thank you."

He stacked her plate with her dad's, grabbed her empty juice cup by the rim, then glanced at her. "You're not from around here."

What? Did she have a sign that said "Outsider" on her forehead? Was she doomed to stick out in this small town? "What makes you say that?"

"I haven't seen you at school."

"Maybe you just haven't noticed me."

"Not a chance," he said, his voice low and gravelly. She shivered. "You, I would have noticed."

She fought a smile. Just because he was seriously cute with his floppy dark hair, blue eyes and broad shoulders didn't mean she was going to flirt with him. She was, after all, getting over a broken heart and had just yesterday sworn off boys forever.

He wiped his hand on the side of his jeans. Held it out. "I'm Andrew Freeman."

She shook his hand. His palm was warm and dry and slightly callused. "Estelle Monroe."

Andrew glanced around, then slid into the booth across from her. Leaned forward. "Did you just move to town?"

"Actually, I'm visiting my father for a few weeks."

He grinned and her breath caught. Okay, so maybe she should rethink the whole "no more boys" thing. Just because Chandler was a major douche bag didn't mean all guys couldn't be trusted.

"Maybe we could hang out sometime," Andrew said. "I could show you around town."

She doubted there was much more to Shady Grove than what she'd already seen. But she didn't mind being proved wrong. Especially when it involved a cute boy. "Maybe."

She didn't like to make it too easy on guys. Not when they so enjoyed the chase.

"Great. Let me put your number in my phone…" He patted his pockets. "Damn. It's in the break room," he said, sliding out of the booth. "I can run back and get it."

"No need." By then her dad might be done with

his call and the last thing she wanted was Kane being overprotective and scary simply because a boy talked to her.

She dug out a pen from her purse, uncapped it with her teeth, then took a hold of Andrew's hand. Instead of writing on his palm where it might get smeared or washed off accidentally, she inked her number onto the inside of his arm, feeling him watching her the whole time.

She capped the pen. "There."

"Table four needs set," the overweight brunette waitress who'd taken Estelle and Kane's order told Andrew as she passed the booth carrying a coffeepot.

"Okay." He picked up the dirty plates. "I guess I'll talk to you later."

Maybe the smile she sent him could be construed as flirtatious. But only slightly. "I guess that's up to you."

As he walked away, she couldn't help but hope they did talk later. If Andrew was around, maybe staying in Shady Grove wouldn't be so bad after all.

KANE'S FIRST TWO calls to Meryl went straight to voice mail. He hadn't bothered leaving messages, just hung up and dialed again. The third time, she finally answered, sounding breathless. "Hello?"

"It's me," he said, walking the length of the building. "Estelle's here."

There was a moment of stunned silence. "What do you mean, here? Where are you?"

"In Shady Grove. And I mean your daughter is here. With me. She got pissed at Pilar and decided she couldn't bear staying there for two weeks, so she got on a plane and showed up at my apartment. I found her there this morning."

No sense worrying Meryl with the events of his accident. Or that, for a good portion of an entire day, neither of them had known their daughter was missing. Sort of.

"Oh my God! Is she all right?"

"She's fine. She—"

"Why didn't Lorena call me?"

"Who?"

"Pilar's mother. I trusted her to take care of Estelle and she couldn't even be bothered to let me know my baby was missing? Wait until I see her at the club when I get back," Meryl muttered darkly. "And to think, I nominated her for PTO president. I'm going to text Belinda and let her know I'm putting my full support behind her election now."

"You might want to hold off on the political intrigue. At least until we find out what exactly happened."

"I suppose." But she didn't sound too happy about it. "What did Estelle say? Did she and Pilar argue?"

"All I got was that she's mad about Pilar and some kid...Carter or Chris..."

"Chandler." Meryl spat the name out as if saying it left a foul taste in her mouth. "Did Pilar try and steal Chandler from Estelle? That little tramp."

The wind picked up, blew his hair back from his face. He shut his eyes and inhaled the clean, damp scent. He had too much to do to deal with Meryl in full mama bear mode. "According to Estelle, it was worse than death."

"Of course it was. My poor baby," Meryl murmured. "Why didn't she call me? Tell me what was going on?"

There was an undertone of hurt in Meryl's voice. He wished he knew the answer to her question. Actually, he wished Estelle had called Meryl instead of seeking him out.

"Ooh, this is all that boy's fault," Meryl said, her accent sharpening. "She must have suspected something was going on between Pilar and Chandler. Estelle hasn't been herself lately."

He glanced at the diner, caught sight of some floppy-haired kid flirting with Estelle. And her flirting back. "She seems fine to me."

Yeah, she'd been upset about him being hurt, but she'd been her usual overly dramatic, chatty self all morning.

Meryl sighed. "She's been so moody the last few months. Always hanging out with that boy at his house and not at home. When she is at home, she locks herself in her bedroom and listens to music for hours on end. When Adam and I ask her to watch a movie with us or help us cook dinner, she refuses. I thought maybe she was jealous of the time I was spending with Adam so I made a point of setting aside girl time, just the two of us, to go shopping or get our nails done and she'd say she didn't want to."

Kane didn't like the sound of that. Estelle had always been happy and social. And she loved being with Meryl. It was one of the reasons he didn't feel guilty about not living closer to his daughter.

She preferred being with her mother.

But she was with him now. "She wants to stay with me until you get back."

"Oh, I couldn't ask you to do that," Meryl said quickly. "I'm sure you're much too busy to have her there."

He *was* busy. He had injuries to heal and a bar to sell. One he had to keep running until that sale went through. Then he had to figure out where the hell he was going next. But Estelle was his daughter. His responsibility. Something he never let himself forget.

"I can call my mother," he said. "I'm sure she'd love to have Estelle visit for a few weeks."

More like Gwen would love having someone to give her attention. But Estelle would be fine there. Safe. Well taken care of and, more importantly, watched over like a hawk.

Meryl made a sound of disappointment. "I don't think that will work. I overheard at the club that Gwen is staying at the Four Seasons while she has some redecorating done."

Damn. Estelle could stay with Gwen there but forcing her to share a suite—even a luxury suite—

with his mother seemed like cruel and unusual punishment. "Estelle says your mother is out of town?"

"Yes, until the end of the month." Meryl cleared her throat and when she spoke again, her voice was hesitant. "Perhaps Estelle could stay with your father?"

Kane gripped the phone so tightly he was surprised the screen didn't crack. "No."

Never. He let his old man be a part of Estelle's life—a small, controlled part. But that was it. No way did he want his daughter under Senior's influence for two weeks.

"Well, then I'll talk to Adam about coming home early," Meryl said. "I'll book the first flight I can find back. I wonder if I can find one with a layover in Pittsburgh," she said, almost to herself. "That way Estelle can fly home with us."

Meryl was willing to cut short her vacation, the first time she'd gone anywhere without Estelle. Meryl had dated over the years, but never seriously, choosing instead to focus on raising Estelle. But about a year ago she met Adam, got engaged a month or so ago. "She can stay with me."

"Are you sure? I'd hate to impose on you."

"It's not an imposition," he told her, raising his voice as a car with a bad muffler pulled into the parking lot. "She's my daughter, too."

"I know it's… You usually prefer to visit her in Houston."

Because he was afraid, always afraid of messing

up again. Of falling off the wagon and becoming a
bad influence on her. Of hurting her. Again.

"I want her to stay," he said, realizing he meant it.
He'd missed her. He'd been so busy working, running
O'Riley's, he hadn't had a chance to fly out to Texas
in almost a year. Yeah, they spoke several times a
week and did the Skype thing, but it wasn't the same.

He wanted to be with his daughter.

"Finish your vacation," he told Meryl, turning toward the diner. "I'll take good care of Estelle."

"I know you will," she said softly.

Her trust in him humbled him. "I'll have her call
you in a little bit."

He disconnected the call as his daughter wrote
something on the shaggy-haired kid's arm—her
number, more than likely. Maybe he could lock her
in his apartment. It would be the only way to keep
her out of trouble. Then again, when he'd been sixteen, nothing his parents had done had kept him from
raising hell.

And in some ways, his daughter was just like him.

Kane shut his eyes and exhaled heavily. And
prayed he'd survive the next two weeks.

CHAPTER NINE

"WHAT ARE YOU doing?" Char asked her sister impatiently as she jogged in place at the corner of Foster Drive and Congress Street.

"Prince is checking out a new smell," Sadie answered as if they had all day to let her dog sniff every sign, telephone pole and tree on the block. Prince raised his head, seemed to grin a doggy grin, then lifted his hind leg and peed on a mailbox. Lovely. "I think he's enjoying his first run."

"First and last run," Char muttered. "At least with me."

She kept jogging in place. She never should have agreed to let Sadie come with her. Wouldn't have if she'd known Sadie was bringing her puppy—who was now the size of a miniature horse and still growing into his big feet and floppy ears.

Plus, Sadie wasn't much of a runner herself. Why, oh why, had she given in when Sadie had asked if she could join her for a quick jog?

She snorted. Jog. Ha. More like leisurely Sunday afternoon stroll. She checked her watch. At this rate, there was no way she'd beat her best time.

"Come on already," she snapped. "How often can that dog pee?"

Sadie raised her eyebrows, strolled over to Char, Prince trotting happily along, his tongue out, his tail wagging. "My, my. Someone got up on the wrong side of the bed. What's the matter? Did you run out of cream for your coffee?"

"I'm not some anal control freak, you know," Char said sharply.

Sadie raised her hands. "Wow. You are a grumpy Gus today. What's the matter?"

Char's face heated. "Sorry," she said. She had been overly harsh. She touched Sadie's arm. Tried to smile. "Can we…let's just get moving, okay?"

But running, or even jogging, was out of the question with those two so Char crossed the street in a brisk walk, her arms pumping, her heart racing.

"You want to talk about it?" Sadie asked, breathing heavily as she and Prince caught up with Char.

"Talk about what?"

"Whatever has you so upset?"

No. Yes.

Argh. She didn't even know.

Oh, she knew why she was upset, why she felt edgy, as if no matter how fast she ran, how far, she couldn't escape these feelings inside her. Couldn't escape one very real, very frustrating fact.

Kane had kissed her.

And she hadn't been able to stop thinking about it. About him.

She'd momentarily lost her mind. That was the only answer to why she'd been even remotely interested in having Kane's mouth on hers. Okay, so maybe there were a few other reasons, such as the way he talked, with that hint of Texas in his voice, how close he'd been to her, how he'd looked at her, as if he'd really, *really* wanted to kiss her.

That was enough to get any sensible, controlled woman to let her guard down.

But she couldn't tell her sister that. Didn't want to tell her.

She wanted to keep the memory, and all these strange emotions the kiss had caused, to herself.

"I didn't get up on the wrong side of the bed," Char said. "I didn't even sleep in my bed."

"Oh?" Sadie asked.

Char glanced at her. "Don't say it like that."

"Like what?"

"Like I did something immoral, illegal or just plain kinky."

"Did you?"

"Of course not."

Mr. Placer, owner of the small grocery store, Jack's Place, drove by. Honked. Both Char and Sadie waved.

"Then you have nothing to worry about," Sadie said. "But now I'm dying to know where you spent the night."

Char should have thought of that before she'd

opened her big mouth. She sighed. Pumped her arms harder. "At the hospital working, and then at Kane's."

Sadie stopped dead. Char kept right on going. Unfortunately, so did Prince, who was jerked back hard by the leash in Sadie's hand.

"Sorry, baby," Sadie murmured absently as she patted the dog's head. She ran to join Char. "What have I told you about playing with someone like Kane?"

Char bristled. "First of all, I can play with whomever I want." Not that she wanted to play with Kane. She just didn't like being told she couldn't. "I'm not a child."

"You just graduated from college."

"Three years ago. Secondly, I can handle Kane."

"Oh my God," Sadie cried, covering her ears. Prince barked. "I don't ever want to hear about your 'handling' of Kane. I'll have nightmares."

"It wasn't like that." They passed a huge brick house with two crab apple trees in the front yard just starting to bud. "He had an accident last night. Wrecked his bike."

She didn't feel guilty sharing that tidbit. It'd be common knowledge in a matter of days anyway. Shady Grove loved gossip.

"What?" Sadie asked. "Is he okay?"

"He's hurt, but he'll be fine."

She quickly filled Sadie in on the accident and Kane's injuries.

"I don't understand what this has to do with you

sleeping in Kane's bed," Sadie said as they turned left onto Fiske Road.

"I slept on the chair. He didn't have anyone to pick him up so I took him home, made sure he was comfortable. Look, it's no big deal. I made him something to eat and helped him get settled. The man was alone. Injured. What was I supposed to do?"

"You could have dropped him off," Sadie pointed out.

"He needed help." She'd thought he'd needed her. That he'd be grateful she was there, taking time out of her schedule, taking care of him instead of going home after a long shift at work.

God, maybe she really did have a martyr complex.

"I guess I was more tired than I thought because I fell asleep," she lied. There was no way she was telling Sadie about Kane asking her to stay. Or about meeting his daughter. She knew when a secret wasn't hers to tell. "On the chair."

"So you're grumpy due to lack of sleep?" Sadie asked, studying her as if she didn't believe a word of it.

"I'm not grumpy." She was confused. Antsy. And irritated with herself for being unable to get Kane and their kiss out of her head.

"I'm glad you didn't sleep with him," Sadie said as nonchalantly as if they were discussing what to have for dinner. "Don't get me wrong. I like Kane. But he's not for you."

Char narrowed her eyes. "Excuse me?"

"He's got an edge. He's the type of guy to love 'em and leave 'em while you're all about strings and attachments and feelings—the tighter the strings the better. He'd break your heart."

Char bit back the words about how James, one of the nicest guys out there, already broke it. But then she'd get a lecture about her mistaken belief that she and James were meant to be together, that she'd loved him. Or worse, that sympathetic look Sadie gave her sometimes when she and James were together in front of Char, as if apologizing for loving him. Having him love her in return.

But she was right about Char wanting more from a relationship than just *wham, bam, what was your name again?* She wanted to be with a man she could build a future with. And that wasn't Kane.

No matter how well he kissed.

But there might be more to Kane than she'd realized. Oh, he wasn't for her. Sadie was right about that. Char wasn't that naive. She didn't want a man who needed to be fixed. A man with a teenage daughter. A man who was a former addict.

She and Sadie continued walking. She didn't want to tell Sadie or anyone what she'd learned about Kane. Wanted to keep his secrets for him.

"How about we turn back?" Sadie asked. "Prince is getting tired."

"Might as well," Char said. She wasn't getting any exercise anyway. "Next time I go for a run, I'm leaving you two at home."

"You can run fast anytime," Sadie said, linking her arm with Char's and swinging them both around. "But how many times do you get a chance to have a leisurely stroll with your awesome older sister and her wonder dog?"

Char stared at the dog in question. "Wonder dog is licking that tree."

While Sadie knelt and told Prince he was going to get splinters in his tongue if he didn't stop, Char heard someone call her name. She looked across the street. Blinked. But it wasn't her imagination, it really was Dr. Justin Louk—complete in running gear—waving at her.

She lifted her hand, bemused to see him in sweats and a T-shirt, his hair windblown. It was a good look for him. Made him seem less perfect.

Not that she minded perfection.

A vision of Kane swept through her mind, of his long hair tangled from sleep, his unshaven face. His kiss.

No. She didn't mind perfection at all.

Squeezing her eyes shut, she shook her head until it cleared of any and all thoughts of Kane. Opened them to see Justin jogging toward her, a smile on his face. "Charlotte. Hello."

"Hi, Justin." She gestured to Sadie, who joined them. "Justin, this is my sister, Sadie Nixon. Sadie, this is Dr. Louk. He recently started working in the E.R."

"Nice to meet you," Sadie said.

"You, too."

Silence. As if none of them had anything to say. Darn it. Why did it have to be so hard to hold a simple conversation with the man she was supposed to end up with? "Uh…I'm surprised to see you," Char blurted. "Here, I mean."

His cheeks were red, though she wasn't sure if it was due to the cold or embarrassment. Though why he would be embarrassed was beyond her. "Since you mentioned how great it was running here, I thought I'd try it. Shake up my routine a bit."

That was the extent of shaking up his routine? For some reason that left her feeling depressed. She really needed more sleep.

"Oh." She didn't actually remember mentioning it to him, but she supposed she must have. "That's good."

More silence. Char searched her brain for something to say, but there was nothing. Nothing. And this was a prime opportunity. She and Justin were away from the prying eyes at work—but were under the curious gaze of her sister.

Prince crept over and shoved his nose into Justin's crotch. Justin looked decidedly uncomfortable and stepped back.

"Why don't Prince and I just wander ahead," Sadie said, tugging her dog back.

They both watched her go. "Well," Charlotte said, unable to stand it any longer. "I guess I'll be going. Enjoy your run."

He smiled again. Nodded. "You, too." She was halfway down the block when he called her name.

She turned and waited for him, wondering at the edge of impatience simmering along her skin. This was what she'd wanted, after all. Justin paying attention to her. She should be thrilled.

Was thrilled, she assured herself.

He cleared his throat. "I was thinking, since you're finishing up your run and all, if maybe you'd like to go get a cup of coffee with me."

Her smile felt frozen. Was he...he was. He was asking her out.

"What about your run?" she asked.

He waved that away. "I've already gone a few miles." He edged closer, lowered his voice. "I'd much rather spend time with you."

"You would?" She grimaced and wished the words back, but they were already out there, proving she was a complete fool and totally inept at this flirting thing.

His grin widened. "I would. Unless," he added when she stood there like an idiot, "you already have plans."

She opened her mouth to assure him she had no other plans, had nothing she'd rather do than spend an hour or two showing him how perfect they were for each other. But that dumb vision of Kane traipsed through her mind again.

And, she realized, she'd never called the pharmacy about delivering his new prescription.

Crap.

"I'm so sorry," she told him, more sorry than he could know, "but I do have somewhere I need to be. I'm free either tomorrow or Wednesday afternoon, though."

He smiled, but looked disappointed. "Wednesday would be great. Shall we say two o'clock? At Brewster's?"

She hadn't been to Brewster's Coffee Shop since she tracked down James there one Saturday last fall. "Sounds good. I'll see you then."

With a wave, she turned and caught up with Sadie.

"Well, well," Sadie said as they waited for a car to pass before crossing the street. "Seems somebody is mighty smitten."

Oh, Lord, was it that easy to tell? "Dr. Louk is just a coworker," she said, sounding defensive even to her own ears.

A coworker who wanted to have coffee with her. Not exactly the most original start to a courtship, but at least it was a start.

"I don't think that matters to him." When Char just stared at her, Sadie added, "It's obvious. He's got a thing for you."

Char stumbled. "What?"

Sadie looked at her as though she'd dropped a few brain cells on her little trip. "He just *happened* to be running in the area? The same area you mentioned to him? Come on. He was obviously hoping to bump into you." As if to illustrate, Sadie bumped Char's hip. "Plus, he was looking at you like he wanted to tie you up in a bow and give you to himself as his very own present. I wouldn't be surprised if he asks you out."

"He did," Char said. Sadie thought Justin had a thing for her? Amazing. Wonderful. For once, she didn't have to do all the work. "We're having coffee Wednesday."

"Good. Just try to have fun without putting pressure on yourself. Or him."

"What do you mean?"

"You're always planning for the next goal, always looking forward. Relax and enjoy where you are now. Don't try to push things. Simply...see where you end up."

But then she wouldn't have any control over the outcome.

"If I don't push, how am I supposed to get the future I want?" The one she'd always dreamed of, planned on having. Sadie didn't understand. She floated through life, taking things as they came, always more than happy to stop what she was doing and try something else.

That wasn't for Charlotte. She liked knowing where she was going, what the end destination would be. And if she didn't navigate, wasn't in the driver's seat, how on earth would she be able to guarantee she got there?

"All I'm saying is every now and then it's okay to

enjoy what you have, who you are in the now. Be in the present."

"Thank you, Obi-Wan, but some of us prefer to know what's coming."

That way, you could plan for it.

"WE'RE CLOSED," KANE said as O'Riley's door opened Sunday evening.

Charlotte walked in, looking fresh and pretty as a summer day in a pair of jeans and bright green top. "Then you should lock the door."

She slid onto a stool as if she owned the damn place and set a plastic bag on the bar.

"Sorry, Red," he said in the tone that always brought out the frown lines in her forehead, "but you'll have to get your booze somewhere else tonight. O'Riley's isn't open on Sundays except during football season."

"Gotta keep those raging Steelers fans happy," she said.

"It's what I live for." There were worse things to live for. Such as where his next high was going to come from.

She looked around and he took the opportunity to study her. She wasn't beautiful; her nose was too pointy, her cheeks too round. So why the hell had he been unable to stop thinking about her all day?

He scrubbed the top of the bar with a damp cloth. Hard. One kiss and he'd lost his mind.

"Where's your daughter?" she asked.

"You're still having a hard time getting used to that, aren't you? Me being a father."

Char set her elbow on a dry spot, resting her chin in her hand. "Well, it did come as something of a shock, seeing as how I don't think anyone had any idea you even had a daughter. Let alone one old enough to drive, gorgeous enough to turn men into even bigger fools and sweet enough to still call you Daddy."

"I'm only Daddy when she wants something. Today she wanted me not to kick her butt back to Houston."

"Is that what you did?"

He sprayed the sink with cleaner, scrubbed the basin, each movement sending jarring pain up his side. He scrubbed harder. "She's upstairs sleeping. Once she goes out, it's tough to wake her."

They'd hung out after breakfast, catching up with each other. Or rather, Estelle had caught him up on her life, chattering nonstop about this friend and that friend, her classes and teachers. He'd kept his comments to a minimum. Partly because it was hard to get a word in edgewise when his kid started babbling.

But mostly because he'd been hurting so bad, he was afraid if he opened his mouth, he'd groan. Or cry. Neither of which would do him any good.

He'd hoped keeping busy would help him forget about the pain. About how much he wished he still had those pills from last night.

"Too bad. I was hoping to get a chance to chat with

her some more," Charlotte said, sounding as if she really meant it. "She's something. And I mean that in the best possible way. You must be very proud."

"I am." Estelle was the best thing he'd ever done.

The best thing that had ever happened to him.

"But you didn't stop by just to hang out with my kid," he said, rinsing the rag and setting it out to dry. "You're checking up on me."

She shifted. "Am I really that easy to read?"

"Like an open book with large print."

She flushed, her mouth a thin line as if she didn't like being open and totally honest. Giving and generous. Traits he didn't understand himself, but they worked on her. "Actually, I stopped by to give you these."

She retrieved a sling from the bag along with a prescription bottle. She set it on the bar between them. He eyed it as warily as he would a bomb, as if one of the pills was going to escape its confinement and leap into his mouth.

"It's your prescription," she said, slowly. "I stopped by the pharmacy and got it for you."

"I'll take this." He picked up the sling, tucked it under the bar. "Thanks, but I don't want the pills," he said, though it was a lie. He did want them. Too much.

She frowned, checked the bottle's label. "It's okay. It's a new script for Toradol. It's non-narcotic. Much less…potent…than the one you had last night."

Potent. She meant addictive.

He pushed the bottle toward her. "I won't take them."

"We talked about this, remember? As long as you take them as directed—no more than the maximum dose per day—the chances of you becoming addicted to them are slim." She gentled her voice, touched his hand. "There's no reason for you to suffer."

Her words blew through him like a fire, burning his resistance. No, he didn't have to suffer. All he had to do was pop a couple of those pills and his pain would be gone.

Temporarily.

He was terrified it wouldn't be enough. That the entire bottle would be inadequate and he'd start wanting more, craving more until he was back to where he was fourteen years ago.

Strung out and desperate only for his next hit. For something to make everything okay.

"I won't take them," he repeated. "Not when my daughter's here."

For the next two weeks, Estelle was fully his responsibility. His only concern. He refused to blow it, to let his past, his mistakes, touch her in any way.

Charlotte curled her fingers around the bottle. "Are you sure?"

He nodded. "When Estelle was little, I promised her and myself I'd never use again." He forced himself to meet Charlotte's eyes, to meet the sympathy there head-on. "I won't take the chance of becoming addicted. I won't take any chances when it comes to my kid."

Charlotte exhaled heavily. "Okay. Okay," she repeated more to herself than him. She tucked the bottle of pills in her purse. "I hope you're at least taking ibuprofen."

"Two every six hours. Like clockwork." They only took the sharpest edge off the pain, but it was all he was willing to do.

"Good." She smiled, as if she were proud of him for not caving to the pain. As if his fears, his past addiction, were to be ignored. She stood, picked up her purse. "Well, I should get going. I'm due at my mom's for Sunday family dinner."

"You have my sympathies."

"For what?"

"Family dinner." Sounded like torture. He should know. He'd suffered through enough of them before cutting himself off from his parents and brothers. Everything and everyone from his past.

Except Estelle.

Charlotte grinned. "Hey, I like my family."

"Even your sister who stole the love of your life?"

Shit. Why had he said that? The comment hit home—her smile slid away and her face lost some of its color. He found himself wanting to touch the back of Charlotte's hand. Found himself wanting to do something a Bartasavich never did. Apologize.

"Actually," Charlotte said, staring at the bar, "I've come to realize perhaps I...overstated my feelings for James."

"Yeah?" Why that made him feel relieved and

sort of happy, he didn't want to examine too closely. "Must suck, though. Having to be around them."

"It's a bit…awkward…from time to time, yes."

Yet she was still willing to go to a family dinner. How many times had she been subjected to seeing James and Sadie together? It couldn't have been easy, not at first. But she did it, had somehow managed to remain close with Sadie, had accepted James as an almost-brother-in-law. She didn't back down from challenges.

That he admired her tenacious spirit and forgiving soul wasn't a surprise. That he found those traits appealing was.

One he didn't like.

"It'll get easier," he heard himself say, then immediately wished he could take the words back. No, they weren't overly sweet or sentimental, were a pat response actually, but he didn't want her to start thinking he might care about her or her feelings.

"It already has. Just as things will get easier with your daughter and, I'm assuming, her mother."

"Estelle and Meryl are very close."

Charlotte blinked. "Oh. I'm sorry. I assumed since Estelle showed up here without your knowledge, that she'd—"

"Run away from home?" He shook his head. "Estelle loves her mother."

"I love my mother, too. But when I was sixteen, there were plenty of times I would have given my right leg to get away from her." Charlotte sat back down, the movement pulling her top taut against her small breasts for a moment before she lifted her hips and loosed the material. Too bad. "Were you and Estelle's mother married long?" she asked, her gaze way too intense. Interested. As though they were two buddies sitting around chatting, getting to know each other.

The interest wasn't bad. He could deal with that, but he didn't want her to get too close to him. Didn't want anyone knowing him too well.

"No."

She looked disappointed, as if his harsh answer had hurt her feelings.

As if she expected more from him.

"Meryl and I were never married," he admitted, pulling bottles of beer from the case he'd slid across the floor earlier and putting them into the cooler. "We slept together once, at a party, when both of us were too young, too stupid and way too drunk to know any better."

He wished he could say that had been his last drunken sexual encounter.

He leaned forward, gave Char his sexiest grin. "I bet you're thankful now I turned you away when you came to my apartment."

"Yes, well, I'm always grateful when someone stops me from making a huge mistake."

His lips twitched at the way she emphasized "huge." Yeah, it would have been a mistake, one he was regretting not making.

He let his gaze drift slowly, deliberately down the long line of her throat to the vee of her shirt, remembered how she'd looked at his apartment, all glowing skin and long lines, subtle curves. He hated that she'd been so willing to debase herself for some guy who wasn't worth her time. He slid his finger over the back of her hand, liked how she froze, the only movement her throat as she swallowed. "Glad I could be of service. Tell me, why did you come to see me that morning?"

She looked startled. "I…" She pressed her lips together and shook her head. "Maybe I wanted to try something new? Do something wild and adventurous and daring."

"Tired of being the good girl, huh?"

"Something like that."

"That may have been part of it, but it wasn't the only reason," he said, watching her carefully. "We both know what you wanted. And it wasn't a walk on the wild side or even to get laid."

She flinched and eased back, sliding her hand away from him. He curled his fingers into his palm.

Wished he could touch her again.

"No, I didn't just want to get laid," she said, color rising in her cheeks. "I wanted…" She sighed. "What's the point? You wouldn't understand."

She got to her feet and for some reason, he didn't want her to go. Not when listening to her chirp on and on actually kept him from thinking of the pain, of those pills in her purse and how much he wanted to take them.

"Try me," he heard himself say.

CHAPTER TEN

CHARLOTTE TURNED, SLOWLY, suspiciously, her shoulders rigid, her narrow waist accentuated by the clinging top. "I wanted to prove something."

"That you were over the carpenter?"

She glanced away. "Maybe."

There was more to it, and he wanted to know what, but he didn't want to push. He hated when people pushed him. But he didn't like to see her morose and defeated. He liked her when she snapped at him, her eyes flashing.

He must be more demented than he'd realized.

"Want a drink?" he asked.

She eyed him warily, but once again climbed back onto the stool. "I thought you weren't serving today."

"I'm not. But you can have soda."

She flushed and he wondered if she was thinking of the first time he'd waited on her, when he'd thought she was underage. "Cola will be fine," she finally said.

He used the hose to pour her drink, then set it in front of her. "On the house for going above and beyond the call of duty."

A smile played on her lips. "Is that your half-assed way of thanking me for helping you?"

"Must be. I'm not usually that nice for no reason."

Charlotte stirred the drink with her straw. Watched the ice move round and round. Sighed. "I wanted to be wanted," she said in a rush. She lifted her gaze to his. "That night when I came to you. I just…I wanted someone to want me. Stupid, I know, but there you have it."

"You were hurting," he said, hating now that he'd added to it.

She snorted. "I was angry. Furious. At myself for being such a fool. At James for not seeing what I wanted him to see, for not having the feelings for me I wanted him to have. And at Sadie for being the woman he wanted. But mostly I was angry he'd messed up all my carefully laid plans for us." Charlotte twisted her mouth to the side. "You accused me of trying to make James jealous, and maybe a small part of me had hoped that would happen, but mostly I thought sleeping with you would make me feel better about myself. Would prove I was…"

"That you were what?" he prodded.

Her cheeks red, she stabbed her straw at the ice in her soda. "Desirable."

She said it so softly, he almost didn't hear, but that one word blew him away.

"I was a late bloomer," she admitted with another sigh. "And then, not much actually bloomed."

He smiled at her self-deprecating humor. "I wouldn't say that."

"You sort of did. When you told me you weren't interested in sleeping with me."

He pressed his lips together. He didn't want to explain himself, didn't want to feel the need to. But he couldn't let her think that. He'd told himself he wasn't interested in her, but she still kept creeping into his thoughts.

"My level of interest," he said gruffly, "may have... changed."

She raised her eyebrows. "I never would have pegged you as a guy to say something he didn't mean just to spare someone's feelings."

Obviously, she didn't think it was a positive trait.

"I'm not," he assured her. "I'm just saying that this morning I was interested." Intrigued. Attracted. "Very much so."

By the way she dropped her gaze, he knew she understood he was talking about their kiss.

"That time..." He wasn't sure where he was going with this, just that he had to say something. "I didn't like that you were willing to sleep with me just to get back at some guy. I don't like being used."

Hated that she'd tempted him to revert to the selfish person he used to be, tempted him to take what he wanted without any thought or care as to how it would affect her.

"And here I thought men were more than happy to be used by women."

"Some are." He put the last bottles of beer in the cooler, shut the door. "I'm not."

CHAR COULDN'T BELIEVE she was having this conversation. It should have been humiliating. It was more than a little embarrassing. But also sort of…liberating. And, if she were to believe Kane, flattering and exciting.

This morning I was interested. Very much so.

She cleared her throat. There was one more thing she had to admit, since this whole confessing thing seemed to be working for her. "You said I'd thank you for turning me down. You were right."

If they'd slept together it would have been…well… she couldn't help but think it would have been pretty damn amazing. She wasn't a fool, after all. But it also could have been life-changing. She would have felt horrible about herself, and was honest enough to admit she would have then put the blame firmly on him.

She didn't want life-changing. She just wanted the future she'd always dreamed of. The one she was planning for. No side trips. No detours. And no one-night stands with the sexy bar owner.

"You're welcome," he said so solemnly she smiled.

The door opened and Estelle walked in chatting on her cell phone. When she glanced up and saw Kane and Char, she waved.

"Sure," she said into the phone as she sat next to Charlotte. "Uh-huh. I will. Okay. Love you, too."

She held the phone out to Kane. "Granddad wants to talk to you."

Kane took the phone and disconnected the call. Handed it back to Estelle.

"Daddy! God—that is, like, so rude. And you've probably hurt his feelings."

"My old man doesn't have feelings. How many times do I have to tell you that?"

Char blinked. "Wait. You have a father?" she asked Kane.

"Most people do," he said, "at least at one point in their lives."

"Right, right, it's just…I hadn't realized your parents were still alive."

"Daddy doesn't like to talk about them," Estelle said as she leaned over the bar and helped herself to a bag of pretzels. "Because they're like, super rich."

Char whipped her head around to look at Kane, her jaw slack. "Your family is well off?" She winced at the shock, the accusation in her tone. What kind of nosy, none-of-her-business question was that?

One she wanted the answer to, she realized.

"They're not well off," Estelle said, ripping open the bag. She crunched on a pretzel. "I mean, my mom's family is loaded, too, but nothing compared to the Bartasavich money."

Kane sent his daughter a narrow look. "Is this what they teach you at private school? To discuss your family's personal finances?"

"What? It's not like I'm bragging. It's not *my*

money." She turned to Char. "You've never really heard of them? Bartasavich Industries?" Char shook her head. "What is this place? Like some kind of alternate dimension where you don't get the news?"

"Only petty things like war, disease and famine. Nothing as important as who Kane's family is."

Estelle, in a pair of yoga pants and a sweatshirt, her face clean, her hair up in a messy bun, was still stunning. And oblivious to Char's sardonic tone.

Kids these days. Too busy texting to pick up on subtle verbal nuances.

"It's okay," Estelle said, patting Char's shoulder. "So, Dad is one of *the* Bartasaviches. From Houston." When that didn't seem to register on Charlotte, Estelle continued. "His father is Clinton Bartasavich. *The* Clinton Bartasavich of Bartasavich Industries."

"Sorry," Charlotte said, "never heard of them."

"Don't be sorry about that," Kane said. "Be grateful."

Estelle rolled her eyes. "Clinton just happens to be one of the top five wealthiest men in Houston, making him one of the top two hundred wealthiest men in America."

Char frowned at Kane. He raised an eyebrow. None of this made sense. He owned a run-down bar and lived in a cramped apartment with second-hand furniture. He'd been in the military, for God's sake. The wealthy didn't let their kids go into combat, did they?

She'd thought he'd grown up on the streets, strug-

gling to survive. Had pictured him poor and neglected because of his drug addiction.

Shame filled her, made the soda turn in her stomach. She'd been wrong. Worse than that, she'd been
judgmental and arrogant to think only the less for-
tunate could have problems.

Everyone had their own burdens to bear.

Estelle looked at Kane. "I can't believe she didn't
know this. She obviously wasn't being nice to you
this morning in the hopes of getting some huge reward."

"She's not usually nice to me," he said.

Unable to meet either of their eyes, Charlotte
sipped her drink, tried to sound natural. "That's
true."

But Estelle had already turned back to Charlotte.
"There's Uncle C.J.—Clinton Junior—he's the eldest
and Granddad's right-hand man—"

"If you consider his right hand up Senior's ass,"
Kane muttered.

Charlotte inhaled sharply and choked on the
soda. She coughed, cleared her throat. "You have
a brother?" she wheezed. Kane gave a quick, jerky
nod. "Dear Lord, there are more of you?" The mere
thought of several Bartasaviches running loose in
the world terrified her.

All that sex appeal couldn't be good for anyone.

"Oh, he has more than one," Estelle said. "Like I
said, there's Uncle C.J., then Daddy." She ticked the
names on her fingers. "Then Uncle Oakes who's a

defense attorney, but Granddad is trying to get him to work for the company. Or at least, get into politics."

"Is that it?" she asked the teen.

"Nope. Next is Uncle Zach who—" Estelle leaned closer to Charlotte and lowered her voice "—knows, like, one hundred ways to kill a person."

"Who told you that?" Kane demanded.

"He did. Uncle Zach's some sort of supersecret soldier with all sorts of nasty skills."

"Not so supersecret if you've heard about it," Kane pointed out.

"Anyway, Uncle Zach's sort of the black sheep of the family on account of he has all sorts of issues. I guess because he's the only Bartasavich son who'd been born on the wrong side of the blanket. But even though he seems all scary and unapproachable, he's actually nice once you get to know him." Estelle frowned. "At least, that's what I've heard. I haven't seen him much. He doesn't visit Granddad very often."

"What he is," Kane said, "is smart."

"Uncle C.J. says he's messed up because Granddad didn't marry Uncle Zach's mom and she took him away."

"Uncle C.J. has a big mouth," Kane growled.

Char's thoughts whirled. She could barely comprehend the truth of Kane's background, let alone try to follow everything Estelle had said.

"I…I don't know what to say." Char couldn't take her eyes off Kane, either; his mouth was tight and a flush colored his cheeks. It was ridiculously appealing. "I'm flabbergasted."

Shocked to hear about Kane's background. Saddened he didn't seem to be close to his family. Didn't want to be close to them. Did anyone in town know about his past? About his brothers? Sadie certainly had never mentioned it.

Unless Kane had confided in her and sworn her to secrecy.

Irritation pricked at Char. Irritation with a healthy dose of envy. She didn't want her sister keeping Kane's secrets.

That was Char's job.

Estelle popped another pretzel in her mouth. "I know. It's because he lives like a hobo. No one ever suspects he comes from money."

"There's nothing wrong with living frugally," he told her, coming around the bar to stand between them. "I'm sure you're in a hurry to get to your dinner," he said to Char.

"Are you kidding?" she asked. "You'll have to drag me out of here. Really. All of this has been fascinating." She turned to Estelle, mostly so she could ignore Kane's darkening expression. "What about your grandmother?"

"Grandma Gwen? She lives in Houston, too. She and Granddad divorced when he cheated on her with Uncle Oakes's mom and got her pregnant. They were married when Granddad had an affair with Uncle

Zach's mom. A few years later, he got divorced again and married Grace—or was it Bambi?"

She looked at Kane. His mouth remained a thin line. A shut, thin line.

Estelle waved a pretzel in the air. "I'm pretty sure it was Bambi then Grace and then Carrie. They're still married, him and Carrie."

Good Lord, Kane's father had been married that many times? And he'd cheated on Kane's mother—on more than one wife? She couldn't help but feel bad for Kane. "And your mother?" she asked him.

For a moment, she didn't think he was going to answer, but then he shrugged. "She never remarried."

"She lives in a house Granddad bought for her," Estelle said, wiping her hands down the front of her pants. "He pays her bills and she pretends to pine for their great love when really, all she misses is his bank account."

"Estelle," Kane said sharply.

The teen blinked at him, as innocent as the angel she resembled. "What? That's what Uncle C.J. says."

"Junior needs his ass kicked."

She batted her eyelashes. "Funny, that's what he says about you."

"Story time's over," Kane said, gesturing for Char to stand up. She was too stunned to do otherwise.

Plus, she really was running late, and Irene Ellison did not tolerate tardiness.

Estelle jumped to her feet. "Before you go we want

to invite you to dinner, to thank you for taking such good care of Daddy."

"We do?" Obviously this wasn't Kane's idea.

Estelle frowned at him, as regal as any debutante chiding the less mannered with one severe look. "Of course we do."

"That's really not necessary," Char said.

"We insist," Estelle said with a big smile. "It'll be fun."

How could it be otherwise with the chatty, bright teen?

"Charlotte works nights," Kane said, and there was that damn tingle when he said her name. "As do I."

It must have been the tingle that prompted Char to say, "I have Wednesday off."

Estelle clapped her hands together. "Perfect. And Daddy, you own this place. You can have someone cover your shift or whatever for you. Where shall we go?"

Kane was watching Char, his expression unreadable. "I'm sure Charlotte would be more comfortable eating in instead of going to a crowded restaurant."

She flushed. What? He read minds now? It was as if he knew she didn't want to explain to anyone who saw them what she was doing with him. People might get the crazy idea she and Kane were a couple.

And she needed Justin to know she was single. Available. Interested.

She just couldn't figure out why, if she was so

interested in Justin—and she was—she wasn't doing more to try to decline Estelle's dinner invite.

Estelle wrinkled her nose. "You want to eat here?" she asked her father.

Kane nodded. "Upstairs."

"Fine," Estelle said, sounding about as far from agreeable as she could get. She turned to Char. "Does seven work for you?"

"Perfect." And if Char was actually looking forward to it, no one had to know but her.

"Fabulous. Speaking of eating," Estelle said to her dad, "I'm hungry. Can we get pizza?"

"Sure."

"I'll wait upstairs." She smiled at Char. "It was so nice seeing you again."

Char couldn't help but grin back. It was like Estelle was half teenager with all the moodiness and chattering that went with it and half adult socialite complete with extreme politeness. "You, too. I hope you enjoy your stay in Shady Grove."

"Oh, I'm sure I will," Estelle said. Then, pushing buttons on her phone, she left the bar.

Kane walked Charlotte to the door. "So…a rich boy from Texas, huh?" she asked, unable to stop herself. Unable to stop from being curious about him. She leaned against the door. "Not how I imagined your childhood."

"I'm a born and bred Texan of the country club set. Grew up in a mansion big enough for five families, was educated in the finest private schools and had my own credit card with no spending limit when I turned twelve."

"Sounds—"

"If you say nice, I may have to rethink you settling for the carpenter and his wages."

"I was going to say indulgent."

He glanced at her in surprise. "It was."

"Must have been hard, growing up like that and not becoming spoiled."

His grin flashed, fast and wicked. Her breath caught. "Who says I wasn't spoiled?"

She laughed. "I can't imagine you being pampered." He was so controlled and hard, independent and aloof. She knew from Sadie he put in sixty-hour workweeks and never complained about taking a shift behind the bar, cleaning up or washing dishes. "You don't seem like the type to ask for someone to bring you what you want on a silver platter."

"I didn't ask for it," he said, his tone cool and dismissive. "I demanded it. I was a spoiled kid, a rebellious teenager. I lashed out at everyone and everything until I realized what I really wanted to lash out against was my entire lifestyle."

"Is that when you became…involved in drugs?"

"I didn't become involved in them. I lived for them. For the next high. The next time I could numb my thoughts. My feelings."

How horrible. She wanted to touch him but didn't dare. Not when he looked so angry and dangerous. "You must have been in so much pain."

"I was bored," he said flatly. "Looking for attention. It's what happens when kids have too much freedom, too much money and not enough interest from their parents. I was an addict at seventeen. By nineteen I'd been to four different rehabs."

"But you're sober now."

"I got clean, joined the service and learned what it's like to work for a living, to make something of myself."

"And you haven't looked back since," she said.

"No sense looking back or forward. Not when I learned it's best to focus on getting through this day, this hour, this minute."

He reached past her and opened the door. She turned. They were close, so close she could breathe in his scent, wanted to continuing inhaling it, if only for another indulgent moment.

She cleared her throat, but when she spoke, her voice was husky. "Are you embarrassed I now know all your deep dark secrets?"

"You don't know half of them," he told her quietly. "You don't know anything about me."

It wasn't completely true, she thought, as she walked out into the twilight, the air cool and crisp. Behind her, he shut the door with a quiet snick. She refused to look back.

Heading toward her car, she dug her keys out of her purse. She'd been wrong about him. More than once, it turned out.

She may not know everything about him, but each

time they were together, she got more glimpses of who he really was, what made him tick and why he was the way he was.

Each time they were together, she wanted to know more.

AT LEAST THE pizza was good, Estelle thought an hour later as she worked on her second slice. Her dad had taken her to a place downtown called Panoli's. It was old-fashioned, and had dingy floors, a few rickety tables in the back and a jukebox. Behind the front counter, an old guy tossed pizza dough in the air, which was pretty cool. And it smelled amazing in there.

So if she ended up convincing her dad she should stay with him, she wouldn't starve. That was a plus.

But there were so many minuses. For one thing, the town was small, not many restaurants were open on a Sunday. And as far as she could tell, there wasn't even a decent mall, which meant she'd have to drive into Pittsburgh every time she wanted to go shopping.

She thought of her brand-new Jeep, her sixteenth birthday present from Granddad, sitting in her garage back in Houston. She hoped her dad would let her bring the Jeep to Shady Grove even though he hadn't wanted Granddad to buy it for her. Oh, her dad said it was because she needed to learn the value of a dollar and how to earn her own way and work for the things she wanted and blah, blah, blah. But the real reason was he hated Granddad and didn't like him doing anything nice for Estelle.

Which was just messed up. Yeah, Granddad had been married, like, five times and he had a hard time keeping it in his pants when he was younger—and she wasn't even going to think about if he kept it in there nowadays because...yuck. But he loved Estelle and she loved him. It should be all that mattered.

She sighed.

"That's the third time you've sighed since we got served," her dad said, sipping his bottle of water. "What's going on?"

She set her pizza down, wiped her fingers on a paper napkin. "Nothing."

He just watched her, as though he didn't believe her. But he wouldn't bug her about it. Her mom would keep at her until Estelle had told her everything, and then she'd try to make her feel better with a shopping trip or an appointment at their favorite salon. But not her dad. He'd wait, let her come to him when she was ready, then he'd just...listen.

It was nice. Oh, she loved her mom, more than anything. But sometimes she liked not having to spill her guts or share every thought she had.

But she couldn't ignore this forever. She'd have to bring it up sometime, and it might as well be now when he wasn't still upset with her surprise visit. Using her fork, she stabbed at a piece of lettuce left over from her salad. "Dad?"

"Hmm?"

"Do you ever…" She set the fork down and clasped her hands together in her lap. "Do you ever think about moving back to Houston?"

She already knew the answer was a big, fat no. She also knew it was a good segue into what she really wanted to ask.

"No," he said. "Why?"

"Is it because of your family?" she asked, though she already knew that answer, too.

Her dad liked to move around. A lot. Plus, it wasn't just his own father he didn't like, it was his mom and brothers, too. Which wasn't fair as Uncle C.J. and Uncle Oakes were both really nice and fun.

Her dad's lips tightened. "It's not someplace I want to be."

Not even for her. But at least she got to see him and he paid attention to her and she knew he loved her. Some of her friends' dads live in Houston and they didn't have anything to do with their own kids.

"But if you lived in Houston," she said, "you could see me every day."

His expression softened. "We'll figure something out, see each other more often."

"Or, I could maybe…move here. With you."

She held her breath. He didn't look angry, more like stunned.

"I don't even know how long I'm going to be in Shady Grove."

"Oh, well, when you move, I could, like, move

with you." Hopefully to someplace warmer with more to do. And a mall.

He leaned forward, studied her as if trying to read her mind. He knew her too well. Knew she wasn't being honest with him. Why couldn't she have regular parents who either ignored her or were clueless when she fibbed?

"You love Houston," he said.

She did love Houston. She loved the weather and the sights and sounds and everything to do there. "I could go back and visit."

"What about school? Your friends? Your mother?"

That's what she'd miss most. Her friends and, of course, Mama. She'd never lived anywhere else, never had to make new friends or be the new kid in school. Although she had already met Andrew. They'd been texting all day, making plans to get together sometime this week.

Maybe she could make new friends after all. She was already almost friends with Charlotte, despite Charlotte being a few years older than her.

"I'm sixteen now," she told him, shoving her plate away. "In two years I'll be at college, and I've never lived with you. This could be our only chance."

He looked confused and, she realized, flattered. Also a little scared. "I didn't know you wanted to live with me."

She didn't. Oh, don't get her wrong. She loved her dad. But he had too many rules. He was always worrying about her making a mistake or a wrong choice just because he'd been wild when he was her age. As if she was dumb enough to get involved in drugs or let some guy get her pregnant.

She'd learned from her parents' mistakes.

"It would be fun," she said, trying to convince herself as well as him. It wouldn't be so awful. Her dad was cool enough, and she really had missed him this past year. "We could move into a bigger place." Because there was no way she was living above a dumpy old bar. "And I'll go to school here. I could even get a job."

He frowned and edged closer to the table. There were only two other tables occupied in the small dining room, one by an older couple, the other a family with three little kids. Still, he lowered his voice. "What's going on? Is this about Adam?"

She got cold all over. "Wha…what do you mean?"

He couldn't possibly know, could he? Had Adam gone through with his threat?

"Your mom said you've been acting strange ever since they got engaged. Are you worried you're losing your mom to him?"

Tears stung her eyes, but she blinked them back. They thought she was jealous. Like some little kid who wasn't getting enough attention. "No. I'm glad Mama's so happy now." It was true. Her mother hadn't dated much until Estelle turned twelve, and then only sporadically. She didn't want her mom to be lonely. And Meryl loved Adam. Estelle had never seen her happier or more content. "I feel like a third wheel. I think they need time together, without me, you know? To really get to know each other and stuff."

Her dad's eyes narrowed. "But you like him?"

She opened her mouth, but the lie wouldn't come out so she nodded. She had liked Adam. At first. She'd wanted him to like her, too. But she'd gone overboard.

She could still hear his low voice; she'd never get his words out of her head.

Who do you think your mother is going to believe?

His question had terrified Estelle. Before Adam, she would have said her mother would believe her. Over anybody. But even if she did believe Estelle, what good would it do? Meryl would break up with him and then she'd go back to being alone.

"I doubt your mother thinks of you as a third wheel," Kane said.

"I know. I just feel it's time for you and me to be together. While we still can. Will you promise me you'll at least think about it?"

He nodded. She didn't need his words to know he'd keep his promise.

And for the next two weeks, she'd do her best to convince him that her staying with him was the best idea ever.

CHAPTER ELEVEN

A FEW YEARS AGO, who would have thought skinny, nerdy Charlotte Ellison would have two dates? And on a Wednesday, no less.

Not that this was a date, Char thought as she climbed out of her car at O'Riley's on Wednesday night. Even though it did include dinner with a gorgeous man. And his daughter.

A thank-you dinner he didn't even want to have.

She picked up the bakery box from the passenger seat, shut the door and pressed the lock button on her key fob. Her car beeped, lights flashing once. She pocketed the keys and headed across the parking lot. There were maybe a dozen vehicles in the lot, and when she grew close to the building, the scent of chicken and tomatoes hit her, followed by a hint of spice. Her mouth watered.

She hesitated at the door leading to Kane's apartment. Looked back at her car. It wouldn't be a big deal to get in it and drive home. She could always phone, tell Estelle she got called into work or had come down with a sudden case of yellow fever. She wasn't sure why she'd agreed to this dinner in the first place. Yes, she'd thought it was sweet of Estelle to offer, but mostly, she'd agreed because Kane hadn't wanted her to.

She was getting to be quite the contrary person.

Char opened the door and climbed the stairs. This may not be a date, technically, but she could definitely count having coffee with Justin earlier as one. The two of them had huddled together in a secluded table in the back corner for two hours. He'd told her all about his family, how close he was to his sister, how much he enjoyed spending time with her kids, how he'd like a family of his own one day. There had been no long, awkward pauses, and she hadn't had to search her brain for something to discuss.

It'd been…nice.

Not magical. Not spectacular or life-changing, which the first date with her intended future husband should have been. It was so frustrating when things didn't work out the way she'd planned.

Made her worry she was doing something wrong. That she was making another mistake.

Her jaw tightened. No. She and Justin weren't a mistake. They were meant to end up together. They had to. She couldn't be wrong. Not again.

Besides, the afternoon hadn't been a disaster. They'd gotten along well, had discovered they had quite a few things in common and enjoyed the same authors and movies. They also shared the same views on the hospital administration and politics. See? Meant to be.

And when they'd finally left, he'd pulled her into

a long, warm embrace. And try as she might, she couldn't work up one tingle, not an ounce of enthusiasm.

Pathetic.

It was just nerves, she assured herself. She'd been too conscious of the mistakes she'd made with James, of pushing too far, too fast. Of expecting too much. She'd been too cautious. Next time, she'd be more relaxed. Stop worrying so much about every word.

She'd make it clear to Justin she was interested in a relationship with him. A future. Their future.

With that thought firmly in mind, she switched the bakery box to her other hand and rapped on Kane's door.

He opened it a moment later.

There was that damn tingle, starting at the base of her spine and climbing her back.

"Red." He opened the door wider. "Right on time."

She brushed past him. "You look better."

His eye had turned purple, but his stitches weren't so red and raw-looking. "I feel like shit."

"Is the ibuprofen helping?" she asked, worried he was overdoing it physically, especially since he wouldn't take stronger medicine.

"Some." He nodded toward the box in her hand. "What's that?"

"Brownies." She lifted the lid showing thick chocolate squares with glossy chocolate icing. "I thought, with Estelle being here, it was a more appropriate hostess gift than a bottle of wine."

"She'll love them. She's downstairs picking up our dinners since I only have one good arm. Mary Susan's making her special chicken fajitas, black beans and rice, and corn bread." His eyes narrowed. "Do you want wine? I can run down and get you a glass."

For some reason, she wasn't as nervous in this tiny, cramped apartment as she had been with Justin at the coffee shop. Weird. "No, thanks. Whatever you have up here will be fine."

"I have water or milk," he said, going into the kitchen. Estelle must have set the table because it was properly done, with a centerpiece of three white candles of various sizes, their flames flickering as Kane walked by. "And some of this juice Estelle picked up at the store."

He opened the fridge door and pulled out a bottle of fruit juice, blended with vegetables to make it healthier. If you ignored the sugar added to make it taste good. "Water's fine," she said, setting the box on the counter. She leaned back, watched him as he pulled a glass from the cupboard. "You don't keep alcohol in your place?"

"It didn't seem like a good idea," he drawled, his accent thicker than usual, "what with my being an alcoholic and all."

"Yet you own a bar. Work there." Serving drinks, being surrounded by it day in and day out. "Isn't it difficult for you to stay sober?"

He lifted a shoulder, poured a bottle of water into her glass. "Some days." His mouth lifting in a self-deprecating smile, he handed her the glass. "Some days it's torture."

"Why do you do it?"

"Let's call it...penance. For my past misdeeds."

She sipped her water, couldn't imagine someone putting themselves in that sort of situation for any reason. "Maybe you've already made up for those misdeeds," she said quietly. "And can stop punishing yourself."

Surely that's what he was doing. And she didn't like it, didn't want him to suffer. Bad enough that he was dealing with physical pain and was too afraid to take anything. But she could respect his willpower. His determination.

How he did it all for his daughter. To be a better man.

"Maybe," he allowed, his deep voice filled with a combination of humor and resignation. "Or maybe I keep adding to that misdeed tally."

Someone pounded on the door and he left Char in the kitchen to answer it. A moment later, Estelle's cheerful voice filled the apartment. "You're here!" she said as if Char had escaped from a maximum security prison. She carried several takeout containers, and Kane held one in his hand, a plastic bag dangling from his arm.

Estelle set down her boxes and gave Char a hug. "I'm so glad you could come."

Char returned the teen's embrace. Grinned down

at her. "Me, too," she said honestly. "Though I'm guessing you don't get your obvious enjoyment of entertaining guests from your father."

"You want entertained?" Kane asked. "Go see a movie."

"Ignore him," Estelle said. "He's been a grump all day. He wouldn't even let me buy decent dinnerware. I mean…look. Nothing matches."

"The table looks very pretty," Char assured her. The dishes may not match, but Estelle had managed to make it look charming by using dark green placemats. The mismatched plates were on top of those—white except one had green checks around the edge and one had a flower design in the center.

"Since it finally stopped raining, I went exploring today and found this cute shop downtown where I found fabric for the place mats," Estelle said, taking the box from Kane, then the bag. "Material Girl?"

"That's a great place," Char said. "It's actually just down the block from my mom's boutique, WISC." Irene loved running the upscale boutique and had made it quite a success.

"Ooh, I remember that store. Awesome front window display."

"I'll be sure to tell Mom you think so." Char really did like this kid. She'd never met someone so open and friendly. It was hard to believe she had Kane's DNA in her. "I really appreciate you going to all this trouble for me," she said, realizing the teen had done just that. Made place mats and set the table, and she had cleaned the apartment, despite her earlier claim that Bartasaviches didn't do dishes and, Char had assumed, other menial household tasks.

Estelle opened the containers and put serving utensils in each one. "It was fun. Even if Daddy doesn't have any proper serving dishes."

"This is fine and it smells fantastic."

There were warm flour tortillas, grilled chicken, a large container of black beans and rice, and another of a crisp, green salad, along with smaller containers of salsa, sour cream, guacamole, shredded cheese and grilled peppers, onions and tomatoes.

"Still, he should have certain things. I mean, he owns only two bowls. What if I want to eat cereal for breakfast and he's used them both?"

Kane set a bag of still-hot homemade tortilla chips in the center of the table. "Then you wash one of the bowls."

Estelle shook her head sadly and sat down, started passing the food around. "That's just silly when it's much easier to buy more." She scooped rice and beans onto her plate. Gave a small shrug. "Oh, well. I suppose it would have been a waste if he had let me buy him proper dishware now. He'd probably leave it all behind when he moved anyway."

Char, in the act of placing chicken onto her flour tortilla, paused. Looked at Kane. "You're moving?"

"Eventually," he said, fumbling to roll up his fajita with his left hand.

"Daddy doesn't like to stay in one place too long. He says he gets bored, but I think he's just running from his past. Literally."

Kane frowned at his daughter. "Have you been talking to your mother's therapist again?"

"It doesn't take a psych degree to know you have deep-seated issues regarding your childhood. Although it might take a therapist to help you figure out those issues so you can stay in one place longer than two years."

"You've never stayed in one place longer than two years?" Char couldn't help asking him.

"Not since I was discharged from the Army." He held her gaze. "When it's time to move on, it's time to move on."

Estelle changed the subject to how crazy her mother's therapist was, but how much Meryl loved the woman and refused to believe she was a complete quack. Char listened and contributed to the conversation as it flowed from one topic to the other, usually due to her or Estelle asking the other a question or bringing up a different subject.

By the end of their meal, Char was relaxed and full, and had had a very good time. Watching Kane with his daughter was enlightening. He obviously adored the girl, and the feeling was clearly mutual. But through it all, Char couldn't help but think about what Kane had said.

When it's time to move on, it's time to move on.

For the life of her, she couldn't figure out why the idea of his moving on bothered her so.

Why she wanted to ask him to stay.

"THE RULE," ESTELLE told Kane as they finished their brownies and coffee, "is whoever cooked doesn't have to clean up."

He leaned back, laid his good arm across his stomach. "You didn't cook. Mary Susan did."

"I would have cooked if you had more than one pot and a frying pan."

"You can cook?" he asked. When he'd been sixteen—hell, when he'd been twenty—he hadn't been able to do anything for himself. Everything had always been done for him.

Estelle hadn't been as indulged as he'd been, but he'd had no idea she was competent in the kitchen. Maybe he didn't know his daughter as well as he'd like to think.

One more reason to seriously consider her request to live with him.

"I'm not as good as Mama, and we both pretty much suck compared to Rosa—that's our cook," Estelle told Charlotte before turning back to him. "But I'm learning. And even though I didn't cook tonight, I did all the prep work. I planned the meal, set the table, ordered the food and picked it up." She pressed her finger against the brownie crumbs on her plate then put that finger in her mouth. "Besides,

Andrew's coming to get me in—" She checked her phone. Made a squeaking sound. "Any minute now."

She leaped up, but at least she took her plate to the sink.

"Who's Andrew?" Char wanted to know.

"Andrew Freeman," Estelle told her. "He works at the diner."

"What about your schoolwork?" Kane asked, standing to block her way before she could slip out of the kitchen. She was fast when she wanted to be.

She rolled her eyes. "I have two weeks to finish it. And I'm on vacation."

"Your mother is on vacation. You were supposed to be in Houston in school, and I don't want you waiting until the last minute to get your work done."

He'd called the school and had them send the next two weeks' assignments to her so she wouldn't fall behind.

"I won't. I promise. Andrew and I are just going to the movies. We'll be back in two hours and then I'll work on it. I've already finished three days of history lessons."

He didn't have a hard time saying no to her, but he liked to think he balanced those times out by letting her have her way, too. "Fine. But be home no later than ten o'clock."

She grinned. Kissed his cheek. "I will."

She scooted past him and out of the room.

"I've never heard of the Freemans," Charlotte

said as she closed the takeout boxes. "Is he from Shady Grove?"

"I don't think so. I met him the other day when he came to get her to take her out for ice cream." Ice cream. Had he ever done anything so innocent at that age? He didn't think so.

"Did you do your best intimidating father routine? Growl at him? Give him one of those scowls you've perfected? Show him your gun collection?"

He realized he was scowling now so he smoothed his expression. Put the boxes of leftovers in the fridge. "I don't own any guns." Being a former Ranger, he was more than comfortable around firearms, but he didn't like having too many possessions bogging him down. Made it too hard to pack up and leave.

"Is that what your dad did?" he asked, not stopping her when she ran water in the sink and squirted in dish soap. It was tough washing dishes with one hand. "Intimidate your dates?"

She laughed. "My dad's about as mild-mannered as they come."

He'd never met her parents, but he'd seen them once when they had come into O'Riley's for dinner. He didn't think his bar was the type of place they usually went to, but Sadie claimed they'd enjoyed their meal.

Irene Ellison was blonde and petite, an older and still beautiful version of Sadie. Her husband, a well-respected ophthalmologist, was average height with a slight paunch and dark red hair.

"Besides," Charlotte continued, rinsing a plate and setting it in the dish drainer, "I didn't have any dates in high school."

"None?"

"'Fraid not." Her voice was light, but she didn't look at him. Embarrassed, maybe? "Like I said before, I was a late bloomer. All arms and legs. The braces and an unfortunate haircut probably didn't help things."

The boys in her school had been idiots. "I'm sure you've made up for lost time."

She flashed a smile at him, her dimple evident, and it about knocked him on his ass. "I've tried my best."

Now that he'd been around her more, he couldn't imagine her spending many weekends by herself. She was too vibrant. Too bright and smart and open to be alone.

"I had a really nice time tonight," she continued, rinsing another plate.

"Everyone has fun around Estelle." His kid was as gracious and charming as her mother.

"I don't doubt that, and I knew I'd enjoy her company. It's yours I wasn't so sure about."

He liked the way she always spoke the truth, no sugarcoating for Charlotte. "I'm wounded."

"You're not. You didn't even want me to come."

True. But Estelle had been right to ask Charlotte over after everything she'd done for them. It didn't seem like enough, but he wasn't sure what else he could do. How much he could give. "I may not have been crazy about the idea." The idea of having Charlotte back in his apartment, around his kid, when he couldn't stop thinking about her. About their kiss. "But I'm glad Estelle did this."

He'd enjoyed himself, he realized with only a hint of trepidation. Had enjoyed spending time with his daughter, yes, but also with Charlotte.

"We're running late," Estelle said as she hurried into the kitchen, "so Andrew's not going to come up."

"But he'll walk you to the door at ten," Kane said, accepting her kiss.

"Yes, Daddy."

Estelle turned and hugged Charlotte, hard. "Thank you for coming. It was so much fun."

"Thank you," Charlotte said. "If you don't have plans Friday, why don't we get some lunch? Maybe head into Pittsburgh?"

Estelle's face lit up. "I'd love that."

"Great. I'll call you tomorrow to set it up."

Estelle left with a wave and a smile.

"You don't have to do that," Kane said.

Charlotte frowned at the silverware she washed. "How else are they going to get clean?"

"No. You don't have to take Estelle to lunch."

"I want to. I like her. You and her mother have done a great job."

Pride filled him. Yeah, his kid was great, but he knew he didn't deserve any credit for it. "Estelle's a good girl." Spoiled and a bit flighty, but with a big heart and a sunny disposition that always astounded him. "Meryl's the one who's done a good job. I've only been a part-time parent."

He hated it. He wasn't the only person who saw their kids a few times a year, but it was still tough.

"I think you may have had a hand in there at some point," Charlotte said, draining the water and wringing out the dishcloth. "I loved watching you two at dinner. You're a really good dad."

Her praise warmed him. "She makes it easy." He pressed his lips together, but couldn't stop the next words from coming out. "She wants to stay. With me. She wants to live with me, permanently, until she goes away to college."

Wiping off the table, Charlotte glanced over her shoulder at him, her eyes wide. "Wow. Does her mother know?"

"I don't think so." He hadn't wanted to say anything to Meryl in case this was just one of Estelle's whims. He didn't want to hurt Meryl.

"Do you want her to live with you? Or are you worried a daughter will ruin your carefree bachelor ways?"

He frowned. Was that what she really thought? Worse, why did it bug him?

Because, he admitted to himself, for the first time in longer than he could remember, he wanted someone to think better of him. He wanted Charlotte to think better of him.

He must have suffered some undiscovered brain damage in his motorcycle accident.

"I'm an ex-addict," he said, his soft tone not hiding the ugly reality of what he'd been. "I already told you that since I left the service, I haven't stayed in one place very long. I've broken laws and went through rehab four times before it finally stuck. Do you know how many women I've slept with? How many I've used?"

She pursed her lips. "I'm not sure if you're confessing or bragging."

"Neither. Just putting the truth you deem so important out there."

"Here's how I see things. Everything you mentioned is in the past. Even if you committed a crime yesterday and slept with four different women last week, it's over. It's what you do from now on that matters."

"A person's past stays with them."

She waved it away as if it were that simple to brush aside his sins. "A person's past shapes who they are, sure. But you can always choose to change. To become a better version of yourself."

Had she been raised under a rainbow by benevolent fairies and happy elves? He wanted to set her straight on the real world, to help her understand you couldn't change the core of who you were, no matter how hard you tried.

He took a step toward her, then another, forcing her back until she was pressed against the counter— shades of the first time she'd come here. "You want to help me become a better version of myself?" He smirked. "You trying to save me, Red?"

She held the dishcloth in both hands in front of her chest, a pathetic shield against him getting too close. "I'm just trying to help."

"Why?"

She opened her mouth then shook her head. "What do you mean?"

"I mean, you must be expecting something, some reward for your time and effort. What is it? Free drinks for you and your friends on the weekends? A picture in the local paper of you with a shiny good-deed medal?"

"You haven't had many people be nice to you, have you?"

He thought of all the people who'd treated him like royalty because of his last name. How eager they had been to please him, to keep him happy in the hopes of getting a hefty tip, entry into his inner circle or a good word in with his old man. "I've had people bowing and scraping to me since I was born. Which is how I know the only reason people do anything for someone else is if they get something out of it."

He could already feel the ropes of expectations, of indebtedness, wrapping around him, growing tauter with every one of Charlotte's small acts of kindness. But he wouldn't fall for it. Wouldn't step into a trap laid with seemingly innocent gestures and outwardly harmless generosity.

Holding her gaze, he waited for her to hiss at him,

to put her thin nose in the air and take a verbal swipe. What she did was way, way worse.

"That," she said softly, "is the saddest thing I've ever heard."

CHARLOTTE WANTED TO hug him.

She wanted to wrap her arms around Kane, pull him close and just hold him. To tell him everything would be all right, that no matter what happened with him and Estelle, things would work out in the end for both of them. That he deserved to have his daughter in his life, as much as he wanted.

She gripped the cloth tighter, the water dripping down her arm. She was losing her ever-loving mind. Hug Kane? It was a crazy thought. An insane urge. He wasn't exactly the hugging type, especially when he towered over her, his face bruised, his gaze cool, his hair rumpled.

Sexily rumpled, of course. She wouldn't expect anything less from him at this point.

Everything about him, from his expression to his words, proved her right. He wasn't a man seeking warm embraces and sympathetic assurances. He was a loner with a bad attitude and a dangerous edge.

Yes, he was suffering—and she didn't just mean his physical injuries. He was suffering on the inside. If ever there was a man conflicted, a man fighting intense personal demons, he stood before her now.

She wanted to help him.

But that didn't mean she was dumb enough to believe she could actually save him.

He inched closer. She knew it was a tactic, meant to put her on edge. She prayed he couldn't tell how well it worked. "You really think I'm a good role model for a teenager?" he asked.

"I think you love her. What more could a child want from a parent?"

He intense gaze pinned her to the spot. Her breath caught, almost choking her. Potent. The man was definitely potent.

"What if love isn't enough?" he asked quietly. "What if I do something to screw it up? Screw her up?"

Char tossed the cloth onto the counter, then, despite her intentions to keep her distance, laid her damp hand on his. "Everyone makes mistakes. There are no perfect parents, believe me, I've seen my fair share at work. More importantly, I've seen you with Estelle. You'd never do anything to hurt her."

He exhaled, the breath seeming to shudder out of him. "That's just it." His voice was ragged, his shoulders slumped. "I did. I hurt her… I almost killed her."

CHAPTER TWELVE

KANE'S WORDS ECHOED in Char's ears. Her blood went cold. Denial, swift and sharp, cut through the haze in her brain. No. He was exaggerating. Or there had been an accident, one of those freak things that happened when a parent, even the most vigilant of parents, turned his attention away for a moment.

Kane would never purposely put his own child in danger.

You don't know anything about me.

Char inhaled, slid her hand away from his. He'd been right the other evening when he'd said that to her. She didn't know him.

She'd managed to convince herself he was some sort of tormented soul. An honorable man doing his best to overcome a dark, troubled past.

What if he wasn't? She'd deluded herself before. Had believed in a fantasy, one she'd scripted from once upon a time all the way to happily ever after.

"What's the matter, Red?" Kane asked, his quiet voice rubbing against her nerve endings. "No words of compassion and understanding? No assurances that I can overcome my mistakes if only I want it badly enough? Or maybe you've realized some mistakes can never be forgotten. They sure as hell can't be forgiven."

His tone was as cocky as ever, his smirk firmly in place, but his eyes were bleak.

"You're right," she said, surprising them both with her admission. "Some things never can be forgotten. But everyone deserves forgiveness."

He deserved forgiveness. Even from himself.

She wasn't sure she wanted to hear what he had to confess, wasn't sure she was strong enough, tolerant enough to listen without judgment. But she couldn't turn her back on him. He needed her more than he had the other night.

And she needed him. Or, rather, she needed to face the truth about him. No matter what that truth turned out to be. "What happened?" she asked.

For a few long minutes, the only sound was the refrigerator running and their mingled breathing. When Kane spoke, his voice was soft and filled with pain. "That car accident I told you about?"

"The one that made you so upset when you remembered it at the E.R.?"

He nodded. "I was twenty. I'd just gotten out of a stint in rehab a few days earlier and had a scheduled visitation with Estelle."

"How old was she?"

"Two. But I'd only known about her for just over a year."

"How is that possible?"

"When Meryl and I slept together, she was home

on break—and engaged to some guy she'd met at college. After that night, we both went our separate ways. She got married and for a year, thought Estelle was her husband's child. When he found out differently, they divorced and she moved back to Houston." He paced the small confines of the kitchen, his movements slow and stiff. "After my second go-round with rehab, I stayed clean for a few months, started taking classes at a local community college. That's when she told me. She hadn't wanted our daughter to have anything to do with me if I was still using."

Charlotte sat down on a kitchen chair, hoping he'd do the same eventually, but restless energy rolled off him like waves. "That must have been hard for her."

"Meryl's stronger than any of us realized. She was willing to raise Estelle alone if it meant keeping her safe from me."

"But you were clean and you did get to know your daughter."

"I stayed clean until Christmas of that year. By July I was back in rehab. When I got out, all I wanted was to spend time with my daughter." He sat on the edge of a chair, his left leg bouncing. "I picked Estelle up. She was so excited to see me, it was like a miracle. No matter how many times or how badly I screwed up, this little person loved me. It was huge, like this weight of responsibility on me. I wasn't sure I wanted it. Knew I didn't deserve it."

He finally leaned back, let his left hand rest between his knees. "We spent the day together, went to the zoo, then to the park. She fell asleep in the car on the way home so I put her to bed at my apartment. I…I thought she'd sleep all night…." His voice dropped off. He cleared his throat. "I took oxycodone. Told myself it was to take the edge off, that it wasn't really using again if I just did it once."

Oxycodone was a highly addictive opioid and could affect people even if they took the recommended dose. "What happened?" she asked gently.

He hung his head. "I thought she'd stay asleep," he repeated. "She didn't. She woke up screaming, said her ear hurt and she wanted her mommy. I couldn't handle the crying so I called Meryl and told her I was bringing Estelle home."

Char was getting a really horrible feeling about what happened next. She laid her hand on his knee. "Kane—"

He shook his head. "About a mile from Meryl's house, I lost control on a curve," he said, his voice flat, his gaze somewhere over Char's head. "We crossed lanes and flipped over before hitting a tree."

Oh, Kane. Her heart broke for him.

"I was knocked out, got pretty busted up— cracked ribs, broken leg, concussion…" He swallowed. "When I came to, they were loading me into the ambulance. I couldn't see Estelle. They had me strapped to the gurney as they took me into the hospital and I couldn't move, couldn't get to her and no one would tell me where she was, if she was okay."

No wonder he'd been so upset getting his stitches,

being in the hospital again. Char edged forward so she could touch him, offer him some small amount of comfort. She gripped his hand with hers, let the other one stay on his knee. His skin was ice cold, his muscles tense. "How long until you found out she was all right?"

"Hours. Finally, after they'd run their tests and set my leg, my father came into my room. Told me Estelle was fine, that Meryl was with her and she'd be taking her home within the hour. I wanted to see her, but he suggested that might not be the best idea," Kane said, his mouth twisting sardonically. He glanced at Char's hand as if surprised to see it on his. Kept staring as he continued, "It was about the only time I can ever remember the old man being right."

"Did you…were you sent back to rehab?"

He shook his head. "The police wanted to press charges against me—reckless driving, driving under the influence, endangering a child. I didn't care. I knew I deserved to be punished for what I'd done. Dad had other ideas."

Kane stood, crossed to lean against the counter, his good arm bent protectively across his sling. "He made it all disappear."

Char frowned. "Made what disappear?"

"Everything. Charges were never filed so, just like that, I was free to move on with my life, as if nothing had ever happened. No consequences. No punishment."

She wasn't so sure about that. Seemed he was still punishing himself. "Your dad has that much influence?"

Kane's face was unreadable. "He has that much power. More than enough to convince a judge, the police chief and a top hospital administrator to alter the reports and make a criminal act go away."

"I can't imagine going to such lengths." Lengths that were not only illegal, but also highly immoral. "Not even to protect my child."

Especially when that child was an adult and obviously needed to face consequences for his actions.

"The old man didn't do it to protect me," Kane said, the fingers of his left hand curling. "He did it to protect the family name."

That, somehow, was so much worse. "I'm sorry."

One side of his mouth kicked up. "Don't feel bad for me, Red. I knew the real reasons behind his actions, just like I knew there would be strings attached if I didn't break free of him for good. I checked myself into another rehab facility, this time paying for it myself."

"When did you join the service?"

"After I was released from the program. One of my counselors was a former Ranger who thought the Army would be a good fit for me. My father hated the idea, which only made it that much more appealing. It hasn't been easy but I've managed to stay clean for fourteen years."

What he'd done had taken incredible courage and

willpower. She'd seen addicts come into the E.R., complaining of a variety of ailments in the hopes of getting drugs. The desperation in their eyes always tugged at her soul. She hated knowing Kane had been like that. That someone so strong had been controlled by his addiction.

"Meryl must have forgiven you," Char said, though she couldn't imagine how difficult it must have been for the other woman. "She obviously trusts you with Estelle now."

"It took time. I wrote them every day while I was in rehab. I think that's what got me through, knowing they were reading my words, seeing my progress, how hard I was working. Meryl let me see Estelle for an hour before I went to boot camp, and during my first leave, they met me in New York for a few days. Eventually, Meryl gave me a second chance."

He sounded shocked, as if no one had ever done that for him before.

Kane's mouth quirked into that smirk of his she loathed, but this time, she wondered if it was self-directed. "Still think Estelle would be all right living with me?" he asked.

"Yes," Char said simply. Emphatically. She stood and crossed to him. "You're not that person anymore. What you did, what you've been through and have now become..." She smiled. "I think you're incredibly strong. And resilient."

And brave. Brave enough to live with his past

mistakes, to face those demons inside him every day and still stay sober.

He looked at her as if she'd lost her mind.

The only reason people do anything for someone else is if they get something out of it.

His words came back to her, made her realize he not only meant what he'd said, but that it seemed to be some sort of personal mantra. As a way to protect himself.

"Now," he said softly, "you know all my secrets." He angled his body toward her, leaned in close. "What are you going to give me for them?"

A chill raced across her skin, foreboding or anticipation, she was afraid to define it. "Nothing's free, is that it?"

"Nothing worthwhile." He scanned her face, his gaze sliding from her forehead to her cheek to chin before settling on her mouth with an intensity, a heated interest that threw her, had her thoughts tumbling round and round in her head. When he touched the indentation above her upper lip, the tip of his forefinger lightly rubbing her skin, she about jumped out of her clothes. "But some things," he continued, his gentle touch hypnotizing her, the lazy cadence of his voice lulling her into believing every word he said, "some things are worth the cost."

Charlotte swallowed. Hard. Holy spit, he was going to kiss her again. She could see the intention in his eyes, feel it in the way his hand slipped to cup her jaw. Sense it with some instinctual, inner feminine certainty she'd never known she'd had.

She wanted his kiss, she couldn't deny it. All she had to do was stand still, maybe shut her eyes and let him do his thing.

But their first kiss had knocked her for a loop, had sent him running from her as if she'd lit his hair on fire. Letting him do that again would be the dumbest thing ever.

His head lowered, his mouth inching closer to hers. Mindful of his injuries, she decided against the hearty shove she should give him, opting to go with the uninspired, yet universal, turning of the head.

His lips brushed her ear.

"Ouch," he murmured, his lips sweeping up the side of her neck. Well, she hadn't exactly pushed him away, hadn't moved at all. "Don't be like that, Charlotte."

The combination of him saying her name and his mouth vibrating against the sensitive skin of her neck made her shiver. "You kissed me the other day and couldn't get away from me fast enough."

His mouth slid up and he pressed a warm kiss behind her ear. "This payback?"

"Yes," she said, shooting for a dry tone, but it came out as a gasp when he gently sucked her earlobe into his mouth. She really, really should back up. "Because the only reason a woman would reject you is because they have been previously scorned."

Finally, thankfully, he leaned back. Watched her

out of hooded eyes. "If it's not payback, then what is it?"

Self-preservation, pure and simple. A woman had to be smart and very, very careful when it came to men like Kane.

"I suppose it could be pride," she said, still unable to move an inch. It was as if he'd put some sort of force field around them, keeping her close. She tapped her forefinger against her chin, pretending to give her next words great thought. "Or it could be that I'm not all that interested in kissing you."

His grin flashed, sharp as a scalpel and incredibly sexy. "That a dare to see if you can get me to prove otherwise?"

She gave a short laugh. "Good Lord, no. I don't need you to prove anything. Even with my limited experience, I imagine you can be very...persuasive. Especially when it comes to getting what you want from a woman."

"You sure this isn't some sort of petty revenge?" he asked, exasperated, irritable and suspicious. She bet he didn't often get turned down. For anything.

"I'm sure." She smiled. How could she not when he looked so put out by her rejection? It was flattering. And went a long way toward stroking her ego, which had taken quite a beating by him not so long ago. "Okay, maybe part of it—" She held her forefinger and thumb close together. "A teeny, tiny, insignificant part was for revenge."

"Like I said. Petty. And beneath you."

"Hey, I didn't say I was proud of it."

His lips curved. The brief glimpse of humor lighting his eyes hit her square in the chest, hard and swift.

Forget self-preservation and pride, she thought.

And she launched herself at him and pressed her mouth to his.

CHARLOTTE KNOCKED HIM back a step and he bumped into the edge of the counter. Pain shot up from his ribs, traveled from his shoulder to his wrist. It was worth it. Any pain was worth it because she was kissing him.

She was kissing him.

God, she was warm. And her scent wrapped around him, beckoning him closer. He wished like hell he could put both arms around her, but he'd have to make do with one. He wrapped his arm about her slim waist, tugging her forward until their bodies aligned. Chest to chest. Hip to hip. Thigh to thigh.

He angled his head, took their kiss deeper, swept his tongue into her mouth. She trembled. He groaned. He loved how she responded to him so quickly, so easily. As though she couldn't get enough of him.

He dragged his hand up her back, trailing his fingers along her spine, pulling her shirt up. He ached with the need to be with her, and he didn't like wanting, not this much, having it be this important to him.

He set out to seduce her, not with flowery words he didn't mean, wasn't sure he'd ever mean. Not with promises he had no intention of keeping or soft touches or long kisses. He wanted her to be inflamed, to be as desperate for him as he was for her.

He wanted to lose himself in her. If only for a little while.

He kissed her hungrily, turning them around and around until they were in the living room. Pushing her against the wall, he kept his hand at the back of her head, held her there. Deepened the kiss, knowing he was out of control, hungry and desperate for her, but he couldn't seem to stop.

Please, God, don't let her stop him.

Her hands went to his shoulders and then up to his head, her fingers stabbing into his hair. She matched the movement of his tongue, of his hips gently rotating against hers. Matched his desire. He kissed her again and again until they were both gasping for breath, her hands caressing his shoulders, his neck, down his left arm and back up again.

He stepped back far enough to slide his hand under the hem of her shirt. She was soft and warm and so receptive to his touch, the way her muscles jerked under his hand, how she gasped into his mouth.

He broke the kiss and somehow managed to pull her shirt up with one hand, helped her tug it off, then tossed it aside and kissed her again. Her breasts were small, but they were big enough to press against him, fill his hand as he cupped her through her lacy bra, his thumb bringing one nipple to a hard peak. She whimpered into his mouth, squirmed, so he did it again. And again, then pinched it lightly.

She bucked against him, her hips brushing his erection, and he growled. Stepped back and ripped open the buttons of his shirt, shoved it off his good arm, then quickly removed his sling and pulled the shirt down his cast. Her hands were there, helping him, skimming against his stomach, his ribs. The material caught on his cast and she was already kissing him again, touching his chest as he yanked the shirt off. He loved the way she touched him, as if memorizing the feel of him, his shape. It drove him crazy. Having her hands on him was better than he'd ever imagined. And he had imagined being with her. He hadn't wanted to, didn't want this strong of a need for anyone. He couldn't count on her to be there, didn't want her to count on him to be there after this was done.

But they were together now. That was all that mattered.

He kissed her again, deep kisses, his tongue rubbing against hers, his hand sliding up and down her side, her back, his fingers trailing across the side of her breast. He walked her toward the hallway, intending on somehow making it to his bedroom, to his bed, but when he got to the doorway, he couldn't help but press against her there, his body holding her prisoner.

He kissed a line down her throat, across her collarbone and to the slope of her breasts. Then tugged her bra down and touched her. "I wish I could put both of my hands on you," he growled in frustration, loving the flush that turned her chest pink.

He lowered his head and took one nipple into his mouth and sucked.

He kissed his way between her breasts, down her stomach to her lower abdomen, his hand gripping her waist. He straightened, kissed her again, hungrier this time, demanding a response from her, an answer to his need. Her hands were hesitant on him, but he couldn't get enough of her touch, the feel of her fingers skimming his shoulders, down his chest.

"Kane," she gasped, tearing her mouth from his. Now she pressed against his chest. Holding him back. He didn't like that at all. "Wait."

It took all his willpower to straighten, to keep his hand on her still, to not kiss her mouth, which was swollen and glossy. "What's wrong?"

He winced. He hadn't meant for that to come out so rough, so accusing.

Her eyes were wide. Still dazed from his kisses, his touch. She licked her lips, the move unconsciously, incomprehensively sexy when she stood before him, naked from the waist up, her hair tousled. "I…I'm not sure this is a good idea."

He inhaled through his nose, tried to calm his heart rate. He needed to slow down. A woman like Charlotte, with her pretty fantasies about what life was supposed to be like, about relationships and happy ever after, needed more than a quick bang against the wall.

She deserved so much more.

He wished he could give her more, wished he could walk away from her, but his need for her was too great. Being with her soothed the ache in his chest, appeased the constant hunger in his soul.

Made him feel less alone.

"Yeah?" he asked, his voice low as he trailed one finger down the long line of her neck. He watched that finger slide over her collarbone, dip into the hollow at the base of her throat before sliding down the slope of her breast. Her nipple tightened. "I think it's the best idea I've had this week. Maybe ever."

Now he had to convince her to agree. He didn't want her to have regrets, didn't want her to think of this as a mistake. He wouldn't force her. But he'd do his damnedest to seduce her.

He traced her nipple, watched as the pink bud tightened, jutting out, waiting for his hands. His mouth. "Do you like when I touch you?" he asked.

Her chest rose and fell heavily to match her breathing. "I… Yes…but—"

He kissed her, nibbling at her lower lip before soothing it with his tongue. Leaned back so their mouths were inches apart. "Do you like when I kiss you?"

Her fingers trembled on his chest, above his heart. "You know I do, it's just—"

He kissed her again, dragged his hand down

her side, traced his fingers back and forth along the waistband of her pants. "I love touching you," he murmured.

"You…you do?"

He'd done too good of a job of convincing her he hadn't wanted her that night. "I do. I want to touch you all over. I want you, Charlotte."

So much. Too much.

Her fingers relaxed, her hands going back to smoothing over his chest. It took some work, but he managed to undo the button of her jeans with one hand, pulled down the zipper, the noise loud in the silence. He slid his hand under the denim and, palming her hip, pushed the material down. He wanted to shove at them, tear off her panties, bury himself deep inside her warmth. Her sweetness. Hunger for her filled him, snapped at his self-control, frayed the hold he had on his willpower.

His hand was unsteady as he slipped one finger under the thin strap of her panties, then tugged them down. She was perfect, all long lines, subtle curves and glowing skin. He wanted to taste her, the most elemental part of her, to hold her against the wall, his hand on her stomach, and kiss her core.

But he didn't want to frighten her, not when she was watching him, her eyes heavy-lidded, her lips parted. He crouched before her, traced light circles over her skin, around her navel. Her skin heated beneath his touch, her breathing grew ragged. Her legs were slim and smooth. Soft. He slid his hand up and down the back of her leg, behind her knee and up her inner thigh.

Her thigh muscles clenched.

He rose. Kissed her neck. "Tell me what you want," he whispered. "Tell me what you like."

"I…I don't know," she said, her breathlessness exciting him even more.

He flicked her earlobe with his tongue. "Let's find out."

He dragged his mouth up and down the side of her neck, settled his lips behind her ear. "Do you like that?"

She swallowed. "Yes."

He touched her core, grazing the coarse curls there. She jerked, pressed against the wall. "Do you like that?"

"I… Yes," she whispered as if admitting some deep secret.

He slipped his hand between her legs. Rubbed her most sensitive spot. She gasped then bit her lower lip. "Do you like that?" he asked.

She opened her mouth, but no sound came out. She nodded.

He shifted to the side, worked her with long, smooth strokes, kissing her breasts, her shoulders, her face before settling on her mouth for a long, leisurely kiss, his tongue lazily touching hers. Continued his slow seduction of her until she relaxed against the wall, until her hips began undulating against his hand.

He moved faster, lowered his head and took one nipple into his mouth, sucking hard. She panted, her hips banging against the wall. When her body tightened around his hand, he straightened. Held her eyes. She shook her head as if denying the pleasure he was giving her. As if afraid of it.

That wouldn't do. Ruthlessly, he worked her. Harder. Faster. Until she came apart with a soft, throaty cry.

EVEN AS THE most potent, powerful sensations swept through her, Charlotte couldn't look away from Kane's eyes. Her mouth rounded and his eyes darkened, his breathing grew unsteady though she was the one who felt as if she were flying. Pleasure coursed through her, wave after wave, the intensity overwhelming, her own response to him terrifying.

As she came down from her orgasm, he kissed her, the heat building again between them. "I want to do that again," he told her, his voice rough, his body vibrating with tension. "I want to make you come again, Charlotte. I want to be inside of you."

Yes. Yes, she wanted that, too. So much. Too much.

He leaned in again to kiss her, but she turned her head, pushed him back. "Wait. Kane…I… God, I'm sorry. I…can't."

He paused. Unlike when she'd stopped him before, it wasn't just resolve that filled his eyes, but frustration and a bit of temper. "Damn it, Red. Why not?"

Yes, she had every right to put the brakes on, but

the least she could do was explain why. "I…I've…
never…" She gestured weakly to herself, then to him,
noted the bulge behind his zipper, how labored his
breathing was. Inhaling, she shut her eyes and forced
the words, the confession, past the tightness in her
throat. "I've never done this before. I'm a virgin."

CHAPTER THIRTEEN

HER WORDS SEEMED to echo in the room. Stark. Honest.

She could feel Kane's stunned silence, could hear the hard rasp of his quickly indrawn breath. Forcing her eyes open, she swallowed. Brought her arms up to cover her naked breasts, hating the shock in his gaze.

She lifted her chin. "I'm a virgin," she repeated because it was a choice, her choice, and nothing to be ashamed of. And she didn't want her first time to be like this, rough and quick against the wall, neither of them sure of where they stood with the other.

"Shit," he muttered, stepping back, staring at her as if she was some sort of act at the freak show. His hair was mussed from her hands, his expression set in hard lines. "Shit. Goddamn it, Charlotte. What do you mean, you're a virgin?"

She winced. Well, he didn't have to make it sound like she was a freaking leper. "I'd say it was pretty self-explanatory." Hurt and mortified, she pulled her panties and jeans up. She scooped up her shirt and put it on, well aware of her braless state, her breasts pleasantly sensitive. Even dressed, she wanted more than anything to dive for the blanket on the couch, to cover and hide herself.

She'd face him, and this latest humiliation, on her feet, thank you very much. She gave him a small, tight smile. Crossed her arms and wished he'd move back, let her leave so she could drown in her embarrassment and regrets. Then crawl into her bed and have a good cry.

"What was that?" he asked, grabbing his shirt and shaking it at her. "What the hell was that?"

"Well, seeing as how you have more experience in this area, I'm not sure how to answer that. But if I had to hazard a guess, I'd say what that was, was a mistake. A big one. But then, you don't worry about mistakes, do you?"

"You came to me," he accused, struggling to yank on his shirt, his broken arm falling heavily against his side. "You came to me last fall, ready and willing to take me to bed. You threw yourself at me!"

After picking up her bra and stuffing it in her back pocket, she met his gaze steadily. "I'm well aware of what happened between us last fall. I'm almost twenty-five years old and, as you've pointed out to me before, it's time…past time…I grew up."

Time she stopped believing in fairy tales like true love and happily ever after.

Oh, she wanted to believe in them. Wanted to believe there was someone out there who would love her forever.

But it was getting harder and harder to do.

"I got carried away," she continued. "We both did."

"You never should have let me touch you."

She shrugged, then sighed. She'd let him touch her because he'd needed her. Wanted her. She'd never had a man want her that much. Had never experienced such a rush of pleasure, of heat and desire. "No, I shouldn't have," she said quietly.

"Look," she said when he remained silent, standing there glaring at her, his shirt open, his mouth a thin line. "There's no reason for you to be so upset. Nothing happened."

His expression grew stormy. "I made you come," he said, the words heated and blatant. "You call that nothing?"

Her entire body grew warm and she remembered, oh how she remembered the sensations flowing through her. The first time a man had made her feel that way. "Yes, you did. Why was that?"

He looked away. They both knew he'd seduced her, taken his experience and her lack of it, and used it to get what he wanted.

To almost get what he wanted, she corrected silently. She was so confused, her feelings for him conflicted. She didn't love him. He wasn't the man she planned on marrying, planned on spending the rest of her life with—and she still would have made love with him. Shame swept through her.

"Can we just…forget this ever happened?" she asked, stepping forward.

Blocking her way, he raised his eyebrows. "I doubt it."

She blushed. "Okay, so maybe *forget* isn't the right word. Maybe we could...move past it? The sooner the better. As in, right now."

"You want to move past this? Move past the fact that we almost had sex against the wall, that it would have been your first time. Now we'll...what? Go on with our lives?"

"Yes, please." She stepped to the right. He moved to his left. In her way again. "If we could go on with them now, that'd be great."

He narrowed his eyes. "What do you mean?"

She linked her hands together in front of her waist. "I mean, I'd really like to go home, so please get out of my way."

He looked as if he wanted to argue, and she prayed he wouldn't because she was vulnerable and unsteady, and if she stayed, even for another minute, she'd break down in front of him. And that would not do.

"This isn't over," he told her through gritted teeth as he shifted to the side.

"Oh, I think it is," she said before grabbing her purse and rushing out the door.

JUST WHEN KANE thought his night couldn't get any shittier, the door to O'Riley's opened and a tall, broad-shouldered man in a three-piece suit and a Stetson stepped inside. Damn it. Kane had come down to the bar after Estelle got home because he couldn't stand being cooped up in that apartment one more minute, not after what had happened between him and Char.

What had almost happened.

I'm a virgin.

Kane's fingers tightened on his bottle of water, denting the plastic. He'd known, somewhere deep in the recesses of his mind, he'd known she was innocent. But it hadn't mattered. He would have taken her, right there in his living room, without a thought or care about anything except his own wants and needs.

Just like the entitled boy he'd once been.

And like that boy, he'd reacted like an angry, spoiled brat when he hadn't gotten what he'd wanted. He'd hurt her. For once, he hadn't meant to. He just wasn't sure how to make it right. If he should even try.

The cowboy's gaze found him. He tipped his stupid hat and jerked his head toward the table in the corner.

Kane ground his teeth together, sent the asshole a middle finger in answer to his silent order and went back to work.

Too bad there wasn't much to do. It was almost time for last call and the place hadn't exactly been jumping after the dinner rush left. Mary Susan and Garret, the twenty-year-old Kane had hired to do dishes, had cleaned the kitchen and already taken off. Just he and Julie were left. Him manning the bar while she wiped down tables.

Usually, this was his favorite part of the night, when things wound down. He liked to do most of the cleanup himself, enjoyed the quiet of it, being alone with his thoughts as he did the mundane chores of sweeping, mopping, washing tables and chairs.

No settling those thoughts down tonight. Not with this visitor from his past sitting in the corner watching him steadily. Not with the feel of Charlotte still on his fingertips, the taste of her on his mouth.

"That guy in the cowboy hat wants to talk to you," Julie told Kane as she came up to the bar.

"Yep."

He felt, more than saw, her study him.

"He can wait," Kane said.

She shrugged, but he saw the curiosity in her eyes, knew she was wondering what was going on. It was only a matter of time, moments probably, before she started asking him questions.

Instead, she surprised him by turning and straight toward the cowboy.

"Sorry," she told him, her voice carrying through the almost empty room. She sounded friendly, but there was a thread of steel under her easy tone that went with the weird hairstyle, neck tattoo and soon-to-be law degree. "We're about to have last call. As the saying goes, you don't have to go home, but you can't stay here."

The cowboy smiled, probably thought it was

charming. "See, here's the problem, darlin'," he said in a Texas twang that grated on Kane's last nerve. "I just sat down."

Julie nodded. "That is a problem," she said all faux concern. Then she leaned forward, had the cowboy's gaze flicking to her dark jeans, which molded her ass, before slowly going back to her face. "But the thing is," she continued, not the least bit upset about some asshole checking her out, "it's not my problem. You need to leave. Now."

Kane came out from behind the bar slowly, knowing the cowboy hated being told what to do.

It was one of the few things they had in common.

The cowboy smirked at him. "You've got yourself a real pretty little guard dog."

Julie, her eyes still on the man before her, asked Kane, "You want me to call the cops?"

"Yes, Kane," the cowboy drawled, amused as hell. "You want the pretty lady here to call the cops?"

"That's not necessary," Kane ground out from between his teeth. "Though I imagine you'd be real popular in jail with that pretty face of yours."

The cowboy took off his hat, ran a hand through his hair, and Julie slowly straightened. Her eyes narrowed as she stared at the cowboy, then at Kane.

"I didn't know you had a brother," she said to Kane.

Clinton Jr. held out his hand. "C.J. Bartasavich." She shook C.J.'s hand. "Just because you're related doesn't mean I won't still call the cops and have your ass kicked out of here."

"Duly noted."

Kane sighed. "It's okay," he told Julie as the last customer left with a wave. "Go on home. I've got this."

"You sure?" she asked.

He nodded.

She touched his arm as she passed. An offering of comfort. A sign of friendship.

He didn't respond. Couldn't. He didn't have friends, didn't want to count on anyone to be there for him because in his experience, they never were. But it was sort of nice knowing she offered.

They watched her go back behind the bar and get her purse, both keeping silent until she closed the door behind her.

"Taking after the old man, I see," C.J. said, standing.

They were the same height, same build, though C.J. had a few pounds on Kane. "Not even a little."

C.J. raised his eyebrows. "Sleeping with your employees? That's Senior through and through."

Kane didn't bother contradicting him. He didn't sleep with people he paid or held authority over. Besides, Julie was gay, and none of it was C.J.'s business. "You're a long way from home," Kane said to his older brother. "What do you want?"

"Checking up on you." His gaze took in Kane's

face, the cast. "Heard you had yourself a little accident. You okay?"

"How did you...? Estelle." His daughter must have told his father about the accident when she spoke with him on Sunday. "I'm fine."

But he wasn't sure how to take his brother's seemingly genuine concern. "Good to know." C.J. sat on a stool. "Now, seeing as how I came all this way to check on your well-being, the least you could do is offer your favorite brother a drink."

"You're not my favorite brother. Oakes is."

"Oakes is everyone's favorite." C.J. went behind the bar and searched the bottles lined up in front of the mirror. "Including mine."

Finding the bottle of Four Roses Single Barrel, C.J. poured himself a healthy amount and sipped his drink neat. They eyed each other, the same way they had all their lives, seeing the other as their greatest ally and biggest enemy. Though C.J. had probably flown from Houston, he didn't look affected by the three-hour flight. His dark designer suit was as crisp and wrinkle-free as when he'd put it on—at some ungodly hour, Kane imagined—the material expensive, the fit perfect.

"Anything else you need to say?" Kane asked. "Because you could have just called to ask how I was."

C.J.'s expression turned thoughtful as he sipped his drink, then leaned back as if he owned the bar and all it entailed, like a king surveying his lands.

Not that it was his fault. He'd been groomed to take over the family business, and he'd eagerly stepped into that role, making the company bigger and better than it had ever been.

"Spit it out, Junior," Kane said, knowing the nickname would only irritate his brother. "Some of us actually work for a living instead of sitting behind a big desk getting fat."

The insult rolled off C.J.'s back. It was hard to get a rise out of his brother on his best day. Guess today wasn't that day.

"Yes, I can see how busy this place must keep you," C.J. said drily as he scanned the empty room. He slid a small, thick envelope out of his inner coat pocket and set it on the bar. "I didn't just come here to check up on you. I'm here on official business."

Kane flicked his gaze to the envelope, his chest tight as he saw the family business name on the upper left corner. His name was written across the front in dark, thick ink. His full name, including his middle, written in his father's hand.

"Not interested," Kane said.

"You might be." C.J. used one finger to slide the envelope closer. "Once you see what he's offering you."

Kane picked it up, turned it in his hand, then tapped the corner against the bar. His father wanted the same thing he'd been after since Kane joined the Army. He wanted Kane back. Back in Houston, back under his control. He thought promising him a prime spot in the company was going to accomplish it, that all he had to do was offer a huge wad of cash and Kane would be scrambling to do Senior's bidding, to give him what he wanted, no questions asked other than, *What else can I do for you?*

Kane had worked damn hard to get away from them all. His mother and brothers and, especially, Clint Sr.

He wasn't going back. His eyes on C.J., he ripped the envelope in two, tossed the pieces into the trash.

"I already know what he's offering me. An office on the top floor, all the perks that come with having fancy initials after my name, my own private secretary—one he's not interested in banging himself— and an annual salary high enough to support a small country. Plus the perk of being under his fat thumb for the rest of my life. No, thanks. Been there. Didn't like how hard he pressed down."

"He wants you in Houston, with your family where you belong," C.J. said, leaning back, out of place in his fancy suit in Kane's run-down bar. Kane was glad. He didn't want his bar to be a place for people like his brother or their family. It was for people who worked hard for a living, who maybe didn't make a ton of money, but they had things the Bartasaviches didn't—integrity. Morals.

But if he moved back to Houston, and Estelle really did end up living with him, he wouldn't be taking her away from everything she'd ever known. She could, for the first time in her life, be close to both her parents, see them every day if she wanted.

He wasn't sure he could do it, though. Not even for her.

"I'm good where I'm at. I'm no man's lapdog." He sent C.J. a pointed look. "Besides, it seems as if that position has already been filled. You may want to live your life in dear old Dad's back pocket, but some of us—or should I say, one of us—has too much pride to be in that position."

C.J.'s gaze narrowed, his shoulders stiffened, and for a moment, Kane thought his brother would take a swing.

But it wasn't going to happen. He could see C.J. fight for control, gain that control degree by degree, the aggression leaving his stance, his fingers loosening on his glass.

Too bad.

"That what you call it?" C.J. asked quietly, a smirk on his face, reminding him of their father. "Pride?"

Kane lifted a chair by its leg, using the momentum to turn it before setting it on a table. He wished he had the use of both hands so he could slam the damn thing down like he wanted. Gave a stiff nod. "You should try it."

"I think I've got pride covered. Pride is doing what's right by your family instead of running off like some goddamn twelve-year-old."

"Leaving isn't the same as running away," Kane

pointed out, though he'd done his fair share of running as a kid.

He'd always been found. Always been brought back.

C.J. laughed harshly. "Christ, but you're an arrogant son of a bitch, you know that? Guess you can't run from genetics."

Because their old man was the same way.

"I'm nothing like him," Kane said, knowing it was true. It had to be. He didn't destroy everything and everyone he touched. He was careful of those in his life, kept his distance from everyone else, didn't take the chance on ruining anyone.

"You keep telling yourself that," C.J. said. He downed the rest of his drink, slammed the glass on the counter. "When we both know the truth. You think you're, what? Settled here? That you belong in this Podunk town at this crappy bar?"

"It being a crappy bar didn't stop you from helping yourself to my liquor."

C.J. shook his head sadly, as if he felt bad for Kane being so damned dim-witted. Kane considered putting the next chair upside his brother's smug head.

"You don't belong here," C.J. told him as he came out from behind the bar. "You never will. People like you, like us, there's only one place we belong, and that's Houston. You can't change who you are inside, what you came from."

"Yeah? Watch me."

"I know you," C.J. said softly. "This place, these

people, they'll soon be a distant memory. You don't stick with anything, never have. You've always run from your responsibilities. You walk away, leaving others to deal with the fallout, to clean up your messes. You've got this bar, but I bet the responsibility of it is weighing on you already. It won't be long before you take off, conveniently forgetting the employees who count on you."

Kane didn't bother denying his brother's words, not when they were too close to the truth. Hadn't he been thinking about moving on again? The only reason he hadn't already contacted a real estate agent and gotten things in motion was because he didn't want to make any plans until he knew whether or not Estelle would be going with him.

"I had to walk away," he said of his decision to join the Army, leaving Houston and his family behind. He couldn't have stayed sober surrounded by his old friends. Couldn't have held on to his pride while accepting handouts from his father.

He'd had to prove he could make it on his own.

"Dad was tough on you," C.J. said quietly, "but think about it. Did he have any other choice?"

No. No, he hadn't. There were days when Kane could admit his father had made a few right decisions, forcing him into rehab, trying to manage his out-of-control behavior. Kane had been on a collision course, one that would have undoubtedly resulted in his death.

"Leaving my past cost me," he admitted to the brother he used to be close to. It'd cost him his relationship with C.J., with his other siblings and his mother. But he'd had to break those ties in order to really be free.

But it didn't mean he didn't think about his family. Didn't wonder how his brothers were doing, if his mother was happy or still chasing money.

He couldn't ask. Wouldn't. He needed a complete break.

"But it was the only choice I could make. I'm not coming back. The sooner you get that through your head, the sooner you can convince Senior of the same, and he can leave me alone."

C.J. sneered at him. Whatever bond they'd had as kids growing up, them against the world, had fractured and then split during their teenage years when C.J. had decided to continue being the golden son and Kane had openly rebelled.

They'd both played their parts. They needed to keep playing them.

"Now," Kane continued, "be a good boy and catch the next flight to Houston and tell the old man you ran your little errand, but I'm not interested."

"No need to go back to Houston for that."

"So call him. I don't care." He just wanted to be done with this little family reunion.

"Not necessary." C.J. raised his glass in a mock toast. "He's right upstairs."

"I'M NOT LEAVING," Estelle's granddad grumbled. "It's not safe for a girl your age to be left alone this late at night. Especially in an apartment over a bar. If your father won't protect you, I will."

He sat on her dad's ratty couch, looking formidable and, unfortunately, unmovable.

Oh, she loved the old guy, even though he bitched about her dad, like, all the time. She just didn't want Granddad here, in her dad's place when Kane got home.

It was best to keep those two apart. Miles and miles and miles apart.

"I'm perfectly safe." Estelle glanced at the door. Was that a sound on the stairs? Crap. Her heart racing, she tugged on Granddad's arm until he sighed and got to his feet. Then she began pulling him toward the door.

"You trying to get rid of me, sugar?" he asked.

"Uh...obviously." *Duh.*

He dug in his heels. Narrowed his eyes. God, it was freaky how much he looked like her dad when he did that. "You're not hiding a boy in here, are you?"

She snorted. "Hardly." As if she was dumb enough to try something like that at her dad's. "I don't have a death wish."

Or a desire to be grounded for the rest of her life.

"I'm just way too tired to deal with you and Daddy going at each other's throats." She hated when they argued, which seemed like all the freaking time. She grabbed the door handle. "So let's just do me a huge favor and put off the start of your latest fight until tomorrow. Preferably when I'm not around."

The apartment door burst open, shoving her back two steps.

Crap again. Too late.

Kane stood on the threshold, looking ready to commit murder.

Not hers, of course. He'd never laid a hand on her. Not even a spanking. No, his glare and fierce scowl were for Granddad.

Sighing, she stepped out of the way. Let the battle begin.

"What the hell are you doing here?" Kane demanded, slamming the door shut with a bang that shook the floor.

Granddad patted Estelle's hand, as if he could tell she was worried. "Estelle told me about your accident. Your brother and I came to see if you were all right."

"Three days later?"

"I run a multibillion-dollar company, boy. I can't just take off whenever the whim hits me—like some people. I have responsibilities. People who count on me. I came as soon as I could clear my desk."

He was worried, too, she realized, surprised to see the concern in his gaze as he took in her dad's bruises and the cast. Heard it in the gruffness of his voice. Granddad had been worried about his son, just like a normal, loving parent.

Her dad didn't see it, wouldn't believe it even if

she sat down and explained it to him in slow, simple sentences.

He was stubborn that way.

He shifted his accusing gaze to her. She widened her eyes. "Well, I didn't know it was some sort of secret."

All she'd done was mention to her grandfather that her dad had been injured. It wasn't her fault he and Uncle C.J. had decided to fly out to Shady Grove.

"As you can see," Kane said through gritted teeth, "I'm fine."

"Fine?" Granddad stepped closer to Kane, his shoulders back, his eyebrows lowered. Even though he was like, pretty old, he was still handsome and tall, his blond hair barely threaded with gray, his body trim. "You call keeping my granddaughter in this…this…hovel, fine?"

"I don't mind," she said quickly, not wanting to be the pawn in this stupid game they played. "It's really not that bad. It's close to downtown and the stairs are good exercise."

"Where I live, where my daughter stays, is none of your concern."

Granddad started blustering, like the wind through the trees in her backyard in Houston during a bad storm. His face reddened. "I'd think *you'd* be a little more concerned about where she was going and who she's with. Out with a boy, and one she barely knows."

Estelle rolled her eyes. She never should have told

him she'd gone to the movies with Andrew. "I have been out with boys before, you know."

"I'd rather not hear that," both men said at the same time.

Then glared at each other, blaming the other for both of them being pretty much the same person. Stubborn. Bossy. Overprotective.

If only they could see it.

Her dad paced the room. He always did when he was upset, as if he had too many thoughts and feelings inside him to deal with. To be still with. "Estelle had my permission to go out tonight. I trust her. She's a good girl."

His praise should have warmed her, used to do so. Now it shamed her. Guilt turned her stomach. She wasn't always a good girl. Had made mistakes she could never tell him about.

They won't believe you.

Adam's voice slithered into her head like the snake he was. She shook it clear.

She placed both hands on her hips. "Do you two always have to fight? It's so annoying. And really immature."

They both gaped at her, but Granddad was the one to recover first. He pulled her to his side, kissed the top of her head. "I'm sorry, baby girl. I didn't mean to upset you."

"Well, it does upset me."

He nodded. "You're right. Your daddy and I will have to work harder on being civil."

The way he said it made it clear he really thought Kane was the one needing to do the work.

"I'll let you two get settled in for the night," her granddad continued, picking up his coat and laying it over his arm. "Tomorrow we can spend the day together." He winked. "See what trouble we can stir up for these Yankees."

"I'd like that." She kissed his smooth cheek.

"Shouldn't you be flying back to Houston tomorrow?" Kane asked.

"I'm staying until Sunday. I want to spend some time with my grandbaby." He sounded defensive. It was a free country, for God's sake. He had to know he didn't need an excuse to stay in Shady Grove. "C.J.'s heading back in the morning, though." He hesitated. Frowned. "Did he discuss that business matter with you?"

Business matter? What business matter? Daddy didn't have anything to do with Bartasavich Industries. Never had.

"I told him what I'll tell you. I'm not interested."

Granddad looked disappointed for a second, but then his expression cleared. "If you change your mind—"

"I won't. And next time," Kane said, opening the door and holding it in a clear sign he wanted his father out of his apartment, "don't send C.J. to do your dirty work."

Granddad stopped on the other side of the door. Looked sad and...old. "I thought maybe you'd listen.

If he was the one doing the offering." He looked past Kane to Estelle. "Good night, darlin'."

"'Night, Granddad."

After her dad shut the door, she curled up on the couch, tucking her legs under her and pulling her sleep jersey over her knees. "What did he mean by a business matter?"

Kane locked the door and sat next to her. Grimaced and readjusted the sling around his neck. "Your grandfather wants me to move back to Houston and work for Bartasavich Industries."

"Oh." She stared at her lap, picked at a piece of fuzz on her yoga pants. If he moved back to Houston, her problems would be over. She could live with him, keep her friends and still see her mom anytime she wanted. "You don't want to?"

"I don't," he said simply.

But she could see on his face if she pushed, he would. He'd do it for her.

And he'd be miserable.

She couldn't do that to him. Couldn't ask that of him. Not when the mess she was in was all her own fault. She squeezed his fingers. "I don't think you'd be very happy at B.I. I can't imagine you wearing a suit and tie to work every day and being stuck in some office.

"Wherever we end up," she said, "whether it's here or Maine or…I don't know…Canada, we'll be fine. Because we'll be together."

"You don't have to do this. Just because you said

you wanted to live with me, doesn't mean you can't change your mind."

Her throat dried. "Don't you want me?"

"Wanting you has nothing to do with it. I need to make sure this is really what you want."

"It is. Really." But don't think she didn't notice he still hadn't said if he wanted her or not.

"Promise me you'll at least think about it some more before we talk to your mom."

She opened her mouth, but couldn't lie and say she wanted to leave everything she knew and live with Kane full-time. So she just forced a smile. And added yet one more lie to her growing list of sins. "I promise."

CHAPTER FOURTEEN

"You're going to be next," Sadie predicted to Harper Kavanagh late Sunday afternoon, as Harper worked to open the bottle of champagne she'd brought to Charlotte's.

Leo had been right. James had proposed to Sadie while they were away. They'd been so excited, they'd come home early that morning to tell their parents. An hour ago, Sadie had called Charlotte and their cousin Harper, and Char had invited them both over for a quick celebration before she went into work.

The cork popped, surprising Harper. Or maybe it was Sadie's comment. "Next? For marriage?" She laughed, as bright and bubbly as the champagne she poured into the flute Char held. Shook her head, the ends of her dark blond hair brushing her shoulders. "I'm not in a hurry. And neither is Eddie."

Eddie Montesano—James's and Leo's brother—and Harper had been together since last fall when Eddie's son was in Harper's second-grade class. They might not be in a hurry, but Char had no doubt that someday she and Sadie would become sisters-in-law.

Charlotte couldn't understand why Harper would want to wait. Then again, the fact that Eddie had

Max and Harper had a young daughter from her first marriage could complicate things.

But if you loved someone, you should want a commitment from them. Should want to commit to them.

Char wouldn't wait, that was for sure. Wasn't waiting, she assured herself as she handed Sadie the glass while Harper poured another one. She veered slightly off track in the pursuit of her five-year plan, hit a roadblock…

A six-foot-tall, green-eyed roadblock.

No, she was not going to think about Kane. It'd been four days since the awful scene in his apartment. She nibbled on the inside of her cheek. Remembered the feel of his mouth on hers, his hand skimming over her. Okay, so it hadn't started out as awful, but that was neither here nor there. It had been a mistake. A doozy.

And she was so very tired of making mistakes.

Harper set the champagne on the coffee table. Char quickly slid a coaster under the bottle. It didn't quite fit, but it should stop any water rings.

"Wait," Harper cried when Sadie raised her glass to her mouth—as if Sadie were about to ingest rat poison along with the alcohol. "We need a toast."

They both looked at Char. Guess since she was Sadie's maid of honor and would be giving a toast at the wedding, they wanted her to practice.

"To Sadie and James," she said, searching for the right words as she raised her glass. Knowing their history, simple and to the point seemed the way to go. "May you always be best friends."

She must have nailed it because Sadie grinned broadly and lightly touched her glass to Char's. "Thank you."

Char had only a small sip, then set her glass aside. She had to work in just over an hour.

"Hard to believe out of the three Montesano siblings in committed relationships," Sadie said, "James and I are the ones getting married first. Is that weird?" She nodded, took another drink. "That's weird."

But she didn't look freaked out by it. She looked... content. Happy. Her sister had spent most of her life searching for excitement, never staying in the same place long, never sticking with one job or one man. Now she was planning her wedding, her marriage and her life, with one of the most settled, grounded men Char had ever known.

"Guess this is the beginning of the end of your adventurous days," Harper said, her pretty face lit by a teasing grin.

"Oh, I don't know about that." Sadie admired her engagement ring, two round white diamonds glittering on either side of a larger blue diamond. "I thought I'd be nervous when he proposed. Unsure. But when he asked me to marry him it was so right. Life with James is...it's everything. Fun and passionate, serious and emotional, and so very easy. I think being his wife, eventually having his babies, is going to be the best adventure ever."

Harper raised her glass. "Well said."

Bitterness coated Char's throat and she wished she could down the rest of her drink, maybe finish off the bottle to wash it away. It wasn't that she was envious of Sadie and Harper—much. She was happy they were both in loving, committed relationships.

Was it so wrong to want that for herself?

Except now she wasn't sure what she wanted. Oh, she'd been sure. Had been convinced she knew exactly what her future looked like: married to a respectable, kind, easygoing man, one who wanted a family, a life right here in Shady Grove, who was nice and charming and socially conscious.

Instead she couldn't stop thinking about a wild-haired bad boy with too many tattoos and a cynical streak a mile wide.

She *would* stop thinking about him. Even if he did slip into her mind every once and again, she wasn't letting it stop her from moving forward with her plans. When Justin had called her Thursday inviting her to lunch that day, she'd readily accepted.

That was how a relationship was supposed to work. A few casual dates so a couple could get to know each other better, followed by dinners out, maybe dancing or a show in Pittsburgh. So far, she and Justin were right on track.

She'd have to make sure they stayed there.

Someone knocked on the back door. Charlotte

excused herself, then walked through the dining room to her small kitchen.

And saw Kane scowling at her through the door's large window.

Her heart did one slow roll. Oh, this wasn't good.

She didn't want to see him. Didn't want him in her house.

He knocked again, a light tap on the glass, then raised eyebrows as if asking her what she was doing. His eye was healing, the scratches fading, his hair falling over his stitches.

She didn't have a choice so she opened the door a few inches, only enough for her message to be clear: he wasn't welcome.

"Kane. Hello." She wouldn't stoop to his level. Would remain calm and polite no matter what. "What are you doing here?"

"You have company," he said, his tone accusing, his eyes narrowed.

She didn't have to wonder how he knew, since both Sadie and Harper had parked in her driveway. "Yes."

He glowered, his hair lifting in the warm breeze. "I thought you'd be alone."

"I'm not. And, as you can see—" she gestured to the mint-green scrubs she was wearing "—I'm going into work shortly so—"

"You've been avoiding me."

She blinked, her hand tightening on the door. "Yes."

Hard to deny it when it was true. So she wouldn't

have to face Kane, she'd even had Estelle meet her for lunch downtown instead of picking the girl up. Afterward, she'd dropped the teen off in the parking lot, then shot out of there like a race car driver after a pit stop.

"As scintillating as this conversation has been," she said, her irritation at him growing—both for his behavior now and for what happened between them the other night. No, it wasn't all his fault, but really, he did hold more than his share of blame. "I need to get going."

"Kane?"

Char sighed and let her head hit the door.

"Hi," Sadie said, coming up behind Char, her glass in hand, a sunny smile on her face. "Did you hear the good news? Come to congratulate me?"

"I'm not here for you," he told Sadie, his gaze on Char. "I'm here for Charlotte."

Her throat went dry, but it was just because of how he said it, with determination and something else, something deeper and hot in his tone. It was the way he looked at her—not even sparing Sadie a glance. It was just her hormones forgetting she'd let them lead her before, and all it had done was leave her feeling confused and hurt.

And, those hormones reminded her, very satisfied.

Stupid hormones.

"I'm sorry," Sadie said with a laugh as fake as their mother's blond hair. "I could have sworn you said you were here for my baby sister."

"You heard right," Kane said. Then he snatched Char's arm and tugged her outside, shutting the door on Sadie's shocked face.

Kept right on pulling her through the yard toward the large oak tree separating her property from her neighbor's. The grass was cold and damp, wetness soaking into her socks as she struggled to keep up, to get free of his tight grip.

She growled in frustration. Seriously, the man had reduced her to growling. "Have you lost what is left of your mind?" she snapped, too irritated to keep her voice down, too embarrassed at his high-handedness not to worry about someone hearing her. Seeing him drag her around like a damn dog on a leash.

Not so much as glancing back at her, he lifted his left shoulder.

She clenched her jaw to stop a scream from finding its way out. While it fit the situation of being forcibly abducted from her home, it also seemed overly dramatic for this particular situation. No sense causing a scene. Or scaring the neighborhood kids racing their bikes up and down the sidewalk.

Someday, she thought, marching behind Kane, her kids would do the same. Ride their bikes with their neighborhood pals, play kickball in the backyard, have picnics right under this tree. It was all part of the plan. The house, her pursuit of a suitable man to become her husband, were all steps she'd carefully laid out, steps that needed to be taken to achieve her goals.

But when Kane stopped at the tree and faced her, eyes glittering, mouth unsmiling, all those plans went *poof!*

And when she imagined her future offspring, those adorable, bright, funny children she someday hoped to have, they all had dirty-blond hair and cool green eyes.

CHARLOTTE WAS RIGHT. He'd officially lost his mind.

Her fault for making it so damned difficult for him to apologize to her. He'd tried calling and texting and had, at one sad, sorry point, resorted to driving past her house. She hadn't been home. So he'd waited, had tried to catch her when she'd dropped Estelle off the other day but he'd been too late.

Now he'd resorted to this, yanking her from her home in just her socks and dragging her across the yard in the hopes of getting a few minutes of privacy.

Yep. Mind gone.

She tugged on his hand again, but he was afraid if he let go, she'd take off. She looked so irritated, her hair spiky, a little wrinkle forming in her forehead. Looking at her made his chest hurt, as though he couldn't take a full breath.

He'd always known someday a woman would be the death of him.

"I'm sorry."

He winced. He hadn't meant to spit the words out that way, angry and frustrated. But apologizing had never been easy for him. Bartasaviches didn't apologize.

"I'm sorry," he repeated, softening his tone to a rough growl, "for what happened the other night. I acted like a prick."

She studied him, trying to decide if she should believe him or not. "Fine," she said, all long-suffering and benevolent. "I forgive you. Now can I please go back inside? I have guests."

"They can wait another minute." Letting go of her hand, he quickly pulled the small box from his front pocket, shoved it at her. "Here."

She fumbled it. Held it gingerly between her thumb and forefinger, as if he'd just handed her a ticking time bomb. "What is it?"

He wanted to smile at the suspicious note in her tone, but didn't dare. "Open it."

Her top teeth sinking into her bottom lip, she lifted the lid. Pulled out the delicate silver chain. The pendant was an irregular circle, as thick as a ring, the bottom flattened.

"This above all," she said, reading the inscription, "to thine own self be true."

He'd made a mistake with her the other night, more than one. The first had been opening up to her, telling her about the accident. He'd been confused by his sudden need for her, his emotions tangled in knots. Angry still, at himself, at his past. He'd taken his anger out on her. This was his way of telling her he respected her decision. He respected her.

"It's…" She stopped. Swallowed, fisting her hand around the necklace. "It's lovely. Thank you."

And she smiled at him, a warm smile filled with understanding. Forgiveness.

It roared through him, blowing away all the bullshit reasons he'd told himself he was here, all the lies and excuses as to why he couldn't stop thinking about her.

"Have dinner with me," he heard himself say, sounding as desperate as some loser who'd never had a date with anyone other than a blow-up doll.

Her smile faded. "What?"

He stepped closer, told himself he deserved it when she edged back, watched him warily. "Have dinner with me," he repeated, softer this time, less a desperate demand and more of a request. "Please," he added when she gaped at him.

See? He could be polite. He'd been taught social graces from the time he was old enough to walk, and at times, he even still knew how to use those charms.

"No," she said.

Did she have to sound so damned emphatic?

"A date," he pressed. "One date. We'll go into Pittsburgh. Hell, we can go wherever you want. New York City. DC. You name it."

"I'm not going out with you."

"Why not?"

"You know why not."

She turned to go, but he stopped her with a hand on her arm. "I want to see you, Charlotte," he said, letting his voice go low and husky. "I want to spend time with you."

"Why?"

How was he supposed to answer that without sounding pathetic? When he couldn't even explain it to himself. "I...I like you."

Christ, that was worse. Now he sounded like a pimply thirteen-year-old sending notes to his crush during study hall.

But it was the truth. He did like her. Liked her humor and her strength. Her honesty and pride.

"Don't," she said quietly. "Don't do this."

"Don't do what?"

"Don't tell me you like me. Don't ask me out. What would be the point? We want different things. I'm looking for someone I can spend the rest of my life with, someone I can commit, fully commit, to. And you're biding your time until you can move on again."

True. He didn't even think about his future, didn't plan on ever settling down with one woman. The idea of marriage, more kids, promising to be there day after day, all the things that were so important to her, left him cold.

"You're right." He stepped back, the cast on his arm feeling heavy, his chest aching in a way it hadn't in days. "Guess I'll see you around, Red."

Her mouth turned down slightly at the corners. "Goodbye, Kane."

He couldn't stop himself from watching her walk

away, the subtle sway of her hips, her long strides, the way the sun glinted off her hair. And wished like hell he had the strength to call her back.

ESTELLE RUBBED HER hands up and down her arms, but couldn't get warm. Chills racked her body, shaking her limbs, making her legs unsteady. The hospital loudspeaker squeaked, then someone paged a doctor. Behind the glass of the little cubicle thingy, a woman with gray-streaked dark hair frowned at her.

Too bad. She probably wanted Estelle to stop pacing, but the movement—around and around the tiny E.R. waiting room—was the only thing keeping her from going crazy with worry.

Where was her dad?

As if she'd conjured him up, the automatic door opened and he strode in, tall and broad-shouldered and strong. She threw herself at him, tears streaking her face. "Oh, Daddy!"

His arms came around her as she knew they would, comforting and warm. He hugged her tight. "It'll be okay."

She leaned back. Sniffed. "You don't know that."

"I know my old man," he told her, leading her to a set of chairs by the window. "He's too stubborn to die." He glanced around at the empty room. "What did the doctor say?"

"Nothing yet." She pulled a tissue from the box on the table next to her. Pressed it against her eyes even though it would make her mascara smear. "They took him back for some tests and said someone would come out as soon as they knew more."

"What happened?"

"We…" She inhaled shakily. Blew her nose. "We were at the restaurant eating dinner." She'd seen her grandfather at least once a day since he got to Shady Grove. Tonight, he was to take a red-eye back to Houston. "Granddad started acting funny. Like, confused. He thought we were back in Houston and then his words started slurring. He said he was having a hard time seeing and he just…dropped his fork."

She'd never forget the way his arm had fallen to his side, as if he had no control over it. How he'd leaned to the right, half of his face drooping.

She'd never forget how scared he'd looked before he'd slumped over.

"Someone in the restaurant called 911," she continued, her voice breaking. "The ambulance picked him up and brought him here. One of the waiters gave me a ride."

Her dad ran his hand through his hair. Exhaled heavily. "Let's see if we can find someone to tell us what's going on."

As they stood, the door next to the cubicle opened and Charlotte came out. Estelle hadn't even known she was working tonight.

She rushed over to Char and grabbed her hands. "Did you see my granddad? Is he all right?"

Char tugged her back to the seat, barely glanced at her dad. Nothing new there. Estelle had noticed there was usually a weird vibe between those two. "They're still running tests. But he's stable."

Stable. That was good, right? Stable meant holding his own.

Stable meant not dead.

"When will they be done? When will they know if he's going to be all right?"

Char squeezed her hands. "I can't give you a time frame. I'm sorry. But I'll do my best to keep you updated."

The last bit she spoke to Kane.

He nodded. "I appreciate it."

"If you need me, have the receptionist page me," she said, standing and indicating the woman behind the glass. "I'll come back out as soon as I hear anything."

"Thank you," Estelle told her, trying to get a hold of herself. Her sniveling and bawling like a baby wouldn't do Granddad any good.

But when her dad wrapped his arm around her and pulled her close, the tears came back. She sobbed against his chest.

And wished her mother were here.

AT MIDNIGHT, CHAR found Kane still in the waiting room, Estelle curled up awkwardly on the chair next to him fast asleep, her head resting on a jacket in his lap.

He looked up when he heard Char come in, his gaze giving nothing away.

She sat on his other side, kept her voice low. "They're moving your father to the ICU. Dr. Lamberson will be down shortly to talk with you, but I wanted to check on you both, see how you were doing."

"You didn't have to."

"I know." She'd wanted to, despite what had happened between them earlier at her house. And not just because she wanted to offer Estelle her comfort. She wanted to help Kane, too.

She'd been working only a few hours when they'd brought Clinton Bartasavich in. She'd known, from her time spent with Estelle Friday, that Kane's father was in town. The EMTs had told her the patient's teenage granddaughter was with him at the restaurant when he'd fallen ill, so as soon as Char had gotten a spare moment, she'd hurried to the waiting room, not wanting Estelle to be alone.

Only to find Kane sitting there, stoic and unemotional.

"It was definitely a stroke?" he asked now.

She nodded. "A blood vessel ruptured and leaked into his brain. He's on medicine to help reduce brain swelling. He's also on a ventilator to assist his breathing."

The doctor would explain all of that and more to Kane, but she didn't want him to sit and wonder what was going on when she could give him some answers.

"How bad was it?"

"We won't know the extent of his injuries until—"

"You know something," he said, his voice low, his eyes tired. "Tell me."

She licked her lips, glanced around, but the only other person in the room was a twentysomething man listening to an iPod. "The damage was severe."

He stiffened. "What do you mean? Brain damage?"

"Possibly." She wouldn't lie to him, not even when the truth was difficult to hear. But telling the truth to the loved ones of patients was one of the hardest parts of her job. "There could be long-term side effects, both physical and cognitive. Paralysis, pain, fatigue. Difficulty with speech, memory loss. The good news is he was brought in right away, which gives him the best possible chances, not only for survival, but for his recovery."

Kane stared down at Estelle, used his forefinger to hook a lock of hair that had fallen over her face and swept it back. In that one simple, incredibly gentle gesture, Char saw his love for her. Though she fought it, her heart softened, threatened to melt in her chest.

"Dad asked me to go with them," Kane said. He turned his head, his eyes not cool now, but sad. "To dinner. It was to be his last night in town."

"You didn't want to go?"

"My dad and I didn't...don't...get along. For the past fourteen years, I've done my best to avoid him. For the most part, he's respected my decision—

though every once in a while he tries to lure me back into the fold."

She knew he wasn't close to his family, but she couldn't imagine not wanting to spend time with either of her parents. "I'm sorry." It was all she could think to say. "For both of you."

He grinned, but it lacked any warmth. "Don't feel sorry for me, Red. The best thing I ever did, besides Estelle, was stay as far away from my family as possible. Especially my old man. He's an adulterer. An arrogant, manipulative son of a bitch. But he's still my father."

"And you're worried about him."

"I don't know what I am," he admitted softly, his words stark, honest and so confused. She gripped his fingers below his cast. Silently letting him know she was there for him.

After a moment, he curled his fingers around hers the best he could and held on tight.

CHAPTER FIFTEEN

THE OLD MAN wasn't dead.

Senior was still alive, though not, at the moment, kicking.

Kane couldn't pretend he wasn't relieved.

The doctor said it was still touch and go. Which was why, after taking Estelle back to the apartment so she could get some sleep and take a shower, he'd come right back to the hospital. Had spent the whole night here, pacing or nodding off in one of the hard, uncomfortable chairs.

It seemed every time he turned around, Charlotte was there, offering him coffee or the sandwich she'd packed for her own lunch. Offering him comfort. Giving him so much more, a sense of hope. Of peace.

She was such a soft touch, he thought, unsure if he pitied or envied her. Even after she'd insisted there was nothing between them, no chance of there ever being anything between them, she was still kind and gracious. Unable to walk away when she thought he needed her.

His steps echoing, he strode down the hospital hallway, turned the corner, then pushed the button to open the doors to the ICU.

Charlotte might be right, and it unnerved him.

He didn't want to need her. Didn't want to need anyone.

He checked his phone. Three missed calls from his mother and an hour-old text from C.J. letting him know he and Oakes had landed in Pittsburgh.

Tucking the phone back in his pocket, he passed the nurses' station, nodded at the two women and one man behind the desk. No doubt his mother had heard about Senior's condition and wanted an update. He'd call her when he ran back to his apartment to shower and change.

Turning right, he spotted C.J. at the end of the hall-way looking out the fourth-story window, his phone to his ear. Though he flew in on a red-eye and had come straight from the airport, he looked as if he'd just stepped out of the country club, his dark dress pants pressed, his white button-down shirt crisp, not a strand of hair out of place. He glanced over, saw Kane approach.

"I'll call you back," he told the person on the other end of the phone and hung up. They sized each other up for a moment, then C.J. nodded. "They won't let me see Dad."

"They're getting him settled, want him to rest." They'd been testing Senior, poking and prodding him most of the night.

"I think we should transfer Dad back to Hous-ton," C.J. said.

And so it started, his brother so much like their

father, trying to control everything. "He's on a ventilator," Kane pointed out. "Do you really think moving him is in his best interest?"

"What's his doctor's name? I want him paged."

There was no sense arguing with stubborn. "Her. You want her paged. Dr. Lamberson."

C.J. was heading toward the nurses' station before Kane was even done talking. Kane caught up with him. "Where's Oakes?"

"He's getting coffee." C.J.'s mouth flattened. "With Carrie. And Mom."

Kane skid to a stop. "You brought Mom? You really are an idiot."

"I didn't have a choice," he said tightly. "It's not like I can ban her from buying an airplane ticket. You think you've had it tough being here all night? Try flying halfway across the country, trying to keep Dad's first wife from ripping his current wife's hair out."

Kane almost felt sorry for his brother. Their mother was a piece of work.

"At least you had Oakes to keep the situation calm." Their younger brother had a way of smoothing rugged waters.

"All he had to do was keep buying Carrie drinks," C.J. muttered. "I spent the entire flight listening to Mom bitch about her new chauffeur, how she's positive one of the housekeepers is stealing the silverware and that she simply can't survive any longer on the pittance Dad gives her each month for alimony."

"Sucks to be you," Kane said. "And I mean that."

"You're just glad it wasn't you dealing with her."

"True." No sense even pretending otherwise.

C.J. went up to the nurses' station and ordered Dr. Lamberson to be paged.

He really was a younger version of his namesake. Demanding. Controlling. Arrogant.

Hard to believe he and Kane had once been as close as brothers could be. They'd survived their parents' tumultuous marriage, watching their mother pretend everything was all right, doing her best to hold on to the life she felt she deserved. Had relied on each other during their parents' divorce when Gwen had tried to pit them against Senior.

Their bond broke when Kane had drifted off into a world of drugs and alcohol.

C.J. had never forgiven him.

Then again, Kane had never asked him to.

C.J. returned a minute later not looking too happy. "The doctor's with a patient in the E.R. She'll come when she's done." Checking his phone, he glanced up, then did a double take. "What the hell is he doing here? I thought he was still in Iraq."

Kane followed his brother's gaze. Zach Castro, their youngest brother, walked toward them resembling the jarhead he was: dark hair buzzed short, camo pants tucked into boots, plain green T-shirt.

"I called him." When C.J. glared at him, Kane shrugged. "He deserves to know."

He'd been surprised to discover that Zach wasn't

still overseas, but on base in Parris Island in South Carolina.

Kane nodded when Zach reached them. "Zach."

Zach returned the nod, his dark, flat gaze taking in Kane's cast. "Fall off your bicycle?"

"Something like that."

Zach turned to C.J., greeted him with a lift of his chin.

Zach had an even bigger chip on his shoulder about being Clinton Bartasavich's son than Kane did, and with good reason. Zach's mother was the only woman Senior had gotten pregnant and hadn't married.

Zach usually kept his distance, physically and emotionally, from his family, especially their father. Yet here he was, at the old man's sickbed.

"He okay?" Zach asked.

"He's going to pull through," C.J. said as if his will alone could make it true. "Sorry to disappoint you."

Zach didn't so much as blink at his older brother's angry tone, nor did he deny he'd been hoping his biological father's prognosis wasn't good. "You told me it was bad," Zach said to Kane, still in that mild tone.

"It is," he said as he spotted Oakes down the hall. "He has a 50 percent chance of pulling through. And even if he does, he could have months of rehabilitation."

"Zach," Oakes said, a grin on his handsome face. He slapped his younger brother on the shoulder with warm affection. "I didn't know you'd be here."

That was Oakes. Always affable. It was hard not to like him, though Zach had spent his entire life giving it his best shot. Zach shifted to the side. "I only came because I thought the old man was dying."

If Oakes was surprised by that, he didn't let it show. Then again, Oakes was a damn good lawyer. They were excellent at hiding their true feelings. "Dad's too stubborn to die." He turned to Kane. Frowned at his cast. "You okay?"

"Had a minor thing. It's all good."

Oakes lowered his voice as C.J. once again was on his phone, Zach leaning against the far wall. "You on anything for pain?"

"I'm good," he repeated. *I'm clean.*

Oakes nodded. The spitting image of his mother with brown hair and hazel eyes, he had somehow managed to not turn out completely screwed up despite having Senior as a father.

He was the only one.

"I'm almost afraid to ask," Kane said, "but where's my mother?"

Oakes tugged on his ear. "Last I saw her, she was complaining to the young girl working in the cafeteria about the coffee. Carrie was in the restroom so I sort of slipped out."

"Smart man."

A middle-aged nurse with cartoon characters on her scrubs came out of their father's room.

"Can we see him?" C.J. asked.

"Two at a time," she said. "Ten minutes only."

The brothers looked at each other.

"Want to draw straws?" Kane asked drily.

Zach straightened from the wall. "Since when does any Bartasavich follow the rules?"

And he walked into the room. C.J. went in next, leaving Kane and Oakes to follow.

Kane wasn't sure what to expect, had thought he could handle anything, but seeing his father in the bed, hooked up to machines, tubing down his throat, it was like being punched in the stomach. It was hard to believe this was the same man who'd been in his apartment just a few days ago. Senior had always seemed bigger than life, but now he looked shrunken. Old.

Senior's skin was so pale it was practically colorless. His hair seemed thinner, grayer, his cheeks sunken. The right side of his face drooped—eyelid, cheek, mouth. Gone was the huge, robust man who used to rule his business and family with an iron fist, taking no prisoners. In his place was a sick old man who couldn't even breathe on his own.

C.J. went to his bedside. "We're here, Dad."

Senior opened his eyes, looked at his sons, couldn't speak with the tube down his throat. But he blinked once slowly, as if their being there was good, exactly as they should be. As he wanted them to be.

Kane wasn't sure what he felt, how he should feel. His father was near death. But he'd won out so far, and Kane had no doubt he'd continue to get better.

Senior held his left hand toward Oakes, who came forward and clasped it.

"You're going to be okay," Oakes told him. "You're strong. You'll get through this."

Senior's gaze went to Kane, seemed to call him. He stepped closer. But when Senior sought out Zach, his youngest son stayed rooted to his spot by the door.

Kane stared at his father. He didn't know if he loved the old man. Definitely didn't respect him. But there was one thing for certain.

He was glad the bastard hadn't died.

CHARLOTTE HEARD THE commotion as soon as she got off the elevator on the fourth floor. Down the hall she saw two women—one a year or two older than her, the other her mother's age—sniping at each other outside the ICU.

She hurried over. "Ladies," she said using her stern RN voice, "is there a problem?"

They both turned to glare at her. Char blinked. It was like looking at two real-life Barbie dolls—both had long blond hair, tiny waists and boobs Char wouldn't be surprised to discover had been bought and paid for.

The younger woman was quite stunning, her hair a shiny golden blond with paler streaks, her wide eyes a light blue. She wore tight dark jeans, knee-high brown leather boots and a fuzzy pink sweater better suited for a five-year-old. The older one was still beautiful, though more conservatively dressed in tan pants, heels and a silky brown shirt. Her hair was a darker shade than her younger twin, her face unlined.

It wasn't natural for a woman of her age not to have any wrinkles. Freaky.

"This doesn't concern you," the older woman snapped, but her expression stayed the same, as if she'd had one too many Botox injections, paralyzing all her facial muscles. "It's between me and this gold-digging little tramp."

Younger Blonde gasped so hard, her breasts swayed. She sneered, not looking so pretty after all. "You're just jealous."

"Jealous?" The older woman sniffed, but the veins in her neck were popping out. She stepped closer to her adversary, towering over the younger woman in her three-inch spike heels. "The day I'm jealous of some cheap, trailer-park-trash whore—"

"Whore?" the other woman shrieked.

"Ladies, please keep your voices down." Char stepped into the fray, praying she didn't end up in the middle of a hair-pulling brawl. "This is a critical care unit. If you can't control yourselves, you're going to have to leave."

"I'm not going anywhere," younger Blondie said with a head toss that should have caused brain damage. "I have every right to be here. Make *her* leave."

"I'm going to call Security," Char said, having

had enough of these two nitwits, "and let them escort you both out."

The younger woman's eyes widened to the point Char worried they'd bulge out of her head.

The older one drew herself up, looked down her nose at Char. "Do you have any idea who I am?"

"Nope," Char said, heading to the nurses' station to call for backup. "And frankly, I don't care."

She was tired and just wanted to go home. But had she? No. After her shift ended, she'd come up here, seeking out Kane. Wanting to make sure he was okay.

She was stupid for doing it, but she knew he wasn't as cold and heartless as he acted. She'd seen him with Estelle. Saw how upset he was about his father.

Kane was a good man. Or, at least, he had the potential to be one.

"What is your name?" the older woman demanded as she followed Char. "I'm going to report you to the hospital administrator."

"Charlotte Ellison," she said as the doors to the ICU swung open. "I'd be more than happy to write it down for you. Just to make sure you get it right."

"Charlotte."

At the familiar drawl—and yes, those annoying tingles again—she turned to see Kane stepping through the doorway. He looked at her, then at the matching blondes.

"Kane!" The older woman frowned. "Darling, you look horrible."

And she wrapped him in a hug.

He looked over her head and met Char's eyes. "I see you've met my mother."

Mother? This plastic Real Housewife wannabe was his mother?

"I'm so sorry," she told him.

Despite the dark circles under his eyes, the green depths lit with humor. He obviously understood her meaning. "Me, too."

It wasn't until someone cleared their throat that Char noticed the three men behind Kane. It was surprising she hadn't seen them, as they were all tall, though the darkest one was shy of six feet. All good-looking. The conservatively dressed blonde on the left resembled Kane so much, he had to be one of his brothers.

Kane's mom let go of him. "C.J.," she said to the man in the white shirt. "I want you to get this wretched hospital's administrator on the phone immediately. This—" she wrinkled her nose at Char "—nurse is trying to force me to leave."

C.J., Kane's mom and the younger woman all started talking at once. C.J. trying to figure out what was going on, the women snapping at each other.

Kane sidled up next to Char. "You kicked my mom out?" he murmured.

"I'm trying," she whispered back.

"Appreciate it."

They shared a smile and she was glad she'd come

here. No matter what sort of busty, overly perfumed crazies she had to deal with.

"Charlotte is a friend of mine," Kane said into the fray, silencing them. "Charlotte, this is my family. My mother, Gwen Bartasavich, my older brother, Clinton Junior," he said, nodding toward C.J. "My younger brothers Zach—" a gesture toward the dark one "—and Oakes."

"Pleased to meet you, ma'am," Oakes said with a charming grin and nod.

"And this," Kane continued as if his brother hadn't spoken, "is Carrie."

"*Mrs*. Carrie Bartasavich," younger blondie corrected, her eyes narrowed. She grinned sharply at Char. "I'm his stepmother."

Poor Kane. She must be five years younger than him.

"If Char thought you needed to leave," he told his mother, "she must have had a reason."

"They were…arguing," Char explained quickly. "And when I asked them to stop, they refused. I'm sorry, but that sort of commotion isn't allowed in the hospital, especially outside the ICU."

"This is all her fault," Gwen Bartasavich said, stabbing a pointy-nailed finger at Carrie. "I came all this way to see Clinton, to make sure he's all right." Her voice broke and she dug out a tissue from her bag. Pressed it to her nose, her mouth quivering. She sniffed delicately, her eyes dry despite all the noises she was making. "I wanted to let him know that I…I forgive him for everything he did. But she told me I couldn't see him."

"Only family is allowed to see him." Carrie glanced at her audience as if looking for support. "That's what the nurse told me."

Gwen drew herself up. "I am the mother of his children."

"If all the mothers of all his children showed up," Zach put in, "we'd have to rent out an entire floor and not just one room."

Oakes ducked his head, but Char was pretty sure she caught him grinning.

"You have no right to dictate who does or does not see my sons' father."

Carrie shoved her left hand—and the huge rock on her ring finger—into Gwen's red face. "See this? This gives me the right. I am his wife."

"Where are you going?" C.J. asked Zach when he brushed past them.

"To my hotel."

"You can't even give us a hand here?"

Zach lifted a shoulder. He looked hard, like Kane, but he also looked mean. "My mother's smart enough to stay away. Seems to me these two are your problem."

And he walked away again, pushed the button for the elevator.

"Look," Char said, using her most soothing, compassionate tone. "This is a stressful, upsetting situation, for everyone. You're worried, you're tired. It might be best if you all went and got a cup of coffee." She eyed the two women. "Separately. Then came back and tried to figure this out when everyone has had a chance to calm down."

"Good idea," C.J. said. Taking his mother's arm, he escorted her down the hall toward the elevator.

Oakes wrapped his arm around Carrie's shoulder. "There's a vending machine in the ICU. Let's get a cool drink and talk about this." Pushing the button to open the door, he sent Char and Kane a wink over Carrie's head.

"That's your family, huh?" Char asked as she smiled at a young couple walking by.

"Minus a few ex-stepmothers. That's them."

"I have no words."

"They have that effect on people." He watched her intently. "Why did you come up here?"

His voice was soft. His tone seeking. Not for the first time she wished she was one of those women who could flirt effortlessly, lie easily. She preferred to tell the truth. "I wanted to see how you were doing. But now," she continued quickly, "I'm heading home."

He walked with her to the elevator.

"I hope your family can figure something out," she said as the doors opened and she stepped inside. To her surprise, he got in as well. Char pushed the button for the first floor and the doors slid shut. "Your mother did come all this way."

"Oakes will convince Carrie to let Mom in. He's a lawyer. He can talk anyone into anything."

She laughed, the sound dying when Kane dipped his head and kissed her.

His mouth was warm, and he tasted like rich coffee and cinnamon. His lips clung to hers, his hands at his side. The kiss was so sweet, unnamed emotions clogged her throat. Had her stomach tumbling.

The elevator stopped and Kane stepped back.

"What was that for?" Char asked, forcing herself not to lift her trembling fingers to her mouth, to somehow try to capture the feel of his kiss.

The doors opened and he gently ushered her out into the hospital foyer. Held her gaze. "Because I really like your laugh."

And the doors shut, leaving her stunned and wondering what she was going to do next.

CHAPTER SIXTEEN

"HOW'S YOUR GRANDDAD?" Andrew asked Estelle Tuesday afternoon.

Sitting on Andrew's bed, Estelle looked up from her math homework. "A little better." Though he hadn't looked good when she'd gone to see him that morning with her dad. As a matter of fact, he'd looked awful, though he'd tried to smile when she'd sat next to him.

Tears stung her eyes, worry sat like a stone in her stomach. She blinked rapidly, swallowed to ease the ache in her throat. She'd wanted to stay longer at the hospital but had been so upset seeing Granddad hooked up to those machines, his cheeks sunken, his body barely moving, her dad had brought her home.

She'd been a wreck all afternoon, jumping every time her phone buzzed. Her dad and uncles all said Granddad was going to pull through but there was no way they could know that for sure.

Please, please, God, don't let Granddad die.

Stressing over things wouldn't help anyone. She needed to stay positive. Granddad would be all right.

He had to be.

She sent Andrew a smile. "You're sweet to ask about him."

Andrew flushed, and she couldn't tell if he was embarrassed by her words or angry.

She gave a mental shrug. She didn't need to know every emotion the boy had. They were friends, possibly becoming something more. Not that he'd made a move or anything.

Too bad. If he did, she'd totally make one back.

But he really was sweet. And funny. She was so glad he'd texted her after school and invited her over. She didn't think she could spend one more minute in that apartment by herself—not without losing her mind. She'd had a horrible day which had only gotten worse when she'd been forced to go to lunch with her grandmother. Talk about cruel and unusual punishment.

And she hadn't even done anything wrong.

Except, you know, run away from Pilar's, fly to Shady Grove without permission and, oh, yeah, totally lie about wanting to live with her dad.

Maybe she should have let her mom come. Meryl had offered to cut her vacation short so she could be with Estelle, but Estelle had told her not to worry. That she was fine.

At this point, what was one more lie?

Restless, she climbed off the bed and crossed to Andrew's bookcase. He had, like, tons of books, which was so weird. She didn't know any boy who read unless they had to for school, and usually they just watched the movie.

Andrew was smarter than most of the guys she knew. That much was obvious even though he didn't act like a nerd or something. But he was always asking insightful questions, and when they talked about stuff, like parents and school, the future or religion, he took his time before answering and didn't mind if she disagreed with him.

Didn't try to get her to think like him.

She snuck a glance at him and sighed. His T-shirt was snug around his arms, clearly showing his biceps. He frowned adorably at his biology notebook, his forefinger tapping the page. His hands were large and tan, his fingers long. She'd like to feel those hands holding hers, or cupping her cheek, his palm warm and dry on her skin as he moved in for a kiss.

She sighed again. Yeah, she'd definitely like him to make a move.

"Your house is nice," she told him.

He shrugged. "It's okay."

Well, it wasn't close to being as big or impressive or expensive as her mother's house, was maybe a quarter of the size of Granddad's mansion. All of Estelle's friends lived in fancy houses, too, usually in cul-de-sacs or the toniest of neighborhoods.

But Andrew's place was still pretty cute. It was one of those old Victorian homes with lots of windows and high ceilings and wood throughout. The furniture wasn't designer and didn't match perfectly; it was a mix of colors and styles, but still looked great.

Very homey. Like you could tell people actually lived there instead of it being a showcase for how much money the parents made with ugly furniture you weren't allowed to sit on and kitchens that were rarely used except when the cook or maid fixed a meal.

His room could use some major work, though. The dark blue walls made it seem smaller than it actually was, and she wasn't a big fan of all the sports posters or the plaid curtains. Guess decorating wasn't his strong suit. Oh, well, she couldn't expect him to be good at everything.

She picked up the baseball glove on top of his dresser. It was heavier than she would have thought and smelled funny. Like wet dog. She set it back down, wiped her fingers on her jeans, hoping the scent didn't linger on her skin. "Are you on your school's baseball team?"

He pressed down so hard with his pencil, the point broke. "No."

She wondered why. He obviously loved sports. Maybe he sucked at them.

Estelle sighed louder this time. Sat on the edge of the bed and swung her legs, her heels sweeping against the carpet.

Andrew stood, then dropped down next to her. The mattress dipped under his weight and she slid toward him. She stiffened, then forced herself to relax.

His knee bumped hers. It was okay, just his knee. He wasn't pawing at her, wasn't shoving his tongue down her throat.

He wasn't like Adam.

But her heart still pounded, hard, in her chest. Her skin got hot. Sweaty.

Maybe she wasn't ready for any moves. But she wanted to be. Didn't want Adam to take this away, too.

Andrew shifted, putting his arm behind her, his hand on the bed. She could do this. She wanted to do it.

She faced him. He swallowed, his gaze dropping to her mouth. He slowly leaned forward. The blood rushed in her ears, her fingers curled into her palms. His mouth brushed hers, his lips were warm. Dry. It was nice, a sweet kiss from a sweet boy. No pressure, no expectations of more.

She forced herself to kiss him back, reminded herself this was what she wanted, but her shoulders were so tight they ached, her breath locked in her lungs.

Andrew edged closer. Their hips bumped, his left hand settling next to her thigh. Trapping her.

Fear clawed at her belly. Perspiration dotted her hairline. Andrew deepened the kiss, his tongue stroking her lips.

Her breath exploding out of her, she shoved him, hard. Right off the bed. He landed on his rear with a dull thud, his expression shocked. Embarrassed.

She leaped to her feet, her hands trembling, her knees weak.

"I'm sorry," she rushed out, hating she'd hurt his feelings. She hugged her arms around herself. "It's not you, I swear."

"Whatever," he muttered as he stood stiffly, then knelt and shut his bio book, gathered up his notebooks. "Look, maybe you should go."

Tears stung her eyes. "No, really. I...I want to kiss you. I just...I freaked out, okay?" She used the heels of her hands to wipe her cheeks. "It's just...a few months ago something happened and...I thought it wasn't a big deal, but I guess it was."

It was the reason she hadn't wanted Chandler touching her. Her coldness toward him was probably why he'd started texting Pilar.

Jerk.

"What do you mean, something happened?"

She sat back down, lowered her head. "It's not a big deal—"

"Estelle," he said softly. "Just tell me."

She wiped her nose with the hem of her shirt—which was gross, but it was either that or let it drip. "A few nights after my birthday, I was in my room when Adam—"

"Who's Adam?"

"My mom's fiancé. He moved in with us after Christmas. Anyway, he came in. I thought it was weird because he'd never been in my bedroom before. He asked me about my day and was just...I don't know…looking around at my stuff." She'd been on her bed, listening to music while she studied chem, already in her pajamas, a pair of shorts and a tank top.

"When he sat on the bed, right next to me, I got nervous, but I told myself I was being stupid." Her throat was so tight, she could barely say the next words. "Then he kissed me."

She'd been so shocked, for a moment, she hadn't been able to move. That shock had cost her because by the time she snapped to her senses, he'd pinned her back against the headboard, his tongue in her mouth, his hand on her boob.

Andrew patted her back, his touch light. He didn't look freaked out that she was telling him this, crying all over him. Didn't seem uncomfortable with it as other guys would be. "Estelle, did he rape you?"

Her head whipped up. "No! God, no." She shuddered. But she'd been afraid he would. "I pushed him off and yelled at him to get out of my room. Told him I was going to call my mom and tell her what a pervert he was."

"But you didn't."

"I couldn't." She'd had her phone in her hand, but Adam had just given her an oily grin. "He told me Mama wouldn't believe me."

"He was playing you," Andrew said firmly, sounding angry. Not at her. For her. "That's what creeps like him do. They're manipulative."

Maybe. "I didn't tell her, I just made him leave

and I locked the door. Made sure it was locked every time I was in my room. And if Mama was out, I left the house, too."

"That was smart." His praise warmed her. He wrapped one arm around her shoulders. "But you need to tell her and your dad the truth."

"I don't know if I can."

He lifted her chin with his forefinger and waited until she reluctantly met his eyes. "You can. You can't let that asshole get away with this. Do you really want your mother with someone like that?"

She sniffed. Wiped her tears away with her fingers. "No."

Andrew nodded as if that was the right answer. "Good. You can do it. You're stronger than you realize."

But Estelle wasn't sure.

There was a quick knock on the door then it opened. "Andrew, could you—"

Estelle looked over to see a woman, Andrew's mom, obviously, standing in the doorway, surprise on her face.

Andrew jumped to his feet. "Mom! Could you please knock before you come into my room?"

"I did." She glanced at Estelle again, stepped fully into the room, crossed her arms as she sent her son a narrow look. "I didn't realize you had someone over."

But it didn't sound as if she was just surprised. She sounded mad. And she looked it, too, her eyes suspicious as she stood in her work clothes, dark pants, ugly sensible pumps and a silky white button-down shirt. She looked like Andrew, or, well, Estelle guessed it would be the other way around. Still, they both had dark hair and complexions, the same mouth and eyebrows, but where Andrew's eyes were blue, his mom's were light brown.

"You were at work," he said, sounding unlike how he did when he spoke to Estelle, always nice and sweet. Now he sounded defensive. Bitter.

His mom raised her eyebrows. "Yes, well that's one of those annoying things I have to do in order to keep a certain someone clothed and fed, and you know, keep a roof over his head."

"If you'd stayed with Dad, you wouldn't have to work," he grumbled in a tone Estelle had never heard from him before.

Mrs. Freeman went white, but then color rushed into her cheeks and she turned to Estelle. Smiled tightly. "I'm afraid Andrew has forgotten his manners. Among other important facts." She held out her hand. "Hello. I'm Mrs. Freeman."

Estelle, knowing full well the importance of a first impression, scrambled to her feet and smiled brightly though she was sure her eyes were red from crying, her makeup smudged.

"I'm Estelle Monroe," Estelle said, working her accent for all it was worth as she shook the older woman's hand. "It's so nice to meet you. I'm so sorry we didn't tell you we'd be hanging out today."

His mother wasn't buying it, that was for sure.

"Well, I like to be informed when Andrew has a… friend over. Especially one he entertains in his bedroom."

"Mom. Jesus!" Andrew said, his hands fisted at his sides. "What is your problem?"

"My problem is that I come home and find you and a girl in your bedroom, on your bed, in an embrace."

Andrew's face reddened; Estelle wasn't sure if it was from embarrassment or anger. He opened his mouth, but Estelle stepped forward.

"I'm so sorry," she rushed on before he could say anything else. "Mrs. Freeman it's, like, totally my fault. My granddad he…he's in the hospital, you see. He had a stroke."

It worked. Mrs. Freeman's expression softened fractionally. "I'm sorry to hear that," she murmured.

"Thank you. He's in the ICU still. I'm afraid it all got to be too much, you know? I'm in town visiting my father and Andrew's just been so sweet to me. I guess he understands what it's like," Estelle continued, "being in a new town far from his friends."

Mrs. Freeman glanced at her son, looked guilty. "Yes. I'm sure he does." She sighed. Smiled which made her look really pretty even though her hairstyle was all wrong for her face structure. "It's fine. How about I order some pizza for dinner before you go?"

She was good, Estelle would give her that. She wasn't having a major fit even though it obviously upset her, Estelle being here with her son. But she wasn't kicking Estelle out. No, she'd invited her to dinner all with the clear hint they finish up what they're doing so after they eat Estelle could get on her way.

"You don't have to go to any trouble for me."

"It's no trouble, really. We'd love for you to stay for dinner, wouldn't we, Andrew?"

"Yeah," he told Estelle. "Stay."

She smiled, not having to fake her relief that she didn't have to go back to her dad's empty apartment. Not yet. That she wouldn't have to be alone for a few more hours. That she wouldn't have to decide, at least for a little while longer, whether or not to tell her dad the truth. "That's so kind of you both. Thank you. Can I help you do anything?"

"I've got it," Mrs. Freeman said. "I'll let you know when it's time to eat, though it'll probably be in about forty minutes or so." She walked out, stopped in the hall and sent a pointed look at the door, her meaning clear.

Leave it open.

When they were alone again, Estelle sat back on the bed. "Your mom is nice," she lied, though, *intimidating* was a better word.

"She's okay."

But he didn't sound as if he meant it.

"Your parents are divorced, right?"

He nodded. Most of the parents of her friends were, too. And the ones who weren't didn't seem to like each other that much.

"Is your dad remarried?" she asked. Most of her friends' parents were.

His expression darkened. "No."

"How long have they been split up?"

"Not long." He sat back on the floor, his back against the bed. His back to her. "We'd better finish up before dinner."

"Oh. Sure," she said slowly, flipping a few pages to find the place where she'd left off.

He didn't want to talk about his family? Honestly, his mom hadn't seemed that bad.

Estelle's mama would have been fine finding them in her bedroom. She trusted her. Mama would have come in, gorgeous as always, smiling and chatting with Estelle and her friends, as though she was one of their crowd. Sometimes it bugged Estelle, how her mom acted as if she was one of her friends, but most of the time Estelle loved having her around.

God, she missed her. And it hadn't even been two weeks. She couldn't even imagine how awful it was going to be without her for the next two years.

Unless Andrew was right and Estelle was brave enough to make sure that didn't happen.

KANE BARTASAVICH WAS not the man of her dreams, Char reminded herself during a lull at work Tuesday night.

But that hadn't stopped her from thinking about him and his sweet kiss. About everything really, their first kiss, how he'd made her feel that evening at his apartment. How she wondered how his father was doing, if his family was driving him crazy.

Wanting to see him.

Which was fine, she assured herself as she finished inputting details into a patient's chart on the laptop. Being a kind, generous person, someone who cared about others, was a good thing. Thinking she could have feelings—real, true, heartfelt romantic feelings—for that stubborn, sexy, someone?

Definitely not okay.

The problem was she needed to keep her distance from him. How hard could that be? Sure, Shady Grove was small, but they weren't the only people in town. She'd managed to avoid him for months before. She could certainly do it again.

If only she could stop remembering how he'd looked before those elevator doors had shut. Tired and almost as stunned by their kiss as she'd been. If only she could stop dreaming about how he'd touched her, made her body come alive, how her nerve endings fairly sizzled just from the sound of his voice.

But that was just sex. She may be a virgin, but she understood how the human body worked. Why she responded to him the way she did. The way she'd expected to respond only to a man she was in love with.

She wasn't that naive—despite popular opinion to the contrary. She knew how powerful sex could be, how good it could feel. She merely needed to forget how he'd looked with his shirt off, dangerous and edgy and ripped. His body leanly muscled, those tattoos begging her to touch them, trace them with her fingertips.

She went hot all over. Waving a hand in front of her face she glanced around to make sure no one noticed. Yes, she was still attracted to him. She wasn't dead, was she? But that didn't mean she should keep making the same mistakes, keep believing there was more to him than a rebellious loner, one who'd never commit, who didn't want the same things she did. Didn't have to keep believing there could ever be a future between them.

And that's what she wanted. A future. Her future, the one she'd dreamed of since she was little. No, she didn't need a man to complete her; she was whole and healthy and just fine on her own, thanks all the same. But that didn't mean she didn't want someone to share her life with.

What she needed was to get back to her plan.

She saved the data, then sipped the bottle of water at her elbow, looked around and spotted Justin at the other side of the nurses' station.

Determined, she circled the counter, put a smile on her face and stepped up to him. "Hi, Justin."

He smiled at her and so what if her heart didn't trip? If her pulse didn't do anything other than keep its regular steady beat? That was all superficial, anyway. He was handsome, kind and smart. Everything she wanted in a man.

"Hello, Charlotte," he said, and she frowned because

the way he said her name was so different from how Kane said it.

Damn it. She wasn't going to think about Kane anymore.

"Are you signing up for the half marathon in Pittsburgh?" he continued, looking at her in a way that gave her the impression he was interested in what she had to say. That he was interested in her.

Then again, what the hell did she know? She'd thought James was interested in her and he'd merely been nice to her because of Sadie. And Kane? Well, she had no idea what his interest in her was.

"I've never run a half marathon before." She'd never run anything other than a 5K, but he didn't need to know everything about her. It was important to keep a bit of mystery in a relationship, after all.

"It's not until the summer. I've run quite a few."

She nodded. Smiled. Waited for him to suggest helping her train, giving her pointers. Anything to prove he was picking up what she was putting down, for God's sake. But he just waited, expecting her to say something, as if it was her turn now. "Uh... that's great."

What else was there to say? Nothing, obviously, because he nodded as if in agreement of his awesomeness and, tapping the file in his hand, said, "I'd better check on my patient."

Char blinked. That was it? She knew their first couple of dates hadn't been exactly mind-blowing but they hadn't been that bad. She thought he'd enjoyed himself, even if he hadn't called since their last lunch date.

Maybe that was her fault. She needed to step up her game, give him more hints, broader ones. Ones even an idiot couldn't miss. How else was she going to let him know she was interested in seeing more of him?

Have dinner with me.

Kane's voice floated through her mind. She frowned. *Not thinking about him or the husky way he'd sounded when he'd asked her out. Remember?*

Still, maybe she needed to start revamping her plan.

She caught up to Justin. "I really enjoyed lunch the other day," she said softly, not wanting it to get around they were seeing each other. Even if it was casual. So far.

"I did, too."

Thank goodness. "I thought maybe, next time, we could go out to dinner? Maybe dancing afterward?"

His grin widened. "That'd be great."

She blinked. "It would?"

"Yeah." They stopped outside his patient's door. "I'm scheduled every night except Saturday."

"Saturday will be perfect." She was supposed to work, but she'd switch with someone. This was important. This was her future.

"Great. I'll pick you up?" he asked.

She tried to work up as much enthusiasm as he had. "Sure. I mean...yes. Yes, that would be wonderful."

He glanced around, then reached out and gave her hand a quick, warm squeeze. "I'm looking forward to it."

Her smile felt frozen. "Yeah. Me, too."

His fingers brushed the back of her hand as he moved to knock on the door.

She felt nothing. No excitement or anticipation. Not even one freaking tingle.

Where was the justice in that?

He walked away, with his perfect hair, perfect smile, perfect runner's body. His skin—insomuch as she knew—unmarred by scars or tattoos.

He was perfect. Perfect for her.

No, her body hadn't responded to his touch, but it wasn't even a full touch, anyway. Just a whisper of one. And it would have been inappropriate for her to get all hot and bothered over his fingers brushing against hers in their place of work. She was sure there would be sparks and fireworks and all sorts of bright lights and explosions once they got to know each other better.

She was sure it would be magical.

Perfect.

Just as she wanted it to be.

KANE WALKED ACROSS O'Riley's parking lot, his hand in his pocket, the fingers of his broken arm cold from the damp air. It'd been a long two days, but his old man was pulling his own. He had a long road ahead of him as far as physical rehabilitation and speech and occupational therapy, but the doctors were optimistic he'd be able to function at 75 percent capacity or more.

Seventy-five percent. The old man was going to hate that, was going to hate not being able to live as he had before. He'd lost the use of his arm and his speech. His right leg was weak. He wasn't helpless, but he'd lost most of his independence.

Kane glanced at the cars in the lot. Not a bad crowd for a Tuesday. He could stop in, work behind the bar or help with cleanup, but he knew the place was in good hands. He didn't have to worry about it going under because he missed a day or two of work.

Besides, Sadie, who usually worked only weekends, was covering for him. Probably talking everybody's ears off about her engagement, her wedding plans.

He wondered how Charlotte felt about it.

He squeezed his keys until the teeth bit into his palm. Every time he let his guard down, even for a minute, she entered his head.

It was the only place he saw her.

Except for his dreams. Hot, sweaty dreams about her pressed against his living room wall, her skin soft and warm under his hand, those little sounds she'd made whispering in his ear.

He stomped up the stairs. Yeah. She really knew how to burrow into a man's head and stay there.

Where the hell did she get off doing it anyway? He hadn't asked her to worm her way into his life. She was the one always worrying about everyone else. Jumping in, making sure he was okay after his accident, bringing him pain pills so he wouldn't suffer. Understanding when he refused them.

He hadn't asked her to be there the night his father had his stroke, to keep coming out and checking on him and Estelle. Holding his hand, sitting by silently while the doctor told him how badly off Senior was.

Then he'd made that boneheaded move of kissing her in the elevator—after she'd made it clear she didn't want anything to do with him—and he hadn't seen her since.

It pissed him off that he'd been looking for her.

He unlocked the apartment door and walked straight to the couch. Leaning his head back, he stretched his legs and shut his eyes. His arm didn't hurt as much, and it no longer felt as though someone stabbed him with each breath, but the remnants of his injuries were still there.

Maybe Charlotte had just been busy working. Was she there now? Her shifts ended late. He didn't like the idea of her walking around the dark parking lot by herself.

Not his business, he reminded himself grimly.

So what if he'd been telling the truth when he'd

stupidly admitted he liked her? Christ, what was he? Eleven?

But he did. He liked being with her. Liked talking to her. So much that he would try to find ways to keep her talking. To get her to stay.

But she still always walked away.

"Daddy?"

Opening his eyes, he sat up. "Hey. I thought you were sleeping."

Estelle tucked her hair behind her ear. "I wanted to see how Granddad's doing."

"No change." He shifted to the right and she curled up next to him, her legs tucked under her, her feet bare. "Did you get your homework done?"

Chewing on her thumbnail, she nodded. "I went to Andrew's," she blurted.

He sat up, speared her with a narrow look. "I didn't give you permission to go there." Damn it, she'd been out with a boy and he hadn't even known it? "I trusted you to stay here."

Maybe that had been his first mistake. Trusting her. But he didn't want to raise her the way he'd been brought up, with demands and lectures and suspicion.

That he'd deserved that suspicion wasn't the point.

Her eyes welled with tears. "I know, and I'm really sorry, but I was so worried here all by myself with nothing to do or think about except the possibility of Granddad dying—"

"He's not dying."

"I know that. But I can't always control my

thoughts." She flopped back against the cushions. "Besides, nothing happened. I was only there for a few hours and it's not like I slept with him or anything."

His entire body went cold. His face numb. The idea of his daughter ever having sex… No. Just no. "You still should have asked me before you even thought about leaving this apartment to go anywhere."

"His mom was there. You can ask her since you don't trust me."

The last thing he wanted was to call some teenage boy's mother and ask her if her son kept his grubby hands off his daughter. "If you say she was there, then I believe you."

Had no reason not to. She'd always been a good girl. Not perfect. She'd had her fair share of troubles—detention for being late to class, out past curfew on a few occasions. Nothing he and Meryl couldn't handle.

Nothing compared to the things Kane had done.

"But this has nothing to do with trust," he continued, "and everything to do with respecting the rules your mother and I have set for you. Including letting us know where you are and getting our permission before leaving the house."

"I know," she said, all resigned and remorseful. "And I really am sorry."

He nodded. "I appreciate that and I appreciate you telling me the truth. But I think it'd be best if you stayed here for the next week, finished up your schoolwork."

"Is that your way of telling me I'm grounded?"

"What do you think?"

She flopped back against the couch, crossed her arms. "I think a week is way overkill. I mean, I did tell you the truth." ▪

He'd give her that. He didn't want to punish her for coming clean. "Three days."

"One seems sufficient."

"If you don't like three, we could always go up to five."

She rolled her eyes. Huffed out a breath. "Fine. Three. But that means I won't be able to go out to eat or shopping with Grandma."

"She's gone. C.J. drove her to the airport an hour ago." They'd managed to talk their mother into going back to Houston, promising to fill her in on Senior's condition at least once a day.

"Oh. If I'd known she was leaving so soon, I would have hung out with her longer after lunch."

Estelle had claimed a stomachache and had Gwen drop her off after they'd eaten.

"No, you wouldn't have."

She smiled. His smile. Seeing it on her face, as always, hit him like a baseball bat to the gut. Love suffused him. So much it scared the hell out of him sometimes.

"Yeah," she said. "You're right. Honestly, I think I deserve a medal for the hour we were together."

"I'll look into getting one made for you." He patted her knee. "It's late. You should get to bed." She slept in his room and he took the couch.

"Actually…" She inhaled deeply, looked worried. Nervous. "There's something I need to tell you."

CHAPTER SEVENTEEN

HER DAD SAT back slowly, his expression concerned. People thought he was some sort of badass because of the tattoos and long hair. And yeah, the past drug abuse. But with her, he was always patient.

Oh, he didn't always give her everything she asked for, and he was sort of strict—at least compared with her friends' parents. Grounded for three days for telling the truth? Please. Estelle knew he was that way because he didn't want her to make the same mistakes he had. Because he worried about her.

He loved her.

Please, don't let him stop.

"What is it?" he asked, his low voice giving her courage. The memory of Andrew's words building that courage up, reminding her he believed in her.

"You remember when I asked if I could live with you?"

"Seeing as how it was only last week, yes, I think it's coming back to me."

She rolled her eyes. He didn't have to be sarcastic. "Well, I wasn't completely honest. About my reasons."

He waited. Then again, he'd known she was keeping something from him. Hadn't he already questioned her on it? Parents. They seemed to have some secret superpower granting them insight into their kids' brains.

"The reason I don't want to keep living at home is because of Adam. But not because I'm jealous or whatever," she added quickly. "It's because of what he…what he did."

Her dad's eyes narrowed. He went still beside her. "What did he do?"

She swallowed, but it still felt as if there was some sort of pebble in her throat. "He…he sort of, you know…"

She dropped her gaze. She couldn't do it. Andrew was wrong about her. She wasn't brave. She was a coward. Scared her parents would blame her. Would hate her.

Terrified Adam was right and this was all her fault.

"Estelle, look at me."

She forced herself to meet his gaze, her lower lip trembling.

"I can't help you," her dad said, "unless you tell me what's going on."

Her arms still crossed, she dug her nails into her biceps. When she spoke, her voice was nothing more than a ragged whisper. "He came on to me."

Kane's expression darkened, and she thought for sure he was going to go to France and beat the hell out of Adam, broken arm or not. Or maybe he'd use his cast to beat Adam over the head.

Her dad's voice got very, very quiet. "What happened?"

She couldn't look at him while she told him. It was too gross. Too humiliating. She stared at her lap. "He came into my room and he…uh…he kissed me."

Just the memory of it made her skin crawl. The feel of Adam's flabby body as he'd pressed her against the headboard, his hard-on touching her thigh. The taste of cigarettes when he'd stuck his tongue in her mouth.

"Why didn't you tell your mother?" Kane asked, sounding mad. She hoped he wasn't mad at her.

"I couldn't. She's never been this happy. I…I didn't want to take that away from her."

Her mother had always put Estelle first. Put their relationship—mother and daughter—before everything else in her life. But in two years, Estelle would be away at college and she hated the idea of her mom being alone.

But Andrew had been right. She didn't want her mother with Adam. He wasn't nearly good enough for her.

"Your mom would never risk your safety, not for anything," Kane said. "Once she hears what that son of a bitch did, he'll be lucky she doesn't skin him alive."

Estelle started crying. "He said if I told her, she'd blame me."

Her dad's head snapped back as if she'd smacked him. "What the hell? You listen to me and you listen good," he said, giving her shoulder a gentle shake, "Meryl would never, ever blame you for this. It wasn't your fault."

"He said it was. That I'd flirted with him. Enenticed him by walking around in my pajamas and lying out in my bikini by the pool." At first, when Adam had moved in, she hadn't thought anything of it, but then she'd catch him watching her. Giving her the creeps. She'd started being more careful about what she wore in front of him. "I didn't mean to give him the wrong idea. I swear. I was just... I wanted him to like me. But maybe," she said hoarsely, confessing her greatest sin, her biggest fear. "Maybe I did flirt with him. Maybe I made it seem like I was interested in him. In that way. That I wanted him to...you know..." A tear dripped onto the back of her hand. "What if it really was all my fault?"

KANE COULDN'T REMEMBER feeling this helpless, this out of control with rage. It filled him, simmered in his bloodstream, raced along his veins. He'd been angry plenty, had spent most of his teenaged years pissed off. Had been scared many times during his time in the service, times when they'd taken on enemy fire or had gone into a possible insurgent's home, not knowing if he was going to make it out alive.

But nothing compared to the bone-deep fear of knowing his daughter had been in danger. The fury pushing him to fly to France, beat the living hell out of Adam, make sure Meryl and their daughter were as far away from the slimy bastard as possible.

But he couldn't let his feelings control him. Couldn't let them lead him into making a mistake. He'd spent too much of his life trying to cover up his emotions, trying to numb himself with alcohol and drugs, lashing out or running away instead of doing the right thing.

His daughter needed him. Here. Now. To help her through this, not tearing out of Shady Grove to track down Adam, not ranting and raving like an out-of-control lunatic.

He shifted to the floor, knelt in front of Estelle, the sight of her tears ripping him apart inside. "Don't you ever say that," he told her firmly, his voice stony. "None of this was your fault. Adam's nothing but a liar. He was trying to intimidate you into not saying anything. Your mother would never believe that crap and I sure as hell don't."

Raising her head, she blinked at him, tears clinging to her lashes, the tip of her nose red. "I don't want you or Mama to hate me."

It killed him that she would even worry about that. "Never. Meryl loves you. I love you. That will never change."

They told Estelle often how much she was loved, but sometimes words weren't enough. Sometimes even parents had to show their kids what they meant to them.

And that was what he was going to do. It was his

job to protect Estelle. Had been his greatest priority and weightiest responsibility ever since he'd found out she was his. "Come on," he said, holding out his hand.

Taking it, she set her feet on the floor, but didn't stand. "Where are we going?"

"You're going to wash your face," he said, tugging her to her feet. He held her close, kissed the top of her head. "And then we're going to call your mother and tell her. Together. And that's how the three of us will get through this. Together."

"I SWEAR TO GOD," Sadie said as she came behind the bar Saturday night, "if that idiot plays 'Love Shack' one more time, I'm going to go *bang, bang, bang* on his fat head."

"He's got at least another hour's worth of quarters lined up on the jukebox," Julie said of the thirtysomething guy doing a shoulder shake next to the entrance to the men's room, his flabby stomach swaying with the movement. "I could accidentally—" she made finger quotes "—knock them off."

Kane sipped his bottle of water, noted the drink in the guy's hand. "Offer him two free drinks if he lets someone else pick the music for the rest of the night."

Julie slapped his arm. "That's brilliant. Must be why you're the boss."

She headed off, winding her way through the crowd to save them all from B-52s overload.

The boss. That was him. Problem was, he still

hadn't decided if he wanted to be the boss. The urge to run was still there, nagging him like an itch he couldn't reach. Had grown stronger since Meryl took Estelle back to Houston yesterday.

They had called Meryl together, as he'd promised. Had woken her up but there was no way Kane could put off telling her that her fiancé was a sick bastard who'd put his hands on their daughter. They'd asked her to go somewhere private and she'd slipped into the living room of her and Adam's suite.

Kane could still remember the shocked silence on the other end of the phone when he'd relayed what Adam had done. How Estelle had clung to Kane's arm as he'd talked, her head bent as if she was the one who had something to be ashamed of.

A moment later, Kane heard the unmistakable low rumble of a man's voice on Meryl's side of the phone. She'd asked Kane to excuse her for a moment, sounding as prim and proper as the debutante she'd once been. But she must have held her phone in her hand because the next thing Kane knew, Meryl called Adam a slimy son of a bitch.

And, if the sound of cracking bone was any indication, she punched the bastard in the nose.

She'd returned to the phone, told Kane she was leaving on the next flight and that she'd be in Shady Grove as soon as possible. He and Estelle had picked her up at the Pittsburgh airport the next evening.

He'd known, as soon as he'd seen Estelle's face when she'd spotted her mother that his daughter wouldn't be living with him. He accepted it. Understood it.

But was still disappointed. Surprisingly so, considering he hadn't been sure he'd been up to the challenge of raising her on his own.

With Senior doing better each day, and since Meryl had kicked Adam's ass to the curb, there was no reason for Estelle to stay in Shady Grove. Kane missed her already.

Now it was time for him to start making some decisions about his own life. Thanks to his cast, though, he had five more weeks before he could go anywhere. At least on his bike.

Until then he'd mull over his options. Look into where he wanted to be. He'd been thinking that instead of going north, he'd head west. Not Houston, but New Orleans might not be too bad. He'd be closer to Estelle. Taking an order for a beer, one of the drinks he could still easily serve, he glanced over as the door opened. Froze.

Charlotte. What the hell was she doing here?

For a moment, one breathless second, he wondered, hoped, she'd come to see him.

Until she turned to smile at the man behind her. The man she was obviously with.

"Kane," Sadie said, bumping his elbow. "Kane."

He frowned at her. "What?"

"The beer?"

He glanced down. Swore at the liquid overflowing from the glass. He shook the wetness from his hand, grabbed a clean glass and pulled another one.

Wiping his hand on a clean rag, he scanned the room until he found Charlotte again. Her date pulled out her chair and she sat, crossed those long legs. She was here. At his place. With another guy.

He strangled the rag, considered wrapping it around her date's neck. Or hers.

Where did she get off coming here, to his place, with another guy, looking like…like that? She wore a skirt. A short one that was snug at her hips and showcased those endless legs. Legs that were bare and even better than he'd ever imagined, her feet in strappy heels. Her top clung to her torso and long arms, the low cut accentuating her neck.

Her date sat across from her, some bastard in black pants and a white shirt, his short hair slicked back, his smile too white, too perfect. That's when it hit Kane, why he recognized the guy. It was the doctor from the E.R.

Son of a bitch.

"Did you just growl?" Sadie asked, watching him intently. She followed his gaze, then deliberately stepped in front of him, matching his scowl with one of her own. "Stop staring at my sister," she said in a low hiss. "I mean it."

Gladly.

Too bad he couldn't seem to tear his gaze away.

He wasn't jealous.

But when the good doctor leaned over to say something to Charlotte, resting his hand on her bare knee, Kane's own hand curled into a fist. His vision took on a definite red haze.

"Hey," James Montesano, Sadie's fiancé, said as he joined them. He glanced between them. "What's going on?"

"Kane is looking at Charlotte," Sadie whispered fiercely. "Make him stop."

James lifted a dark eyebrow, a beer in his hand. "How do you suggest I do that?"

"I don't know," she said with an irritable shrug. "Punch him or something."

"You want me to punch your boss, while you're at work?"

She poured vodka into a shot glass, her mouth pinched. "Fine. Wait until after I'm done working."

James and Kane eyed each other, much as they had when Kane had deposited a drunk Sadie on James's doorstep last year. They were close in height, but James had weight on Kane. Then again, Kane was meaner and a dirty fighter—something C.J. could attest to.

But James wasn't a brawler. And he didn't have anything against Kane once James had realized Kane wasn't trying to sleep with Sadie.

"If I punch him," James said mildly, "I might spill my beer."

"Good call." To reward him, Kane opened another bottle of his favorite brand. Handed it to him. "On the house."

Sadie slapped her hands on her hips. "Really? You won't fight to defend my sister's honor and all for the cost of a beer?"

"Your sister's honor is fine," James soothed. With that, and a silent toast with both bottles, he headed back to join his brothers at the pool table.

"Relax," Kane told her. "Your sister is safe from me."

She may not be safe from Dr. Handsy, though.

Not his business or his problem.

Refusing to look their way again, he went back to work. Pulling beers, pouring shots, mixing drinks. For over an hour, he managed to not look Charlotte's way.

And then she sashayed up to his bar as if she had every damned right to do so.

"Kane," she said, looking nervous. Good. "Hello."

He nodded, which only seemed to unsettle her more. Perfect. Why should he be the only one who was a mixed-up mess? "Uh...you remember Dr. Louk?"

She was introducing him to her date. He'd been dreaming of her, missing her, and she was rubbing his face in it.

He'd never known she'd had a mean streak.

Smiling, his bedside manner obviously not just for show, but a part of his everyday charming, polite, happy-go-lucky life, the doctor reached his right hand across the bar.

"Justin," he said, as if Kane wanted to be on a first-name basis with him. "How are you doing?"

Kane raised his cast to show he wouldn't be shaking his hand. "I'm healing."

Justin gave a self-deprecating laugh at his handshake blunder. Settled his hand on Charlotte's waist. "Good to hear." He turned to Charlotte, his fingers curving along the slope of her hip. "Excuse me for a minute?"

She nodded, stood there looking all bright and out of place in his dim bar. Her lips a glossy red, long silver earrings dangling from her ears.

The damn necklace Kane had bought her hanging from her neck. A guy bumped her as he came up to the bar and ordered a draft. She stepped to the side, had the silver pendant swinging.

"Do you need a drink?" Kane asked, his voice a low growl.

She startled as if surprised he was asking that of her. She was in a goddamn bar, wasn't she? She must have been sipping on something for the past hour.

"No. Thank you." She moved closer, set her sparkly bag down. "Justin saw you and wanted to come over. To see how you were doing after the accident."

Well, that explained it. Though she didn't have to. It also made it clear she would have kept her distance if it was up to her.

Yet she was the one who'd come to Kane's bar.

Since he had nothing to say, he kept silent. Gave

the customer his beer. Took another order, all the while aware of her there, close enough to touch.

"How's your father?" she asked when he came her way again.

"The same." Carrie and C.J. were trying to decide where Senior should have his rehab, in Pittsburgh or Houston. Zach had gone back to base after his two days off and Oakes had flown home the same day as Meryl and Estelle, needing to get back to a court case he was working on.

Charlotte ran her finger back and forth across her bag. "That's good. That he hasn't taken a turn for the worse, I mean. What about Estelle? Is she still hanging out with Andrew?"

"She's gone. Her mother took her back to Houston."

Now she looked sad, disappointed, as if she'd miss his kid. "I thought she wanted to stay with you."

He lifted a shoulder. "She changed her mind."

Charlotte touched his arm. "I'm sorry."

He didn't move, simply stared at her fingers on his skin. She slowly drew her hand away. He wished he could drag her out back where they could be alone, but he wasn't going to play the jealousy card. Wouldn't let it, or these confusing, conflicted feelings he had for her rule him.

Not when he was afraid she had too much power over him already.

"What are you doing here?" he asked, angling his

body over the bar so he could speak quietly and still have her hear him.

"What do you mean?"

"I mean, I kissed you in the elevator and haven't seen you since, and now, you just happen to come here with a date?"

Color washed up her neck. "We…we were at dinner and we came in for a couple of drinks. That's all."

It wasn't. It couldn't be. They could have gone to three different bars, all within a mile of here.

"Whatever you're trying to prove," he told her, "you've proved it."

Her eyes flashed with building temper, and for a minute, he thought she'd whack him with that beaded purse of hers. Almost wished she would. Seeing her here, after wanting nothing more all week than to talk to her, touch her again, made him feel tight with tension, antsy with unnamed emotion, the kind that built up in a man until the only way to rid yourself of it was to explode.

"I'm not trying to prove anything," she insisted.

"You think the doc is safe?" Kane asked, his gaze holding hers. "You think he's the perfect guy for you, someone to fill the role of future husband?"

"I think he's a nice man, an intelligent, handsome man who is interested in me," she said softly. And Kane wondered, worried, that she hadn't brought the doctor there to make him jealous.

That she was with Justin because she was moving on with her life. Moving away from Kane.

And that was even worse.

He straightened. Smirked. "My mistake." Tossing down his rag, he called across the bar to Sadie. "Switch sides with me."

She did as he asked, looking at him curiously as they passed each other.

A few minutes later, Justin returned and he and Charlotte walked out.

Hand-in-hand.

For several long moments after they left, Kane stared at the closed door, his back teeth ground together so tightly, his jaw ached. He wanted to run after her, demand she quit playing these games. Tell her to give the doctor his walking papers.

He wanted to beg her to stay with him. To give him a chance.

He whirled around. Beg. She'd reduced him to this. Turned him into a jealous, pathetic loser willing to toss aside his pride.

He took an order for a kamikaze from a pretty brunette, poured vodka into a martini glass. He'd never been a fan of vodka, but when the potent scent of it hit him, it was all he could do not to raise the glass to his mouth and down the shot in one swallow.

His hands shook, his body craved the alcohol like his lungs craved their next breath. But he knew what would happen if he gave in. One drink wouldn't be enough. It had never been enough.

When faced with his greatest weakness, the best

thing, the smartest thing a man could do was get as far away as possible.

He slowly, deliberately, added lime juice and triple sec to the drink, set it on the bar, took the brunette's money and did what he was best at.

Walked away.

"I HAD A NICE TIME," Justin told Char as they reached her back door.

She smiled, hoped it looked more natural than it felt. "Me, too," she lied. But really, one harmless fib could be forgiven between them, right? They were... perfect together. Everyone who'd seen them tonight had told her so, especially after they found out he was a doctor.

Doctors and nurses. Nurses and doctors. God, you'd think they were peanut butter and jelly.

But at least they hadn't run out of things to talk about as she and James had last year. Nope, they'd had plenty to say. Interesting medical cases they'd come across, their time at college, his years at med school, their coworkers and patients and the town. He was happy in Shady Grove, ready to stay here and settle down. He was handsome and nice, and while he didn't seem to get her sense of humor, that was okay.

You think the doc is safe? You think he's the perfect guy for you, someone to fill the role of future husband?

Her fingers curled. So what if she did? There was

nothing wrong with making a plan or wanting to be with a certain type of person.

"Thanks again," she said as she unlocked the door. She kept her hand on the knob, smiled up at him, the porch light illuminating his features.

"Thank you," he said. She ground her teeth together. One of them had to stop thanking the other. At least their kids would be polite. Polite and cute with his warm brown eyes and brown hair. Polite, smart and taking care of all their friends, making sure everyone around them was happy and healthy. They'd excel in school and never cause their parents any trouble.

A sudden vision of a little boy with her fiery hair and freckles and Kane's green eyes and wicked smile filled her mind. He'd come home with holes in his best jeans and marks from playground scuffles. He'd charm his teachers and have his mother wrapped around his little finger. Or what about a little girl? One with strawberry-blond hair and Charlotte's eyes who'd boss around all her classmates and adore her daddy and be his little princess.

She shoved the visions from her mind. They weren't real. This, the man in front of her, was, and she was going to make things work with him. It didn't matter that, while there hadn't been any lulls in their conversation and she found him to be perfectly nice, Justin hadn't been able to truly hold her interest tonight. Her own fault for stupidly suggesting they have a drink at O'Riley's.

Whenever Kane was near, she didn't, couldn't, think straight.

Whatever you're trying to prove, you've proved it.

She'd been doing nothing of the sort. Justin had suggested an after-dinner drink and she'd complied. O'Riley's just happened to be the closest establishment to the restaurant. Her sister worked there, for God's sake. Char had every right to go in there with anyone she wanted.

But it had been hard to focus on Justin when she'd felt Kane watching her. She'd ignored him as much as possible, until Justin had wanted to check on his well-being.

She had wondered about the possessive look in Kane's eyes. As if he'd been…jealous.

Which was ridiculous. He'd almost ruined her date with his snarky comments and bad attitude. But she refused to let him get to her, refused to let his behavior upset her or let herself dwell on the questions running through her mind. Such as why he'd said those things he'd said. What it meant, if anything.

Justin smiled at her, held on to the door frame above her head, leaned forward. "I hope we can get together again."

See? He was sweet. Patient. Not pushy or confusing at all. With him, she knew where she stood.

Sort of.

"Of course."

Next time it'd be better, she assured herself. They'd stay far away from O'Rileys. Maybe go into Pittsburgh where they could spend a few hours over a leisurely meal, get to know each other even better. They'd date for a while, get engaged, then she'd plan the perfect wedding for them, the perfect life.

Just as she'd always dreamed.

His smile widened and he seemed really pleased. "Great. I'll call you."

"Okay." Why was he still standing there when all she wanted was to go inside and crawl into bed so she could replay her conversation with Kane? Analyze how he'd looked at her. How he'd sounded.

Justin leaned forward and her eyes widened. Her fingers tightened on the door handle but she forced herself to remain still. He kissed her, his mouth firm and warm as it moved over hers. It was…nice.

Nice. And absolutely, positively without any heat, fireworks or tingles on her end of things.

She could have cried, wanted to, badly. Wanted to bawl and scream and, yes, stomp her feet in a full-fit tantrum.

He pulled back, straightened. "No, huh?" he asked, looking disappointed.

She opened her mouth to lie, to pretend she had no idea what he was talking about. To assure him it was great, the best kiss she'd ever had.

"No," she said then winced. "I'm sorry."

"Me, too." He stepped back, ducked his head. "Is it because of that guy? Bartholomew?"

"Bartasavich. Kane Bartasavich." She cleared her throat. "No… Yes… I don't even know."

"That's what I thought." He stared out at the dark night then faced her again. "I really enjoy spending time with you, Charlotte. I think we could be good together. So, if things don't work out between you two—"

"They won't," she said with a harsh laugh. "I mean, they haven't. I mean…" She inhaled. "We're not…we're not together."

"I'm not sure he knows that." Justin took her hand. "I saw how he watched you tonight. If you change your mind, you know where to find me." He kissed her knuckles, then gave her hand a gentle squeeze and walked away, disappearing into the night.

She went inside, not bothering to turn on the light as she slumped into one of the kitchen chairs. Held her head in her hands and tugged at her hair. What was wrong with her? She'd just sent away the perfect man. She had no doubt Justin would be a great husband and father, and she couldn't work up the slightest interest.

She knew why. Kane. He filled her thoughts. She'd been such a fool to think she could ignore her feelings for him. That if she tried hard enough she could pretend she didn't want him.

Oh, God, Kane was right, she realized, bile rising in her throat. She had gone there to prove a point. To prove to herself there was nothing between them, that anything she thought she felt for him was nothing more than physical attraction.

Shame turned her stomach. She was such a fool.

Before she could talk herself out of it, she stood, grabbed her keys and purse, and headed out to her car.

If she was going to be a fool, she might as well do it big.

CHAPTER EIGHTEEN

SHE'D COME FULL circle, Char thought, staring at Kane's closed door. Right back to where she'd started this journey all those months ago.

She knocked, stepped back and waited. A moment later, he opened the door, looking dangerous and untamed, his hair wild around his face, his shirt no longer tucked in.

Those damn tingles she hadn't felt with Justin washed over her body, causing her scalp to prickle, gooseflesh to rise on her arms.

Her throat was dry, her head spinning. Oh, God, this was a mistake, her thoughts, her feelings... they were all wrong. Worse, they were going to get her into an even bigger mess than before. But she couldn't stop herself, couldn't stop what was going to happen any more than she could stop being a redhead.

Some things were beyond control.

It was scary as hell, but it was worth it. Kane was worth it.

"You were right," she said, pushing the words out, hoping they were enough to stop him from slamming the door in her face. "I came to O'Riley's tonight to prove something. But not to you. To myself. It didn't work."

His eyes gave nothing away. "Where's your date?"

"Home." She didn't dare step forward, not when he was so cool toward her. "I guess. He dropped me off and left."

"Ah, the perfect gentleman. Don't tell me, he walked you to your door then gave you a chaste kiss good-night. One you could think about for the rest of the night."

"His kiss—" She wouldn't say the other man's name, not now, not when things between her and Kane were so intense. "It doesn't have to be the last thing on my mind," she whispered.

His gaze heated and he took a step forward, only to stop. "What are you doing here?"

"I…" Taking her courage in hand, she met his eyes. And told him what was in her heart. "You. I'm here for you."

After a long moment, he held the door open and she stepped inside. Without a word, he shut and locked it. But he didn't touch her, and she wanted desperately for him to do just that. For him to take away her nerves and her doubts.

Then again, the last time she'd let her body determine her actions, it hadn't worked out so well.

She'd make sure this time was different.

He cupped her head with his good hand, dragged her to him slowly, giving her plenty of time to evade. To pull away. But she couldn't stop him now, didn't want to, truth be told. Not when he was standing so close to her, his mouth tight, his eyes hot with want. With need.

She laid her hands on his chest, slid them up to his shoulders and tipped her head back for his kiss. It was soft. Gentle. So unlike the first time when a fire had raged between them, heating her insides, taking her thoughts and her sanity. This time he kept the kiss in control.

It was lovely.

But she wanted the heat, that flash of desire and need she sensed inside him as if he were barely holding it together, holding on to his control. Having no idea what she was doing, only knowing she didn't want him to treat her like some damn china doll, as if she'd break at the slightest hint of desire. Didn't want him to treat her like a quivering virgin. She wanted him to treat her like a woman. A woman he desired. And if he wasn't going to go there, wasn't going to let their passion have free rein, then she'd have to.

She gripped his head on either side, her hands fisting in his hair, and rose onto her toes, pressed against him fully, heard his grunt of surprise. She had no idea what she was doing, how to get a man to respond to her, but it wasn't rocket science. It was sex. Human nature and instinct. She'd just go with the flow. God help her. The last time, their only time, the problem arose because she'd been overwhelmed by her feelings. Her doubts and fears and how much she'd wanted him.

But tonight, she'd be the one in charge.

She proved it by deepening the kiss, her hands tugging on his hair, her tongue sweeping into his mouth. He made a sound in the back of his throat, one that told her he liked what she was doing, so she did it again, now smoothing her hands over his shoulders, up his arms, but she couldn't feel enough of his skin so she leaned back enough to work on the buttons of his shirt.

He kissed the corners of her mouth, his touch incredibly sweet. Seductive. "You know this is a mistake."

"A doozy." She didn't like to make mistakes. Was afraid one of those mistakes would be irreversible. It was better, safer, to stick with the tried and true. To plan, to think of every contingency, every possible outcome—good or bad.

"Some mistakes, though," she told him, "are worth it."

He brushed another kiss over her mouth, raised his head to meet her eyes.

She could hardly believe this was happening, that she was here, about to make love with Kane Bartasavich. This man with the broken arm and bruised face, stubble covering his chin, his hooded gaze. He was dangerous. Not the type of man she went for, not the type of man she dreamed of being with, of having a future with.

But it didn't feel like a mistake.

It felt right.

He kissed her with a heat and need that burned through her. She deepened the kiss, clenching his shoulders.

He made another sound, this one half laugh, half groan, and grabbed first one wrist, then the other, circled them both in his large hand. Holding her away, he broke their kiss. "What's the hurry?"

"No hurry," she said, testing by tugging, but he held firm.

"Worried you'll change your mind?" he asked with that grin of his she'd come to adore.

"Worried you'll change yours," she heard herself say honestly.

His expression softened. "Not a chance. I want you. I dream of you, of your skin and that bright hair. You, Charlotte," he said roughly, softly, "are under my skin. In my head. I can't get you out."

He wanted to, it was clear. Wanted to rid himself of her. She wasn't sure how she felt about that, couldn't worry about it. Not now. Later, when she had time to think things through, she'd sort through all of these conflicting feelings inside her.

Much later.

"You're in my head, too," she admitted. But held back her greatest fear. That he might just be in her heart as well.

He let go of her and she stripped him of his shirt, finally touching him the way she wanted, her hands smoothing over his cool flesh. She placed kisses along his collarbone, let her hand trail down his ribs to his stomach, felt the muscles there quiver.

He gave a low, rough curse and yanked her to him, kissing her hungrily as he maneuvered them down the hallway and into his bedroom, backing her to the bed where she sprawled on her back. Kane flipped on a lamp.

Gaze intense, mouth unsmiling, he walked toward her, bare chested, his body a piece of art, his face so handsome. Her stomach did one slow roll as she drank in the sight of him. This hard man with his demons and past sins. This man who adored his daughter, who fought each day to be better. And she knew, as long as she lived, she'd never forget this moment.

The moment she fell in love with him.

He lay beside her, kissing her, his hands roaming over her, memorizing every detail of her face and body, every slight curve and angle, every dip and slope. He slowly undressed her despite her need for him to hurry up, but she knew it was her nerves pushing her to want this over quickly.

Even as she prayed every second would last a lifetime.

She helped him take off his jeans, pull off his briefs.

"Stop thinking," he whispered as he settled next to her on his right side, his head resting on his arm above his cast. He trailed the fingers of his left hand over her breasts, circled her nipple with his forefinger.

"I never stop thinking," she said, knowing it was an impossibility.

"Let's see if I can help with that." And he scooted down, bent his head, took her nipple into his mouth and sucked.

Sensations flowed through her, building higher and higher. His hand swept over her, leaving trails of pleasure in their wake, his mouth working magic. Her body heated. "Aren't we going to…" She gasped as his hand traveled down her stomach to trace a line above her pubic bone. "You know…"

"We're definitely going to you know," he said, brushing his mouth down her rib cage, "but first you deserved to be cherished. Worshipped."

She let her head fall back. "Oh. Well, you're the expert, after all."

And he proceeded to prove he was as he slipped his hand between her thighs. Her hands curled into the sheets, her head tipped back. Her hips rose of their own accord as pleasure built and built until finally, she exploded into a million pieces. When she was able to open her eyes again, she smiled. "I was right. You really are an expert."

KANE HAD NEVER seen anything like Charlotte. Her long limbs supple and almost glowing in the dim light, her hair a bright contrast to his white sheets, her skin flushed prettily, a look of surprise and satisfaction on her face.

He'd put it there. It made him feel powerful. And

scared the shit out of him because he wanted to be the only man to do so.

Because being with her, touching her, loving her and bringing her pleasure brought him a sense of rightness that he'd never had before. As if this was where he was meant to be. With her. Always with her.

But that wasn't real, wasn't what she was here for. Yes, he liked being with her. Yes, he enjoyed talking to her and listening to her, liked seeing her smile and hearing her laugh. None of that meant he had to start spinning fantasies about what this was between them. About imaginary feelings that weren't real.

This, he thought, skimming his hand over her hip, was real. The feel of her soft skin, the scent of her arousal and perfume, the way they sank into the bed together. The feminine smile on her face, the teasing glint in her eyes. He'd absolved himself of his mistake with her, of the first time they'd been together.

But he wasn't done with her yet.

"Not an expert," he said, sliding his lips over her shoulder. "Experienced."

"It came in handy," she said, pulling him closer. His erection nudged her outer thigh and she raised her eyebrows. "Guess I'm not doing too badly at this, either."

He kissed her. How could he not when she looked so damned pleased with herself? When he was so happy to be with her?

The kiss soon heated. He loved the way she responded to his touch, the little sounds she made as if amazed and very, very pleased by what he did to her. She grew emboldened as they kissed and touched each other, their skin heating and growing slick with sweat. Her hands roamed over him, seeking and curious, and he couldn't let her do anything but explore to her heart's content, even if it did drive him crazy having her soft fingers encircling him, stroking him.

Finally, when he couldn't take it any longer, when he knew she was ready for him, he sheathed himself with a condom. Kissing her, he rolled them both so that he was on top of her, holding his weight on his left arm. It was awkward and not easy, but it was worth it to be with her.

She looked uncertain. Nervous. He didn't mind the uncertainty, liked that he could put her on edge. He was feeling the same himself. As if a stiff breeze would push him over, stumbling down a path he wasn't sure he wanted to take.

But he didn't want her nervous. Not now.

He kissed her again until her body lost its stiffness. Until she was writhing underneath him. He entered her slowly, watching her face for any signs of distress or that she'd changed her mind. But there was nothing but pleasure. Her gaze held his and what he saw in the blue depths humbled him. Trust. She really did scare the hell out of him. He wanted to be worthy of her but he wasn't. Still, he had this moment and he could be worthy of this.

He slid deeper inside her wet heat. She was so

tight, he had to stop so as not to go too fast, too hard, but she groaned and lifted her hips. He set an easy motion, his hand gripping her slim hip. She met him, thrust for thrust, her hands moving over his shoulders, down his arms. He felt her body tighten and heat beneath his. He shifted, angling his body to give her even more pleasure, going deeper and deeper until she climaxed, her body tightening around him.

As she came down from her orgasm, he buried his face in the crook of her neck, pressed his mouth there as he increased his pace. Her nails dug into his skin; her breath was hot and came out in short gasps next to his ear. "Kane," she gasped. "Kane…"

The sound of her saying his name pierced him. He had a sudden and vicious need to hear her say it again and again. To wake up next to her. To see her face before he fell asleep. To hear her voice, the sound of her laugh every day. The want hit him with the force of a baseball bat, the ensuing images of her with him, day and night, forever, threatening to knock the breath from his lungs.

She licked his earlobe, sucked it into her mouth and scraped her teeth against it. "Kane," she whispered yet again.

With a roar he came, emptying himself.

Later—could have been hours, though it was more than likely just a few minutes—he managed to roll to the side, taking her with him, holding her against him. She snuggled close, laying her head on his shoulder, her hand resting above his heart.

"So," she said after a while, sounding content and pretty damned pleased with herself, "that's what all the fuss is about, huh?"

He smiled against the top of her head. "That'd be it."

"Is that pretty much how it always is?" she asked.

"Pretty much," he lied, though he'd never experienced anything quite as earth-shaking as what had happened between them. But if he believed that, if he bought into it, then he'd have to believe all the bullshit about sex being better with someone you love, someone you wanted to spend the rest of your life with.

Pure fantasy, that.

Char traced the lettering above his heart, Savage, the nickname he'd been given in the service due to his last name. Could she feel the way his heart tripped under her touch? How unsteady it—and he—was? Did she have any idea how unsteady he felt around her, as if he had to be extra careful of his next step.

"I guess I'll have to take your word for it," she said lightly, her voice a bit sleepy. "Seeing as how I have nothing to compare it to."

He frowned. Realized that, eventually, she would have something to compare this to. They weren't forever. They weren't even exclusive for right now. If he let her go, *when* he let her go, she'd find someone else, another man to make love to her, to touch her and make her come, to hear the sounds she made.

Some other lucky bastard who'd get to hold her afterward and see her smile.

Kane rolled her onto her back. Her eyes flew open. She laughed. "What…?"

He kissed her and, for the next hour, did his damnedest to prove that despite his words, when it came to what they'd just shared, nothing else would ever come close.

KANE WOKE SLOWLY, the morning sun shining in his eyes. He rolled over, brushed against a soft, warm weight.

Charlotte.

He pulled her closer, kept his hand on her hip. She sighed. "G'morning," she murmured, her eyes still closed.

He kissed her. "Good morning." Then, because she was warm and sleepy and sexily rumpled, he kissed her again.

And again. And again. Soon their bodies heated, their breathing grew ragged. She was so soft, so sweet. He wasn't used to sweet, wasn't sure it was something he wanted to be around too often. It could mess with a man's head, make him think stupid thoughts. Make him believe someone cared about him enough to put him above their own needs or welfare.

He knew better.

But he couldn't let her go. Not yet.

He tugged her over so she straddled him.

She nibbled on her lower lip, placed her hands on his chest for support. "Are you sure about this?"

He grinned. "Positive." He covered himself with a condom, then lifted his pelvis. It only took a moment for her to catch on and she slid up and down his length. She quivered. Gasped.

"Lift your hips," he told her, hating that he couldn't do it himself, couldn't grab hold of her as he wanted.

She rose onto her knees. Fast learner that she was, she gently wrapped her hand around him and guided him inside her. He watched her face as she lowered her hips, her mouth opened, her eyes dark.

"What...what should I do?" she asked when he was firmly embedded in her tight heat.

His groan turned into a laugh. "Whatever feels good."

Her forehead wrinkling in concentration, she moved forward. Then back. He arched, shut his eyes against how good it felt. He didn't want to rush her, didn't want to take anything away from another first experience.

Her pace was slow. Steady. It about killed him. But she took his advice, kept working him, her face glowing with pleasure, her skin heating.

Her breasts swayed, her face flushed. "I...I think...I want to go faster."

God, but she was something. Innocent and so sexy at the same time. "Are you sure?" He licked one taut nipple. "Maybe what you really want is me deeper?"

He lifted his hips. Her eyes widened. She licked

her lips. "Yes, that's…that's good but I think…maybe if I just…"

She dropped to her elbows, pumped her hips faster. Harder. He met her thrust for thrust. Their bodies grew slick with sweat. She pressed her face to the crook of his neck, her breathing ragged. He knew she had to be close, wasn't sure how much longer he could hold out on his own orgasm.

He turned his head, captured her mouth in a heated kiss, one where he tried to tell her everything he was feeling, everything he thought about her. She pulled away, began making those sexy noises that told him she was close to coming.

She straightened, her hips pumping, her fingertips trailing against his stomach. "Oh…oh…" Her eyes darkened and she held his gaze as she came, her body tightening around him.

Knowing he'd never see anything more beautiful in his life, he followed her over the edge.

She collapsed on top of him, her heart racing against his. After catching her breath, she lifted her head. What he saw in her eyes humbled him.

Terrified him.

He knew what was coming before she spoke, but he couldn't find the strength to stop her.

"I love you."

Her words were like a cold dose of reality, one he didn't want to face. Not now. Not ever.

But it was too late.

"You don't love me."

She slowly sat up, moved away from him. He immediately missed her warmth. "You mean you don't want me to love you," she said, her voice shaking.

A muscle in his jaw worked. He sat up, swung his legs over the side of the bed, his back to her. "You don't love me," he repeated. "We're..."

"Oh, no. Please, go on. We're...what? Friends with benefits? Sex buddies?"

"It doesn't matter," he said, yanking on his jeans from last night, not bothering to button them. When he turned, he found she'd already put on her bra, was sliding on that tiny skirt. He wanted to rip it off again, to go back to the way they'd been last night. The way they'd been a few minutes ago.

"You don't want to love me," he said as she tugged on her shirt. "I'm not the guy you're looking for."

"You're the guy I want. And what do you mean, not the guy I'm looking for? I want a man to be my partner. Someone who's caring and generous. Who makes me laugh. Makes me think. Who pushes me to be better. Stronger. Who encourages me to take risks." She crossed to him, laid her hands flat against his chest. His heart tripped. "You may not be the man I always thought I wanted, but you're the one I want now. Don't push me away because you think it's best for me."

CHAR HELD HER BREATH. Under her fingers, Kane's heart beat quickly. She did that. Made his heart trip, like he did hers. He had to care for her. He had to.

He was doing this as some lame attempt to put her back on her path to her perfect future.

Her perfect future was with him.

"Don't try to turn this around," he snarled, his expression darkening. "I'm not some good guy here doing the right thing out of honor or whatever."

"But you are honorable. Can't you see that? You're a wonderful father, have a fabulous relationship with the mother of your child and have spent hours at your sick father's bedside. The same father you claim you don't want anything to do with. You want, so badly, to keep separated from everyone and everything, to be isolated emotionally, but you're not."

"I'm an addict," he said harshly. "You can't ignore that. Can't pretend my past doesn't happen."

"Your past will always be a part of you, but you're more than your addiction, so much more than your mistakes. Tell me," she said, turning him so she could swipe her hand across his back, "why did you choose this for one of your tattoos?"

He stiffened. "No reason."

"Please. You expect me to believe you just happened to spend hours upon hours having a phoenix inked into your back? It's a symbol for what you've gone through. Except you weren't reborn from flames, you were reborn because you turned your life around. You did that, all on your own." She laid her hand on his arm, held his gaze. "You're a good man. You overcame your past and are now a member of this town, you made O'Riley's bigger and better.

You're more honorable than you think." She swallowed, knew she had to share with him what was in her heart. "Those are all part of the reasons why I fell in love with you."

He flinched. The man actually flinched at her declaration. She'd be pissed if her stomach didn't feel so sick, if a cold sweat hadn't coated her skin.

He stepped back. Looked hard and unyielding. "It's just sex."

"That's it? Nothing else. No feelings involved?"

"Look, I care about you—"

"Yay. You care about me," she said flatly. "That is so reassuring. I mean, I just told you I'm in love with you and you…you come back with you care about me? Wow. Talk about putting yourself out there."

Which was what she was doing. What she always did. And, once again, it was coming back to bite her in the ass. You'd think she'd be used to the pain and disappointment, but this time, this time seemed so much worse.

Like she might not ever recover.

"You're confused," he said almost desperately. "You're messing up sex with feelings."

"Well, silly me, being so sentimental and emotional when it comes to sex. I'm glad you're here to set me straight on how and what I feel and how wrong I am about those feelings."

"That's not what I meant," he grumbled. He scrubbed a hand through his hair. "Look, we're both tired. Let's just…talk about this another time."

Char froze, felt as if everything inside her had turned to ice and one wrong move and she'd shatter into a million pieces. "You really don't want me."

"I don't see any reason for us to go round and round on something that doesn't matter."

She laughed harshly. It was either that or curl into a ball and cry like a baby. "I see. So my feelings, my wants, they don't matter." She hugged herself, but she was still so cold. "So what happens now? You'll call me later? We'll hook up a few times—a few or a dozen, whatever you prefer—and then when you're tired of me, you'll just walk away."

"I'm not in a good place right now for this conversation and I wasn't…I'm not…looking for a relationship. That was always clear. Families, relationships are nothing but a pain in the ass. Eventually, everyone shows their true colors. Guess you're just seeing mine sooner rather than later."

Char hated that Kane saw family—the love and commitment that came with it—as a noose slowly tightening around his neck. "I can show you what it's like to be a part of a family that loves and respects one another. I can show you how wonderful it is to be in a relationship with a woman who truly loves and respects you. A woman who'll be by your side no matter what, who'll support your decisions, cheer you on and be your lover, friend and partner for life. Someone who'll never walk away from you." She closed the distance between them, lightly touched his jaw, his cheek and lowered her voice. "Someone like me."

The panic on his face might have been comical if it didn't tear her heart out and rip it in two.

He caged her wrists, pulled her hands from him. "I can't. There's nothing between us except sex. You're mixing up attraction with feelings, making more of our physical relationship than what's really there."

He believed that. He really, truly believed what he was saying.

That was what hurt the most.

"I can accept that you're going to stand there and try to reduce what we have to lust," she said, her voice unsteady, tears stinging her eyes. "That you're going to deny your feelings."

He didn't want her. All of the fears and doubts she'd had since she was a skinny teenager came rushing back.

She opened the door, held it until she could get her thoughts under control. Her feelings. "I can forgive you for not loving me," she said quietly. "But I'll never forgive you for hurting me this way."

She shut the door behind her with a soft click and gave in to her tears as she hurried down the stairs.

CHAPTER NINETEEN

"YOU CAN COME out during Easter break," Kane told Estelle as they chatted over Skype. She and Meryl were back to normal. As soon as they'd gotten to Houston Meryl had packed up Adam's things and set them on the curb. Estelle was back in school and she and Pilar had made up.

All was right with his daughter's world again.

Wish he could say the same for his own life.

"But that's, like, three weeks from now!"

Estelle wanted to come back to Shady Grove since Senior was going to transfer to a Pittsburgh hospital for his rehab. Why Carrie decided on that instead of sending him back to Houston, Kane had no idea, but it pissed C.J. off but good.

"You've already missed two weeks of school," he reminded her. "Your granddad will understand."

"I hope so." She checked her nails, dipped the brush into the nail polish bottle. "I was thinking I could also come out at the beginning of summer."

"Sure." He'd put off selling O'Riley's, at least for the next year or so. He couldn't live near Estelle, but he could give her that much permanency.

"Maybe I could stay for the whole summer," she said, looking hopeful.

"You don't have to do that." He was worried she felt guilty about not wanting to live with him.

She rolled her eyes. "Duh, Daddy, I want to. It'll be fun. We can hang out a lot and I can see Andrew and Charlotte again."

Charlotte. He hadn't seen her since she'd left his apartment a week ago. For the best, he told himself. She was confused. Thought he was something he wasn't. Some sort of hero.

A man worthy of her.

"She called me, you know."

His mouth tightened. "Charlotte called you?"

Estelle nodded. "Two days ago. Said she visited Granddad and he looked a lot better."

Charlotte had visited his father, then had called his daughter to tell her Senior was looking better.

He didn't want to think about her, didn't want to talk about her. Couldn't fall asleep at night without reliving their lovemaking. Without seeing the hurt in her face before she'd left.

Hurt he'd caused.

I love you.

They were just words. They didn't mean anything. In a few weeks, she'd move on, go back to looking for her future husband, a doctor or an accountant, someone clean-cut and boring.

Lucky bastard.

She didn't want Kane. Not really. He had a past

and history he was ashamed of, not to mention no matter how hard he tried, he couldn't separate himself fully from his crazy dysfunctional family.

"What if I shut the bar down for a few weeks when you visit," he said, needing to get Charlotte out of his mind. "We can travel up the coast."

Estelle's eyes widened and she clapped her hands. "Yes! Oh, I know. Charlotte can come with us."

He fisted his good hand. Imagined Charlotte on the beach, her long, lean body in a bikini, a blue one to bring out her eyes. "I'm sure she wouldn't want to."

"Of course she would," Estelle said as if he was an idiot to even doubt it. "Besides, she has a thing for you. I'm sure she'd love to go away with us."

His daughter had seen that? "Trust me. She doesn't want to go anywhere with me."

"You did something," Estelle said, looking at him with suspicion. "What is it?"

"I didn't do anything." Except hurt Charlotte's feelings. Let her go. No, he hadn't let her go. He lost her. "Look, there's nothing going on between me and Charlotte."

"Oh, my God, she dumped you," Estelle said, hitting her desk with the palm of her hand. "What did you do?"

"She didn't dump me. We were never together."

"Okay, okay. Obviously you messed up," Estelle continued blithely. "You can get her back. First thing you need to do is send her flowers but, for

God's sake, don't write the note yourself or you'll just blow it." She picked up her phone and started typing. "Let's see… Dear Charlotte, these flowers don't compare to your loveliness…" She wrinkled her nose, tapped another button—hopefully the delete button. "No, you'd never use loveliness. She'd see right through that."

"I'm not sending her flowers—"

"Right. Good idea. Skip right to jewelry. Nothing too showy and nothing as predictable as diamonds."

"I'm not giving her jewelry, either. There is nothing going on between me and Charlotte. There never was and there never will be so just…drop it."

"Why not?"

He frowned. "What?"

Estelle rolled her eyes. "Why won't there ever be anything between you two? It's obvious you're into each other."

"I'm not having this conversation with you."

"Daddy, please, I'm practically an adult."

She wasn't. She was his little girl. Always. "Charlotte and I want different things."

She wanted a fairy tale and all it ensued—marriage, kids, weekend dinners at the in-laws. Strings and commitments and promises of forever.

He wanted… Hell…he wasn't even sure anymore. Three weeks ago he would have said freedom. Solitude. But being able to jump on his bike and take off to places unknown didn't hold the appeal it once had.

And solitude felt more like loneliness.

Estelle shook her head at him disappointingly. "Daddy, I love you, but sometimes…you're a real idiot."

She hit a button on her laptop and the screen went blank.

The apartment was eerily quiet after Estelle's chattering. He went into the kitchen, got a bottle of water from the fridge, opened it but didn't drink. Stared out the window at the starry sky. Ever since Charlotte left his bed, left his life, last week, he hated being here. Felt trapped in the small rooms, as if the dingy walls were closing in on him.

Everywhere he turned, he saw her. Every night he dreamed of her.

He missed her. More than that, he ached for her, physically ached, as if a piece of himself were missing.

She was an addiction, more dangerous than the one he'd had fourteen years ago, and that one had almost killed him. These feelings he had for her were dangerous. Terrifying. He didn't love her. Couldn't.

Loving someone meant trusting them. It was too big of a risk. One he wasn't strong enough to face.

The truth shuddered through him. He hung his head, squeezing the water bottle so tightly it exploded in his hand. He didn't move. After everything he'd done, after everything he'd faced, after he'd busted his ass turning his life around he was still nothing but a damned coward. An idiot, as his daughter had so helpfully pointed out.

He didn't have to keep punishing himself for his past. Didn't have to be alone.

He could be with Charlotte. Have her by his side, in his bed, in his life. They might not last forever, but however long they did—months, weeks or days—it was better than letting his fears push her out of his life.

It was better than simply letting her get away.

He tossed the bottle into the sink then strode to the door.

And prayed like hell he managed to convince her to give him a second chance.

CHARLOTTE STEPPED OUT of her car, still in her scrubs, only to stop when Kane, sitting on the stoop of her back door, straightened and stood.

What was he doing here? Hadn't he done enough? Hurt her enough? "Skulking around someone's house is not an attractive trait," she said, reaching back in for her purse and bag. She swung her purse onto her shoulder, used her key fob to lock her car. "Not to mention it's just plain creepy."

"I want to talk to you," he said as if he had any right to be at her house this early in the morning with his hair all mussed and his snug shirt clinging to his broad shoulders and flat stomach. He had dark circles under his eyes and at least two days' worth of facial scruff.

She only wished she didn't find it, didn't find *him*, so annoyingly appealing.

"Well," she said, brushing past him so he either had to move out of her way or take an elbow to the ribs, "as I've recently learned, we don't always get what we want." She unlocked the door and faced him with a mean smile. "Now, all I want is to get inside, get something to eat, shower and maybe read for an hour before I try to get some sleep. So, goodbye."

He kept the door open easily—too easily—just by holding it. "I want to talk to you, Charlotte."

"Again, we don't always—"

"Please," he said gruffly. Damn him, he knew she couldn't refuse when he was all polite and his accent came out.

She stepped aside. "You'll have to talk while I eat," she said grumpily. "I'm hungry."

She turned her back to him, set her items on the table then crossed to the cupboard. While he watched her like some scowling, wild-haired poster child for rebels everywhere, she poured herself a bowl of cereal. Scooped up a bite as Kane paced her kitchen. Ignoring him, she sat at the stool at the counter and ate, tried to pretend a big, hulking man wasn't circling her kitchen like some damned specter of boyfriends past.

She wouldn't ask why he was here. Told herself she didn't care, not one bit. Not after he'd hurt her that way. Not after she'd opened up to him. Trusted him with her feelings. So, no. It didn't matter why he was here or that he more than likely walked the three miles from O'Riley's just to see her.

She'd have to be a complete and utter fool to let him back in her life. And Lord knew her mother had not raised any fools.

Finally, when she was fishing out the very last of her cereal, he stopped, faced her. "I may have been premature in ending things between us."

Char snorted. "Uh, you didn't end anything. If I remember correctly, I did the ending. And I'm pretty sure it was a really good decision. Especially if you came here to try to tell me how you may have made a mistake. May have? Really? Could you get any more indecisive? God." She stood, rinsed her bowl because there was no way she was going to let that cereal dry on it. "If you came here to waffle about whether or not you want to be with me, you've wasted your time and mine. "So," she continued, pointing rather dramatically toward the door, "since you're unsure of your feelings for me, I think you should leave. And when those feelings do become clear, please, please do me the courtesy of staying gone because I do not want to go through this again with you ever."

To her horror, her voice shook, tears threatened. She swallowed them back. She'd cried enough over him the past few days. She refused to do so anymore.

He walked up to her, his face set, and she thought he was going to listen to her, that he was going to do as she asked and leave her be. Instead, he grabbed her shoulders, yanked her to him and kissed the breath from her lungs, the doubts from her mind. She sank into him—how could she not when she'd thought of nothing but him ever since she left him the other day?

But then, thankfully, she found her strength, her resolve, and tore away from him. Shoved him. Hard. "No. Damn it, no. You don't get to do this to me. We're done. You may not have made that decision, but it was ultimately your choice."

He moved as if to walk away, and her heart broke, the thought of shutting him out again was hard, but she knew she had to do it to get past this. To get over him. To keep her heart safe.

Kane whirled around. "I've been miserable," he said lowly.

She nodded. "Yeah? Welcome to the club, buddy. And don't think for a moment I feel sorry for you, either."

"I…" He rolled his head side to side. Exhaled heavily and pinned her with his intense gaze. "I've missed you. I've left my family, have gone months…years… without seeing them. Have made and lost friends and have never, not once, missed anyone the way I've missed you these past few days. It was like…"

She bit into her bottom lip. She wouldn't ask. Wouldn't give him any more of her time or thoughts.

But she couldn't stop the words from coming out any more than she could stop herself from loving him.

"Like what?" she asked after a moment, her breath lodged in her throat, her heart racing. She tried not to hope, she really did. He'd hurt her too much for her to think there could be anything between them. But the thought formed all the same.

He looked miserable. As miserable and unhappy as she'd felt this past week. It shouldn't please her, but it did. It really, really did. Knowing he'd suffered the way she had, that he regretted—as he should—his stupidity, his mistake—made her own pain that much easier to bear.

Made it that much easier for her to want to forgive him.

She sighed. Guess she was a fool after all.

"It felt as if a piece of me was missing," he said quietly. He lifted his hand, touched the ends of her hair just above her ear. "Like it was hard to breathe without you there. I crave you, Charlotte."

Oh, that was good. Really good. But she had to be smart. She had to protect herself. "What if you were right? What if it was just sex?"

"It wasn't. I lied when I said that, when I said it was always that way. I didn't want to admit how great it was, how much it meant to me. I was stupid. Scared."

"Scared? Of me?"

He nodded. "You have the power to hurt me. You have my heart in your hands."

"And you don't trust me not to crush it?" She shook her head. "You don't trust me at all, do you?" she asked quietly.

"I was an idiot not to."

She crossed her arms. "You were. But maybe you were right. Maybe we're not meant to be."

"Don't say that." He sounded desperate. Shaken. "Please, Charlotte. Give me another chance."

"I'm not sure I can," she whispered. "What if you decide you can't trust me again? What if you get scared? I don't want us to be sex buddies or 'sort of' seeing each other. I love you. I'm in love with you, and for me, that means forever."

"I'm not the man you wanted," he pointed out, and she saw, for the first time, that knowing she'd wanted James and Justin, by her thinking she had wanted them, she'd hurt him, too.

Maybe they were both idiots.

"You're not the man I thought I wanted. You're better. You're real and not some fantasy I concocted in my head. But if you don't believe that, if you don't trust in that, in me—and in us—there's no point in us trying anything."

He swallowed visibly. "I can't let you go again," he said raggedly. "I'm in love with you and that's the best damn reason I can think of for us to try. I want to spend the rest of my life with you, and the way you discuss disgusting medical cases over meals. Your plans and goals, your smile and laugh." He took her hands in his, and she noted his were unsteady. "Charlotte, I want you. Only you. Forever."

Tears threatened again but they were the good kind. It was scary to hope. Terrifying to trust. But in the end, the heart wanted what the heart wanted.

And her heart wanted Kane. Only Kane.

Half laughing, half crying, she threw herself into his arms. "I want you, too. You're not who I envisioned, but you're the perfect man for me."

He held her tight, pressed his face against the crook of her neck. "Damn right I am."

And when he kissed her, they were both smiling.

* * * * *

Be sure to check out the other books in
Beth Andrews's IN SHADY GROVE *series!*

TALK OF THE TOWN
WHAT HAPPENS BETWEEN FRIENDS
CAUGHT UP IN YOU

All available now from Harlequin Superromance.
And look for a new IN SHADY GROVE *book*
from Beth Andrews later in 2014.